THE
GREAT
HARLEQUIN
GRIM

www.kidsatrandomhouse.co.uk

THE GREAT HARLEQUIN GRIM

Gareth Thompson

DOUBLEDAY

London • New York • Toronto • Sydney • Auckland

THE GREAT HARLEQUIN GRIM
A DOUBLEDAY BOOK
978 0 385 60920 3 (from January 2007)
0 385 60920 5

Published in Great Britain by Doubleday,
an imprint of Random House Children's Books

This edition published 2006

1 3 5 7 9 10 8 6 4 2

Papers used by Random House Children's Books are natural,
recyclable products made from wood grown in sustainable forests.
The manufacturing processes conform to the environmental
regulations of the country of origin.

Set in Mrs Eaves by Palimpsest Book Production Limited,
Polmont, Stirlingshire

RANDOM HOUSE CHILDREN'S BOOKS
61–63 Uxbridge Road, London W5 5SA
A division of The Random House Group Ltd

RANDOM HOUSE AUSTRALIA (PTY) LTD
20 Alfred Street, Milsons Point, Sydney,
New South Wales 2061, Australia

RANDOM HOUSE NEW ZEALAND LTD
18 Poland Road, Glenfield, Auckland 10, New Zealand

RANDOM HOUSE (PTY) LTD
Isle of Houghton, Corner of Boundary Road & Carse O'Gowrie,
Houghton 2198, South Africa

THE RANDOM HOUSE GROUP Limited Reg. No. 954009
www.kidsatrandomhouse.co.uk

A CIP catalogue record for this book is available
from the British Library.

Printed and bound in Great Britain by
Mackays of Chatham plc, Chatham, Kent

To the loyal family few,
and for John Murray

'Fireworks are an art form that use the
night sky as the canvas'
Larry Crump

'He who hath smelt the smoke is ne'er again free'
the motto of *American Fireworks News*

PART ONE

Blackrigg Valley,
the Scottish Borders;
November 5th,
five years ago

ONE

The boy giant lumbered over sparkling meadows. His great boots kicked through green grass, with long wet strides. Then he skidded on a frosty patch of mud. His tall frame tumbled and crunched down on one side. He lay quite stunned until his lungs could suck air again.

'Urghh! Bugger! Hate you, mud!' he cried. He pulled down the sleeves of his huge red jumper. They covered his cold hands, which were bigger than a grown man's.

Now the boy giant's jeans felt dewy damp. He was only thirteen, but already stood well over six feet. There wasn't much fat on his lanky bones. His fair hair straggled over a bright red face.

On the main road, beyond the fields, he saw a bus disappear. The white faces of schoolkids were pressed at each window. He knew they saw him fall, and felt their laughter echo inside him. He staggered up like a newly born calf and ran to a foggy stream.

Bright early sunshine slowly burned away the mist. The sheep fields lay green and golden. Trees on the low slopes were yellow, pink and black.

The boy crouched by the water. He splashed his bony hands in icy ripples. Pulling them out, he watched clear drops drip slowly down his fingers. Then his long elastic limbs began to contort. His legs reached upwards and stretched back, until his feet were locked behind his neck. He was all tucked up, head between both knees. The toes of his wellies rubbed an itch along his spine. His arms folded round the backs of his thighs, making a human egg shape. He sat and rocked gently forwards.

Breakfast would be ready by now. He had been up for two hours, helping around the small farm. There were cows to milk, then pigs to feed. He had a name for every animal. Just little things that made each one stand out: Long Tail Calf, Bully Big Balls, Great Fat Arse, Lazy Last One; Pinkest Pig, Snotty Snout, Long Pisser, Mr Mudbath.

Someone called him. His ears pricked up like an owl's.

'Haitch! Haitch!'

The boy giant's name began with an H. The stern bark of his dad's voice yapped out.

'Haitch! Breakfast!'

It was a sharp order, like a dog being called inside at night. Haitch unfolded out of his body knots, then flopped back home in his green wellies.

The old farmhouse stood in a valley called Blackrigg, ten miles north of the Scottish border. The house itself was made from dark wood. Right beside it were two low barns, to shelter the animals, also built of black timber. Haitch's bedroom looked right over them. At night he could hear the calming shuffle of hooves on hay.

Badger, the black and white sheepdog, waited by the door. He leaped up to paw the boy's chest, but could only reach his belt. Haitch grabbed Badger's legs, kneeling to have his red runny nose licked.

The house was the kind a child might draw, with four windows and a smoky chimney. It had just a kitchen and a dining room downstairs. Up the creaky wooden stairs were two bedrooms and a little bathroom. Haitch went indoors and held up his hands.

'Look, Mum!' he shouted, too loudly. 'All clean. Done in cold river. Bloody froz!' He jumped on the spot and clapped heavily.

'Aye, but hush now,' sighed his mother. She sat down beside her thin husband, who was already seated. Haitch's parents, Walter and Jean, were both gangly beanpoles in their youth. But years of backbreaking farm work had made them stoop. Their shoulders and spines ached, so at night they needed tablets to help them sleep.

They never expected to have children. Haitch came along when his mum was forty-six. They knew soon enough he'd always be a burden. But there was no special school close by to take him. The nearest one was in Carlisle, down over the border in Cumbria.

So they kept him at home and watched him shoot up. By thirteen he could carry big bales of hay, but couldn't count them. He could climb fruit trees in seconds, but couldn't spell 'apple'.

Walter cupped a coffee mug with hands like old shovels. Curly white hair rolled under his brown cap. Jean put three boiled eggs in front of Haitch. The boy giant sat perched on a rickety stool, cutting toast into soldiers. His lean face was always rosy from being outside all day.

'Bonfire tonight!' Haitch shouted. He scooped a whole egg and ate it in one munch. 'Don't forget bonfire, Dad. Dad? *Dad?*'

'No, I won't forget.' Walter's voice was gently Scottish, though he came from south Cumbria. 'Just be careful when—'

'Got fireworks!' Haitch burst in. He giggled loudly and looked around the room. On the sideboard were three big boxes. They were covered in red and blue stars and stripes. Boxes full of mystery and magic. A white packet of sparklers lay on top.

'Don't swear and shout so, Haitch,' said Jean. 'Do try and remember.'

Walter crunched some toast, heaped with marmalade. His only child ate noisily beside him.

'Fireworks, bonfire,' said Haitch quietly. 'First time ever.' His voice rose to a shout. 'Man full of straw! Burn his bloody head off!' He jiggled about on his hard round seat.

Jean closed her eyes and sipped warm tea. Walter chewed his toast, gazing into space, grazing like a cow. Haitch dropped a knife. Leaning down for it, he crashed off the stool. Plates on the sideboard shook as he met the floor. A cardboard box jumped off the edge, spilling three Roman candles. One rolled gently into a shadow under the dresser.

Jean stroked her forehead lightly. 'What a shock for the animals tonight, Walter,' she said, 'when you start letting those stupid things off. Rockets and God knows what.'

Walter nodded. 'Aye. Wish I'd never bought them,' he said. 'But he shouted so loudly in the shop. Everyone was looking.'

Haitch took his wobbly seat again. He threw a toast

soldier down for Badger. He whispered to himself and the nibbling dog, 'Sshh! Gonna burn bad man.' He bashed at an eggshell. 'Got fireworks, Badge.' His voice became harsh and excited. 'Wait 'n' see. Got big . . . hot . . . *fire*! Burn all night.'

Badger whined softly and licked the boy's green boots.

Jean began clearing away the breakfast plates. 'Never again,' she mumbled. 'Why did we ever bother . . . ?'

Walter crunched quietly and stared at his wife. But whether she'd meant the bonfire party, or their only child, he couldn't tell.

TWO

At half past four the school bus came past again. Three lads got off half a mile from the farmhouse. All wore purple blazers and black trousers.

'He ain't really our age,' said the stoutest of the three. 'He can't be.'

'He is,' said a blond boy. 'He's only thirteen.'

'Bloody freakshow, man.'

'Wait until he speaks. It's well gaga.'

'How tall is he?'

'Ten foot, I've heard. That right, Donnie?'

A lad with striking red hair clamped a hand over his mates' mouths. 'Hush your wild words, boys,' he said. 'When Donnie Turnbull tells you this mutant oddity is a mere six foot four, what do you say?'

'I'd say he's twice the size of Tommy. Short-arse.'

'Up yours. Ouch! What's that for, Donnie?'

'For crudeness beyond your tender years. Now let's march.'

Blond Davy, tubby Tommy and redhead Donnie took a muddy path. A high brambly hedge ran beside it. Their decent school shoes were soon mucked up. Daylight was dimming into smoky early evening. The air blew cold and crisp from their mouths.

The path swung left over more fields, through a farm gate to a boggy track.

'Lift your sweet eyes yonder,' Donnie said. 'The main attraction lurks.'

All three peered across to a grassy bank that faced them. It ran on and on, rising and dipping like a great breaking wave. A tall boyish figure stood on the slope. Treetops behind threw deep shadows around him. He seemed to be watching the visitors. Then he picked up what looked like half a forest. He dragged it down the bank to chuck on a large dark heap. Broken crates, leafy branches, sawn-up logs, old cardboard.

'Trot along,' Donnie said. 'Let's offer our services.'

'I'm cold,' moaned Tommy, rubbing his plump blazer sleeves.

'So let hard work set your heart a-blazing. So march!'

Donnie led the way, the other two shoving chilly hands in holey pockets. They squelched over soggy turf, their socks growing damp.

Haitch saw them coming and hid behind the cold bonfire. He peeped through smashed twigs and boxes.

The higgledy heap was tall and wide. But his huge red jumper was like a rising flame. The growing dusk wasn't enough to cover him.

The gang of three stopped a few metres away.

'All right there, big man?' Donnie called out. 'We've come with helping hands for the great bonfire activity.'

Just then the faint snarl of a tractor engine cut in. The three boys looked away to the right and saw the farm vehicle wobble off. Its grubby red body and huge black wheels made for a distant field.

At this, Haitch ran out from hiding. He jumped on the spot, flapping his arms madly.

'That's Dad!' he shouted. 'Dad, Dad, Dad!' He made a joyful squealing, clapping his hands up high. The tractor growled back from a distance. Haitch yelled again, still jumping, now slapping his cherry cheeks.

'Jesus,' muttered Tommy.

Donnie stroked his chin. 'It's a terrible shame,' he mused.

'I've seen enough,' Davy said.

Donnie smirked. 'Och, you've seen nothing.'

Haitch came to a rest. He wiped a snotty nose on his big red sleeve, looking down over the three boys.

'Over there,' said Haitch, pointing at the rolling bank behind. 'Them trees is cut up. I did. Did like this.' He made a chopping action with both hands.

'Ch! Ch! Ch!' he said as each stroke sliced the air.

'Aye. Awesome strength, big man,' Donnie said. 'So let's go carry it here. Lads?'

'Right,' came two tired grunts.

Haitch stared into all three faces. He tugged his bright blowy hair. Then he lifted a large elbow, showing a rip in his king-size jumper.

'Got hole,' he said, sniffing deeply. 'Bloody bugger.'

Davy snorted loudly.

'Pig,' said Haitch. 'Got pigs here. Long Pisser, Snotty Snout.'

'Watch it,' breathed Davy.

'Easy, man,' Donnie whispered. 'Play along.' He walked towards the dark green bank. The slope was gentle but it fell away steeply beyond. A yellow roof of treetops glowed on the other side from a thicket of oaks. 'This way, good sir?' Donnie said.

Haitch suddenly galloped after him. His knees kicked high in the air like a wild stallion. His great green wellies wobbled. 'Follow me!' he yelled. 'Giddy up!' He slapped his legs, tearing past Donnie.

'No way,' said Tommy. 'He's got an axe over there.'

'Aye,' Davy said. 'And Donnie's got steel fists. Make tracks.'

They huffed upwards, then slithered and stumbled all the way down.

Near the foot of the humpy bank, before the small forest, was a stack of logs and branches. Haitch gathered a pile of wood and strode back up the sharp hillock.

'Easy!' he shouted back. 'I'm Superman. Look!'

'Aye,' Donnie murmured, 'you soon best had be.' He barked a command, rubbing his palms together. 'Right, boys, gather winter fuel though the frost is cruel.'

Each lad grabbed cold timber, scraping it on his purple blazer. By the time they'd reached the bonfire, gasping, Haitch had made a third trip.

Davy and Tom chucked their bits at the great stack. 'Fun's over,' Tom panted. 'He's just dumb. Big deal.'

Donnie held up two fags. He lit his own, then gave the others one to share.

'Not so hasty,' he said, blowing out. 'Look busy.' He started poking around the base, shifting bits of cardboard. Haitch came charging back down, arms full of dead forest.

'Hey, hey!' he squealed. 'Get off that. Get logs. Now.'

Donnie stood back up. 'Sorry, kind sir,' he said. 'I was just seeing if you had a Mr Guy Fawkes here to burn. Thought he's mebbe trying to escape.'

Haitch gave a wide red smile. With huge finger jabs he pointed at the shadowy farmhouse. 'At home,' he said. 'Mum did make it. Big straw head.'

Donnie wiped his hands on Tom's blazer. He glanced up at a white shaft rammed into the bonfire like a flagpole. 'Is that so?' he said in a slow Scots drawl. 'You see, we lads have this old Highland game. You take it in turns and pretend to be the Guy. Your hands are tied and everything, just like poor Mr Fawkes.'

'Donnie . . .' mumbled Tom, but was waved to silence.

Haitch rubbed his big blue eyes, leaving dark streaks below. 'Yep, yep,' he said. 'Gonna burn bad man.' He squinted at the dark distance, where a tractor still rumbled. 'Tea time soon. Got piggy bacon. Dad killed Runny Bum last week.'

'Poetic,' said Donnie, blowing smoke rings. 'Quite poetic. Shall we show him the rules, lads?'

Tom and Davy stared back in cold protest. 'Aye,' said Tom finally. 'Remind us how we play, great master.'

Donnie's red hair glowed in the gloom. He scrambled up the planks and boxes, snapping fistfuls of twigs. Davy followed glumly, splinters burying into his hands. Donnie sat against the white pole fixed at the centre. The wooden clutter on all sides held it firm. He put both hands behind his back, winking at Davy.

'Tie my hands, o jailer!' he cried. 'And may God have mercy on my sizzling arse.'

Davy made a show of tying the old rope. 'Can we naff off now?' he muttered.

'No,' said Donnie quietly. 'Not until we've all had a turn.'

'You'll scare the big wuss witless.'

Donnie gave an ugly grin. 'Weep not for life's victims, Davy boy. For the dull and the dumb. Just make sure they . . . get what's coming.'

THREE

'Guido Fawkes!' Donnie shouted. 'The only person ever to enter parliament with top intentions. Born in York, 1570. Executed this day in 1606, after the Gunpowder Plot against King James the First and his crippy club foot.'

Below him, Davy threw an unlit match on the stack.

'Whoosh,' said Tom weakly. 'Look at the terrible flames.' He kicked a stray branch and yawned mistily.

But Haitch wasn't bored. He began jumping and shrieking wildly. He ran right around the bonfire, blowing big breaths at it. 'Die, you bad man! Bad man die!' he cried, clapping huge hands. He held up his palms as if the cold wood were alight. 'He burns and burns! He screams!' He put a finger in each ear and ran on the spot. Faster and faster he went, his long legs in a blue blur. He shook his head until his cheeks rattled. A long cry whined from his open mouth.

'And now I croak!' Donnie yelled. 'See my sweet soul

fly to hell.' His head sank onto his chest as he sat dead still.

Haitch stopped, looked up and chewed his hands.

'OK, big fella,' Tommy said, grinning. 'The deed is done. You need mourn no more.'

Haitch took out his long fingers and pointed at the heavy clouds. Tommy gazed up after him, rubbing his tubby tummy.

'Oh aye,' he laughed, 'he's dead. Brown bread. Gone to that great shepherd's pie in the sky.'

Donnie slithered back to earth. 'See me up there, big man?' he said. 'Feel the history shiver through ye?' He gave Haitch a friendly punch, though there was force within it.

Haitch returned the thump from a great height. 'Me up there,' he shouted, towering above Donnie, whose eyes narrowed after the blow. Then the boy giant spoke softly, as if to a small animal: 'Me up there.'

'I'm not sure now. Have we time?' Donnie asked. He touched a throbbing shoulder. He made a big show of checking his watch.

Davy huffed. 'Get a shifty on then, it's well dark.'

But Haitch could see clearly enough. He climbed the rickety bonfire like a squirrel scaling a tree. He parked himself on top, beside the pole, and sang out. 'Ready! Mr Fawkes is ready!'

'OK,' Davy shouted. 'Whoosh, there goes a match. Right, we're off now, Long Legs.'

Davy felt a hand on his arm. 'Less hasty,' Donnie said. 'Hold on, big man,' he cried. 'I'll bring this pagan pageant to life.' He began moving up the dark mound, his damp feet slipping. The mass of wood shifted and slid below him.

Haitch gave a huge grin. 'Can see Dad!' he yelled, his warm spit flying.

'Aye, big man. And hear Daddy's tractor close by? So close that no harm could ever befall ye?'

'Dad, Dad, it's me!' squealed Haitch. He started waving, but Donnie reached for his hands. He pulled them against the white pole and looped the rope into strong knots. He lurched back to the frosty earth, arms out wide.

'Can you hear us in the dark night, big man?' he called up.

'Down there! Down there!'

'That's it, Daddy-Longlegs. We're right in front.' Donnie reached into Tom's pocket and snatched a book.

'Hey, leave off. That's my maths homework.'

'And a right pig ye've made of it.' The book's middle pages were ripped out.

'Donnie! Bloody pack that.'

'Get away with ye. And your fractions are shite, man. An eighth of ninety-four is . . . twenty-three over two.'

Haitch pulled at the post like a chained-up dog. 'Cold!' he called. 'Dark now. Can't play now. Tea time.' He moaned quietly. 'Got bacon, got beans . . . want Badger.'

A match flamed into life. Donnie touched it onto Tom's torn sheets. He shouted to the large lurching shadow above. 'Sit still there, big man. We'll get a barbecue going.'

He dangled burning pages over the bonfire. The whites of his eyes gleamed like a cat's.

And that's when Haitch began to wail. He blew a jet of cold frightened breath. He yanked his tied hands, bashing his head back on the pole.

'Leave it, man,' Davy said, stamping his feet. 'Let's away for the bus.'

Donnie's left hand made a finger gesture. His right hand held the torched paper, joining its tip to a wedge of cardboard on the heap. The brown board smoked.

Haitch screamed for his dad. His big body rocked as if in the grip of a nightmare. The tractor clattered, quarter of a mile away.

Donnie wafted the cardboard. It spat sparks like fireworks. Donnie took two slow steps up the wooden mass, chanting slowly, 'Remember . . . remember . . . the fifth of November.'

He laid the blazing board on a branch. Dark twigs began to roast. Donnie jumped back, wiped his hands in Tom's hair and strode off. A long desperate cry followed from above.

Davy shoved Tommy aside in panic. He grabbed a frosty log. Stepping up, he bashed the burning cardboard. He stood sideways and stamped it. His holey sock scalded. Davy screamed. The board slid into the bonfire's dark heart. There it found a box of old newspapers. One dry corner of a *Daily Record* grew warm. The heat steamed in. The front page began to curl and catch.

A flame flashed below the boy giant's feet. His wellies lashed out but the rope held him fast. His rubbery legs rose up, coiling round his neck. But he couldn't prise the pole out. His limbs went down again, thrashing over hot wood. He gave a long whimper like a beaten dog. Then came a gasping breath. Then a raw animal howl. It shivered through the bleak air like a blade.

PART TWO

South Cumbria,
the English Lake District;
five years later

FOUR

Two of us rode in the front of a large white van. There was room for a third but no matter. The third one, my mum, wasn't coming with us. No one had said why, and yet something felt very wrong.

So it was just me and my wordless dad. He was driving, though he hardly looked awake. I saw him yawn and rub his unshaven face. His quiff of dark brown hair was all slicked up high. His thin sideburns were styled with care. But his eyes were red and for once he hadn't cracked a bad joke all day.

The gearstick rattled in the gap between us. I glimpsed myself in the mirror. My large wide green eyes glowed back. I always thought they made me look demonic. But Mum called them gooseberry eyes, as they were so round and bold.

Hers were a bit like that, only blue, and I got my fair hair from her. Mine was all spiky blond and cut short. I wore a stud in each ear, and was normal height for thirteen and a half.

Glenn Jackson, that's me. Glenn — my dad took the name from a song by legendary Manchester band The Smiths. The double 'n' often fools people, but that's how it is on the lyric sheet, so that's how it is on my birth certificate. Just one of those daft quirky tricks parents play.

As we drove north from Lancashire, the landscape changed. We left the towns behind and saw mountains creeping up. We were moving from Burnley to a Lake District village called Torbeck. The main roads grew smaller, less busy, and Dad kept stopping. He got out a map and peered at it with a sigh.

'All right, Dad?' I asked softly.

He stroked his temples as if to ease a hangover pain. He shoved the map back under the front window. 'All right, mate,' he mumbled. 'Be patient. I'm a bit lost.'

I looked through the wide windscreen. The bright sky was blue and summery. Sunlight dazzled off the grey-green hills.

'What's that orangey stuff?' I asked. 'It's growing everywhere.'

Dad steered the van from a lay-by. 'Bracken,' he said. 'It's a tall fern. Grows green in summer. Turns reddy-brown in the autumn.'

It was the most he'd said all journey. As we pulled away, something slid in the back. I looked round at our worldly goods: Dad's precious rock record collection; his battered acoustic guitar covered in peeling protest stickers — CND, STOP THE WAR, COAL NOT DOLE; my paints and brushes in a plastic box; crates of clothes, books, frying pans. Mum's things were mostly back in Burnley. So was she.

I looked at Dad as he yawned again, his brown eyes glazed and sad. He must know why, at the last minute, Mum had left us to move on our own. But he still hadn't said. I kept checking the rearview mirror, expecting to see Mum catch us up in our old blue car. There wasn't much other traffic on the road. I finally got fed up with being treated like a stranger.

'No sign of Mum,' I said, craning my neck to the van's back window. 'When did you say she's leaving Burnley?'

'I didn't,' Dad said, jerking the clunky gearstick. 'She'll come when she's ready. And not before.' He put his foot down and the speedometer soared.

Dad finally muttered something about his best friend Geoff, who'd be following on behind. Geoff had been out with Dad and their mates the previous night, on a leaving do. Dad wasn't a big drinker. He didn't need to be, as he couldn't take his beer. I drank him under the table on my thirteenth birthday.

He'd looked all upset and bleary as we left Burnley. It was eight months since the town had been hit by a wave of race riots. There'd been clashes between gangs of Asian and white youths, and mad panic on the streets. Armed police had waded into the rioters, who in turn got heavy with baseball bats. A war veteran aged seventy-six was attacked, for no real reason. A taxi driver got beaten with hammers, and his battered face made the next day's papers. TV helicopters throbbed high above the smoking streets. The town was labelled a national disgrace. A fascist hellhole. Both sides of the race divide blamed each other.

I wasn't allowed out for two days, not even to school. After that, my parents wanted to move away. I didn't mind going. We'd only been in Burnley for five years after I'd started life in Oldham. I'd got no special friends and was up for new adventures.

Mum had also dropped hints about having a second kid. So it looked like being a clean start all round. Somewhere quieter for me, and for whatever little brother or sister might happen along. After thirteen and a half years as an only child I'd better get used to sharing.

'Why now?' I'd asked Mum, as me and her did the weekly shop in Booths.

'Why not?' she'd said, nudging the trolley against me. 'About time you had a playmate of sorts. Too much time locked away on your own, sweetheart. A martyr to your art, that's what you've become. A martyr to your beautiful art.'

I was five when I began drawing, and soon found I had some sort of gift for it. Nothing dead special, but enough to make people look twice. Since then I've always painted and sketched.

That night before we moved to Torbeck, I was watching a TV art show on BBC2. Some beardy presenter was painting in the style of the great masters. He was doing Vincent Van Gogh's famous painting *Sunflowers*. It looks pretty easy to begin with, just orange and yellow flowers in a wonky vase. But then you try to get the same stunning light and colour; the same simple warmth and beauty. It's impossible.

I'd been watching closely, taking notes. The gas fire spluttered. Stuff sat around in cardboard boxes. Mum knelt in front of me, her hands on mine. I briefly looked away from the TV and caught a watery gleam in Mum's eyes, like she'd been out in the cold.

'Glenn, love,' she whispered. 'There's an important letter for your dad. In the kitchen.'

'OK,' I said, turning back to the beardy man. He was mixing some colours. I leaned forwards to see better. Mum tugged her wavy blonde hair then stroked my spiky golden crop. I moved from her gentle touch. 'Mum! Leave it! Did he use yellow there?'

Mum's voice was low and husky. 'Sorry, sweetheart, I didn't hear.' She tried clearing her throat but still sounded hoarse. 'Listen, I'll see you soon, darling. Dead soon. Your dad's back any minute. OK? Glenn?'

I nodded, hardly hearing a word. Beardy was going on about Van Gogh cutting off an earlobe. He gave it to a prostitute. Two years later he borrowed a gun to end his life. His final self-portrait shows a tortured soul in terror. I stared at its grim gaze on the screen. I could feel Mum's round blue eyes watching me.

'Glenn?' she whispered. 'You're everything to me. Never forget.'

The pain in her quiet voice made me give a nervous glance. She relaxed her chubby cheeks into a smile and I smiled back.

'My funny artist,' she sighed. 'Your talent doesn't come from me. Wish it did. What have I given you?'

I put a finger on my lips to shush her. Beardy was plugging next week's programme, on Picasso. Mum squeezed my knees firmly, then rested her forehead there. She knelt a moment longer, as Beardy waved goodbye, before padding quietly into the hall. I heard her pick up something. The front door opened.

'Mum?' I called after her. 'Bring us a Mars bar.' The

door closed with a soft click. I shrugged, sat back and made a rough sketch of some sunflowers.

I'd gone upstairs by the time Dad came back. I heard a plate smash on the kitchen floor and guessed he was legless. Stretching out on the duvet, I thought about life after tonight, up in back-of-beyond Cumbria. I pictured myself by a lake, all posey at an easel, paintbrush in hand. And there'd be a barefoot farmer's daughter, lying nearby in summer bracken. Some chubby chick, with corn-coloured hair, and a right dirty mouth on her.

Dad slammed the front door, making my heart jump. I couldn't tell if he'd gone back out or not. I sat up and drew a quick self-portrait before bed. I often did them, like freaky Vincent Van Gogh once had. After we moved to Torbeck, those pictures changed. They became wilder, darker and scruffier. So did I. Then for a while I stopped my art altogether. It was only after the terrible chaos that I took it up again.

FIVE

On the way into Torbeck a large stone sat by the road. 'VILLAGE OF THE YEAR' was carved on the face. Broken bottles lay in the grass below. There were ancient hills to the left of us, modern homes to the right.

It was easy to find the block of council houses. They looked basic and modern, like homes that local people could afford. There were two rows facing each other. Down at the end, the road through curved left and took you to another lot. Our new place looked like the one we'd left in Burnley: pebble-dash front, bit of a garden, three up, two down. Only here was much quieter. Hardly anyone was about. The Village of the Year was lying low.

Saturday afternoon and it started to spit with rain. Dad flung open the van, jangling some door keys. We were moving into number twenty, down on the left. We began lugging boxes of stuff. This wasn't how I'd imagined it. I'd thought the whole tiny place would turn out and greet us with apple pies and cups of tea flowing. But not even a curtain twitched over the way.

Back up the road we'd come down was a wooden bus shelter, on the left. A few kids loitered inside, smoking and bouncing a football. Right across from there was a small green in a triangle shape. Beyond it lay a main road that curved through the village from end to end. And along this was a row of smarter houses, with a few cafés and shops. Cars went past on their way to nearby campsites, or in the other direction to the posh village of Hawkshead. People in bobble hats and walking boots poked around. Feeling stared at from the wooden shelter, I headed back.

And then someone came riding by, up from the bottom block of council homes. Some bullish lad a bit older than me. He was big and burly. His hair was rusty and cut short. He was on a bike, with his legs splayed out wide like a clown riding a tricycle. Glancing back at me, he spat onto the pavement. He cycled on, lifting his hefty arse clear of the saddle, past the bus shelter, where someone shouted. Swerving onto the main road, he gave two fingers to a car that hooted a warning.

I helped Dad carry his big record collection in. Manchester bands mainly, or Northwest groups and singers. He was loyal to his roots.

He swept back his high quiff of hair. We were both sweating in the mild October day and I wanted to ask if Mum was coming later. But the sight of Dad's drooping shoulders made me leave it. He rolled his forehead in a sorry way on the van's grubby side.

I lugged in some of his hi-fi gear. A plastic bag fell off it, onto the pavement. My scruffy mascot bear dropped out. He was yellow, with a red jacket and green cap. One of his paws held a paintbrush. I called him Rembrandt, after the famous Dutch artist who'd looked like a bashed-up bear by the end.

I blushed and looked around. But no one had noticed my daft old teddy. That youth on his bicycle was well gone. My arms were full with Dad's record deck, which I dumped in the kitchen. I hurried back outside to fetch my fallen toy before the whole village saw him.

But someone had beaten me to it. A girl about my age stood there like she'd shot up through the pavement. She wore glasses of an older style. Not trendy rimless, or modern thin lenses. These had clear plastic frames and looked cheap as chips. But the girl's eyes were warmly brown behind them. Her cheeks were pale; her red lips almost smiling. Her hair was dark and all tangled.

She held Rembrandt in one hand, dusting him down with the other. She nuzzled his tatty face. Her lips brushed his black nose. Then she handed him to me, rubbing her palms on her old jeans.

'There,' she said. 'That's better now.'

My face was red with awkward shyness. 'Thanks,' I said, feeling daft holding Rembrandt like I was five. 'The things we keep, hey?'

The girl's eyes widened behind granny glasses. 'Precious things,' she said. 'Priceless.'

She turned away before I could answer. Her witchy raven hair was quite long. I wondered if she ever combed it. I thought of Dad, gelling and brushing his quiff every morning before showing himself.

The girl crossed the little green, where an old man smoked on a bench. Then she was gone. I wanted to follow and see where she lived, when Dad's mate Geoff finally turned up in our old blue car. I shielded my eyes to see if Mum was with him. But Geoff was alone.

SIX

Geoff had got lost around Kirkby Lonsdale. Unlike Dad, Geoff could take his beer and had a belly to show for it. He wore a claret and blue Burnley football top. We'd unloaded most things by the time he arrived with a last lot. My room was quite small, at the back of the house. Sticking my head out of the window, I could see up the winding road to some shops.

Dad shut his bedroom door, though I could hear him talking to Geoff. I listened outside but they spoke softly. My guess was that Mum had a problem at work. She'd been with Booths, the northern supermarket chain, for years. When we decided to move they changed her branch to a Cumbrian one. A council house came up in Torbeck and that was it, we were all set.

Dad hadn't got a job to come to. He'd worked for the council in Burnley, dealing with tenants' problems. But Dad said Cumbria's towns always needed such staff.

So the wheels were set in motion and off we were supposed to go. All three of us.

Mum and Dad met at a Pulp gig in Blackburn when they were both twenty. A year later they got married. Janet and Nick. Then I came along a bit before planned. Mum worked from nine till four in school terms, and mornings during my holidays. Like Dad she was thirty-five now. Unlike Dad she probably acted it.

'You never grew up much past eighteen,' she'd often tell him. She used to laugh when saying this, or ruffle his curly quiff. Last time I heard her say it she did neither. And that last time was the Thursday before we moved.

Dad was going to a fancy-dress do at The Phoenix that evening. It was a Burnley pub which did theme nights, comedy and karaoke. Dad loved it but Mum wouldn't go any more. She was taking me to the cinema instead.

Dad got ready in the kitchen. He took shiny sheets of tin foil and wrapped himself from head to toe. The crinkly slinky stuff even went round his shoes. He kept the foil in place with Sellotape. Even his head and bushy hair were covered, except for eye and mouth holes. He was going as a jacket potato.

So we two went off to the movies. And then there

were three. Outside the Odeon, Mum introduced me to Ray. She said he worked for Booths in the wine section, buying stock from abroad. He wore a casual white suit and a yellow tie with little red roses on. He was all smiles under short brown hair. His shoes had bright buckles.

'Ray's coming with us,' Mum said. She had a bright blue dress on below a black jacket. She wore long leather boots. I'd never see any of this gear before, or maybe I just hadn't cared enough to look.

Ray bought us popcorn and orange in the foyer. Mum sat by him in the plush darkness. When I looked over, they weren't watching the film. They were busy whispering, heads together. Later we all went out for supper. Ray told us the countries he'd been to, tasting and buying wine: Chile, Argentina, New Zealand, Portugal.

'We went to France once,' I said, licking pizza sauce off my fingers. 'We normally go somewhere like Blackpool or Whitby. But Mum deserved a real holiday, so we drove down to France and camped. Then Dad and me got ill from the tap water. Dad wouldn't have the local wine and lived off cans of Guinness. Mum ended up just looking after us both. She was fed up and kept saying so.'

Ray gave a forced laugh and reeled off some top

French wine regions. Mum played with her wavy blonde hair. She kept giving me short looks to see if I was enjoying myself. I was thinking what Ray would be like to sketch. Pretty boring really . . . too busy smiling and talking.

But Mum didn't seem to find him dull. I'd never seen her look so flirty and full of herself. She pressed Ray's hand when talking to him. She laughed at his naff takeoff of a Spanish wine dealer. When we said our goodbyes, they embraced and she whispered something to him. He nodded and held her hands out in front. I walked away all puzzled and stared through a Blockbuster's window.

If Ray wouldn't be much fun to sketch, then my dad was always good to draw. He still looked youngish, with a strong jawline and thin sideburns. His brushed-up brown fringe made a nice quiff. He had that 1950s teddy-boy look and a wide smile. His hair was cut short at the back and squared off. He wore colourful shirts and a leather jacket with the collar turned up.

Now there we both were, in Torbeck, minus Mum. Dad was still locked away with Geoff. I finished unpacking my clothes and made a sandwich from the few kitchen bits we'd brought. Then I slipped out into the unknown village alone.

SEVEN

Mountains were things I'd only seen in the distance before. They seem so remote through the windows of a car, or a train. As if they're over the border of some country you can't enter.

But they circle Torbeck like a rocky fortress. I stood in the quiet road looking up at them. Now they were dizzily close and I felt my head spin. It was up in the misty clouds, lost among those high, swirling peaks.

I crossed the little triangle of grass. The old man smoking his pipe on the bench gave me a nod and a 'Howdo'. Shops over the road sold rucksacks, waterproofs, hiking boots. There were tearooms and guesthouses. Window signs read VACANCIES or NO VACANCIES.

I went past a pub called the Queen's Head, with a large tarmac outdoor area. Nearby was a real cosy shop. The windows were full of sweet and lollipop jars. They had displays of local beer, jams and sticky sauces.

Next door stood a place full of touristy tat. Cowpats

made of toffee. Little stone gnomes, baring their bums. Chocolate raisin 'sheep droppings'.

There were pubs everywhere. I looked at their menus in window cases outside, gasping at the prices. Only the top restaurants in Burnley charged anything like that.

There was no sign of a chippy. I felt hungry for George's Plaice, back in Burnley. And for George himself, being large and loud over the hot, hissing fryer. Fresh fatty chips, each one as thick as your thumb, glowing with golden oil. Sometimes I'd get them in a white cob, so the butter just began melting. Or they might be doused in roast-onion gravy.

But then George's business got gutted in the riots; burned to a charred shell. George did well to escape with his life by leaping from an upstairs window at midnight. Luckily his lardy arse landed on a stolen BMW's roof. I think the car needed more repairs than George.

Back opposite the green I stared up and down the quiet main road. A girl my age came out from one of the nice houses on that side. A tall one with several storeys. The girl's long brown hair was immaculate. Her face was slender and dead pretty. But her mouth had a surly stiffness, like she'd forgotten how to smile. She wore a white fur-lined jacket and black trousers with sharp creases. She also carried two collecting tins. As she came nearer I heard them jangle and thought I was being invited to give money.

'Hi,' I said. 'What you collecting for?'

She stopped right in front of me. She looked into my green eyes then gave me the full once-over. Her slim face was freckly around the nose. It went bright red when I smiled.

'What?' she asked. She knocked the tins together, her brown eyes still racing over me.

I smiled and tried again. 'What you collecting for?'

'Um, couple of things,' she began. 'One's for a youth-club we're trying to get started. The other's a mental-health charity.' There was a nice northern twang in her voice, but she sounded pretty cultured.

'Oh right,' I said, digging in my pockets. 'Here's fifty pence.'

'Um,' said the girl again. 'Well, you need a raffle ticket then.'

'That's all right,' I said. 'Put it in the youth-club one. Might end up hanging out there myself. I'm Glenn.'

'Oh? OK.'

I raised my eyebrows like, *Uh . . . you got a name?*

'Lavinia,' said the girl, running a hand through her lush brown hair. She went all red again, like I was the first boy she'd ever talked to. She pointed up ahead towards the village centre. 'I have to go,' she said. 'That way. Up there.'

'OK. Bye, Lavinia,' I said, waving her off.

Nice bit of posh, I thought. Bit nervy and gawky. Nice tight bum, perhaps a touch on the bony side. Maybe not a farmer's daughter. Then Lavinia turned her head round and saw I was watching still. She twisted away, bashing a tin against her leg for being caught out.

I'd met two girls in two hours. Not a bad start, even if they were like chalk and cheese. I tucked in my blue T-shirt. It said 'I LOVE MAD-CHESTER' in white letters. I mooched back to number twenty unseen. There was nobody around the facing rows of council houses.

Dad and Geoff were at the kitchen table, with mugs of tea. Dad looked worn out and rubbed his face. He wore a maroon jumper over a yellow and pink shirt. The bright colours glared in the bare little room. I sat at the table. Three white envelopes lay in a heap. Each had one of our family's names on: Nick, Janet, Glenn.

'What are these?' I said.

Dad sighed. 'From the district council, to welcome us. Found 'em by the doormat earlier.'

I opened mine. The card had a painting of water rushing over rocks. My artist's eye liked the bold use of colours. There was a printed 'WELCOME' inside.

'Nice touch,' I said.

Geoff took it from me. 'Pretty,' he said. He stuck out his bulging bellyful of Burnley shirt. 'Got some new places to draw now, Glenn.'

'Yeah, I have. And maybe some new faces.'

Dad rolled his brown mug around. He spoke down at the table.

'Listen, um, your mum's away for a bit, Glenn. Staying with some . . . friends. Needs a break, y'know? From us. From everything.' He glanced up now. 'From me.'

I frowned at the hurt on his face. The strong jawline made him look both tough and tender. The swept-back hair exposed his brown eyes below.

'Oh?' was all I could say. 'So . . . I see.'

'Don't know how long for,' Dad said. 'Can we manage between us? Until things mebbe straighten out? Until Mum . . . whatever?'

I looked at Geoff, who gave a thin smile.

'Guess we'll have to,' I said. 'But what about, y'know, what about shopping? And my new school? And getting things done?' I felt a sudden claw of panic.

Dad ducked his head again, tilting and rolling his empty mug.

He knew what I meant about 'getting things done'. Mum even used to fix the car for him, not to mention rewiring house plugs. Dad just went to work, came home, played his records (loudly) and guitar (badly), then lazed on the couch until Mum stirred him.

I went upstairs and sat on my bed, trembling with worry. Alone with just my scatterbrain dad I felt orphaned. Mum was the foundation that we all based our lives on; a warm and reliable rock. Now the promise of a new school and a new start was more of a terror. That claw of panic dug around my insides again. I held Rembrandt close and thought of that sweet scruffy girl nuzzling him, then handing him back. I went down to the kitchen again, trying to breathe slowly.

Dad and Geoff were out in the road. I put their mugs in the sink and lobbed soggy tea bags into a white bin. They landed on something. I bent down to look. Something that was all torn up now. Mum's welcome card from the council – ripped into four big bits.

EIGHT

After Geoff left in the hired van, Dad went into his room. I tapped on the door. Bedsprings creaked and feet padded over the floor. Dad's eyes were all red and his quiff messed up.

'Sorry,' I said. 'It's just there's nothing much in to eat. Dunno when the shops shut here.'

Dad sniffed loudly and stepped back. He got his wallet and handed over some notes. He sniffed more deeply and fished out a hanky.

'D'you mind going?' he said. 'I mean, going shopping?'

'No, that's cool. Um, shall I get some Hobnobs? Mum's favourite bickies for when she turns up? Yeah?'

Dad just closed the door quietly. I heard him lie on the creaky bed. I knocked firmly. 'Or shall we treat Mum and get some KitKats? Maybe the chunky ones?' There was no answer.

I trudged out into a sunset of hazy woodsmoke from home fires. That nice local gaff was closed, but I found

a supermarket open late. 'YOUR CARING, SHARING CO-OP'
it said on the door. I filled a basket with basics — bread,
butter, biscuits, beans. Some kid about my age was on
the till. He sat reading a comic behind the counter. When
I coughed, he finally took my money in silence and got
the change wrong.

'There's, like, two quid missing,' I said.

A gleam of panic lit his eyes. Either he'd been trying
it on, or just couldn't count. He bashed the till again
and silently paid up. The receipt told me I was 'happily
served by Dougie'.

'Thanks,' I said, checking the details. 'Bye, Dougie.'

I heard him cough and hack something up in his
throat.

The evening was a long one. I did beans on cheese
on toast for two. Dad made a show of getting organized. He got the TV all set up in the front room. He
bumbled about with kitchen stuff and looked in my
bedroom.

I sat on the sofa, glancing at a hospital drama. 'Is
Mum phoning tonight?' I asked.

Dad was trying to wire up his hi-fi stuff. He knelt
on the floor with his back to me. He grunted something.

'What?' I called, over the TV noise.

'Don't think so,' Dad said.

I leaned forwards. 'You think so? What time?'

Dad grabbed the remote off the floor, pressing mute. He spoke sharply, staring at the wall. 'I . . . don't . . . think . . . so.' He pressed the sound back on. Two nurses were arguing loudly. I reached for the remote and cut the noise again.

'Tomorrow then?' I asked. 'D'you think she'll phone tomorrow?'

Dad was using a large hammer to straighten a wall plug's nail. He tapped it gently then banged harder. Flakes of paint flew off. He cursed quietly. I stared at his back, feeling shut out.

'Or the day after?' I said quietly. 'Or can I phone her?'

Dad bashed the wall, making a dent. He didn't look round, just knelt there all hunched up.

I slunk upstairs and got a sketchpad. I drew myself first — just how I was feeling. I looked at the finished work, at my plain pale face and spiky short hair. My mouth a touch droopy like I was hearing sad news. I drew the first girl I'd met earlier, all witchy hair and old specs. I put a heart shape in the top corner, but crossed it out. Then I drew Lavinia with her collecting tins and slim blushy face. I tried to get her surly gawkiness in there, but couldn't manage it.

I slipped into my cold new bed about eleven. Football

highlights were booming downstairs. There was no noise from the road outside, unlike the drunken weekend shouts back in Burnley. Here it was all owl hoots, not car horns. No one taking a quick piss in our front garden. No one dragging their screaming girlfriend along by the hair.

I dreamed of me and Mum sitting in the cinema with her smarmy mate, Ray. He had a plate of Hobnobs on his lap. When he whispered to me, his face was furry and worn like my Rembrandt bear. He hissed, 'I'm your daddy now, Glenn. And we're all moving some place far, far away . . .'

NINE

We didn't get up early. I lay in bed, aware of the crushing quiet. When church bells began tolling I opened my curtains onto a cloudy day. The houses opposite looked unlived in, but there were cars outside.

We both moped around trying to arrange this new house. Dad went out of his way to avoid me. He scrubbed inside the oven for ages, though it was clean, just to stick his head somewhere quiet.

I hovered around him with questions about Mum, but it wasn't easy talking to someone's arching spine. About one o'clock, he asked if I'd seen a chippy.

'Nowhere,' I said.

'Really? Thought there would be. There anything else?'

'Couple of shops. One looks nice. Don't trust the other yet. Stacks of pricey pubs.'

Dad still hadn't shaved, which was rare and meant

he wasn't planning to go out. He was vain enough to look decent even when unhappy. He got his wallet, then tapped it slowly.

'Best be careful with cash,' he said. 'Until things are more settled. Can we make do with beans again?'

'I guess. Though Mum won't be happy we're living on quick snacks. Look, Dad, what's going on? I've got new school tomorrow. What do I do, just turn up? How long's Mum staying away?'

Dad handed over three pound coins. 'Get a few loaves,' he said. 'We can always freeze them.' He sat in an armchair, biting his nails. His dark blue jeans were crumpled like he'd slept in them. His big toes poked through sweaty yellow socks. No sign of his normal cherry-red Doc Martens shoes. He never wore anything as dull as carpet slippers.

I walked up the empty pavement and crossed the little green opposite the bus shelter. Over the quiet main road, the Queen's Head pub had a full car park. Sunday lunch tangs wafted through its open windows. The front door was hidden by a curve where the road twisted. Then round this corner came the first girl from yesterday, the helper of dropped bears.

She walked towards me, dressed just like before. Old sweatshirt, old green jeans, old trainers. Old-style specs and that witchy broom of black hair. Her lips were twitching happily ten metres off. They made a broad smile as we got close. I saw a flash of white teeth. The smile filled her face from brow to chin.

She was almost past me when she slowed up, and I stuck out a hand. It brushed against cold fingers. Cold hands, warm heart, my mum says. Me and the girl stood facing each other.

I jumped in and said, 'Thanks for helping yesterday. Y'know, when I dropped . . . something.' I lowered my voice to a strong whisper. 'Oh, and it's hush-hush about the bear. He's a lucky mascot.'

The girl nodded slowly and solemnly. She spoke very softly. 'I can keep secrets,' she murmured. 'I've got this freaky teddy thing. He's called Creepy Crawly. Some nutty family gave it me years back. When you unzip his tummy, loads of slimy plastic bugs drop out. He's meant to be infested with them. And Crawly's only got one eye — an enormous thing stuck on the left side.' She nodded thoughtfully again. I did the same.

'Unusual,' I said, fiddling with an ear stud.

The girl sighed. 'I'm stuck with him now, I guess. He's pretty manky. I don't take great care of things' — she pulled her tatty top — 'as you can see.'

'Me neither,' I said. 'I've just moved here, by the way. It's only me and my dad right now. You'll soon see him around. Can't miss him with his Elvis quiff.'

'He sounds cool,' she said. 'You both do.'

I smiled and stared shyly at the pavement. 'Cheers,' I said. 'Um, you always lived here?'

'Ooh no,' she said. 'No, no. It's a long and strange story.'

'Why strange?' I asked, my eyes now roaming all over her.

'Heavy stuff,' she said, rubbing her pale cheeks. 'Too much to tell. Hey, do you paint? There's red stains on your fingers. And on your trainers.'

'Yeah, quite a lot. Do you?'

'I sure do. Oh look, I'd best be off . . .'

Somebody eased me out of the way from behind. It was Lavinia, with her well-groomed long hair. She took my new friend by the arm, carrying two collecting tins again. I could just make out the details printed on each. One said MIND — MENTAL HEALTH AWARENESS, the other YOUTH CLUB FUND. She rattled them as if expecting another donation, then hauled the scruffy girl away. Lavinia turned back to me with a freckly frown, raising her eyebrows. She tossed her long brown hair. It was a real contrast to the scrambled black mop of the girl beside her.

I watched until they both went left through a garden gate, into the tall house Lavinia came out of yesterday. The painter snuck a glance back at me just before she went indoors. I felt my heart swell and start burning up. It went like a balloon with a jet of hot air inside.

I hadn't even asked her name, or told her mine. But when you get a sudden *thing* for a person it hardly matters. You start by imagining their name, with whatever seems right. She looked like a Jenny to me, or something dead casual like a Vicky.

I walked past the pub door, my head all floaty. Then came the cushy-looking shop and it was open. A sign above it said HENDERSON'S. I went in. A woman sat behind a till in the corner. For a few seconds I couldn't look away. Bright fair hair, a cosy figure, blue eyes, rosy cheeks. It could've been Mum's sister, if she had one.

The far end had a meat counter. By it was a big dairy section, gleaming red and yellow with cheese. At the bread shelves I took about three quid's worth.

Mum's cheery double beamed as I put down the basket.

'Hiya, love,' she said.

'Hiya.'

'You on holiday?'

'What? Oh . . . no. Just moved here.'

'Ohhh . . . Oh right. Yeah, someone said.'

'They did?'

'Yeah. News don't hang around long here.'

'Guess not,' I said, feeling edgy.

'That's three nineteen, love.'

'Oh damn. Dad only gave me three.'

'That's all right. Bring the rest next time.'

'God! You sure?'

'Course, that's fine.'

I stared at her kind homely face. She was a bit younger than Mum, but so like her. The sort little kids always ran to with a cut knee. I felt a lonely ache and stared far too long.

A limping old man came into the bright shop. 'Hello, Val,' he called. I snapped out of it and left, walking home quickly, feeling suddenly geed up.

We ate in silence around the kitchen table until Dad took his plate through to watch a cruddy cowboy film. He hated westerns so I knew he was avoiding me. It felt dull and unhappy staying indoors, and I had new places to explore. Those gritty mountains were calling me — crying out to be drawn. I did the washing-up, knocking plates around noisily. Dad turned up the TV. I slammed the front door and left.

In the end I was only gone for about three hours. Yet nothing in my life, and no one ever after, would seem quite the same again.

TEN

I lifted my face to a flood of autumn sunshine. The village was busier now, after lunch. A minibus pulled up near the bus shelter, letting out a noisy gaggle of hikers.

I had no local map to follow. Val waved at me from the bright shop window. I waved back with my free hand, the other holding a sketchpad. Some pencils filled a jeans pocket.

A road going by the caring, sharing Co-op rose out of the village. It came to a barbed-wire fence forking left and right. Left went into the hills, over a cattle grid on a rutted road. Cars crunched back and forth on their way to a youth hostel at the foot of the mountains. Climbers in heavy boots came and went. I looked at my torn trainers. You heard stories of people walking the ridges in rubbish footwear. Some never made it back.

So I went the other way, following a stony footpath.

It twisted through woodland, with lower hill slopes up on one side, and a busy main road down on the right. I walked quickly over sharp white stones. Felled trees lay around the jungly hillside banks. Grassy trails were trampled into the fells above. Bracken shone like fresh fire under the sun.

A silvery blur flashed up a tree. I lifted my eyes to meet hostile black ones. A grey squirrel. I knew the French called them tree rats. It stared harder, then with a sudden twitch was lost in the puzzle of branches. I looked back in case I had anyone for company. But the white woodland path was empty and the only sound came from hissing hillside streams.

The track through the forest came out at a cross-roads. Down on my right stood a farm, set some way back from the road. If I followed my path further along there was a turn-off from the main road. It rose up through trees that were speckled in red and yellow. But instead I took another rough left turning nearby, also going upwards somewhere. The craggy slope lay strewn with rocks. Now the noise of rushing water was louder.

The potholed track, the width of a car, rose quickly. I felt the strain on my city legs. My left ankle gave way in a sudden rut. Fresh cold air knifed up my nose.

I went through a gate with a stile. Now I could hear and see the rapid river. Way down below, on my right, it roared like a high-speed train whooshing through.

I stayed on the rising trail, where a drystone wall crumbled beside me. I stood in a gap and looked at the abyss far below. If you slipped here, you'd tumble until the river took your soul. A sheer drop to wild water that clattered down from the distant hills. Big boulders lay in its path like a giant's stepping stones.

I moved clear of the edge and went on. Trees grew from the deep ravine that narrowed in gradually, like a long arrow. On the high path I was right among their spreading crowns. Some were like fairy-tale trees. They had tiny yellow leaves, as if the branches were dripping gold.

Now the stream was higher, where the valley rose below me. Finding a break in the trees, I saw the heart of the giant water machine: two pounding waterfalls. They looked as cold as crystal and just as pure.

Close behind them was a flat bridge. A hollow arch, like a train tunnel, took its weight. Through this the river rushed down from the mountains far above. The white surge got dragged over great slimy slabs. At the point where the water fell, the rock formation rose from the riverbed. It stood like a cliff. Here the surge split into those two cascades. They poured into a whirlpool and bubbled and frothed. I made some pencil sketches using dots and short lines, standing on the bridge where spray sparked up from the wild water.

Crossing over, I met another old route, guarded by warm woodlands. It must be the same track I'd seen from the crossroads earlier, which veered up off the main road. It was heavily holed and just wide enough for one vehicle.

I kept struggling uphill, past fields and meadows. Finally a broad, primitive clearing opened out. A thick autumn forest glowed on my right. But everywhere else was like an old war zone. A vast grey rubble of rocks. Some were the size of bombs; others had cracked into stony shrapnel. It looked as if a nuclear warhead had blasted. And I even saw a site where it could have landed.

My eyes didn't accept it at first. This great pit in the earth, looming like an underworld. This yawning opening, like a comet's crater. Shrill winds whistled over the wasteland. Something crashed about in the yellow-orange trees behind, but I never looked round. My gaze was on the massive chasm up ahead. I was drawn towards it, even as I felt its deep-sunk danger.

ELEVEN

I felt exposed on this desolate plain. The wind played like a spook among the rocky ruins. In the distance were red-brown mountain ridges. But just here it was all flat and grey. I'd never felt so utterly alone.

I picked a way through the fragments of stone. The closer I got, the wider the crater stretched. One slithery slope had been eaten away. This took you down to the very brim. There was only a withered bush there to cling to.

So I stood above on a grassy ledge, staring to the far side. The whole oval void was like a Roman stadium. But the sides were a sheer breakneck drop. You'd have to be right on the rim to see the bedrock base.

I lay down flat and crawled closer. I squirmed forwards a bit. Now my nose was two metres from the edge. I sat up and knelt. My knee scraped a thick lump of stone. I lobbed it over with real force. It sank into the stiff breeze. I waited and kept counting. It seemed an age. I got up to nine. Then a faint splash came back. Water! What the hell was this place?

Across the great divide before me, clumps of trees were shedding copper leaves. Maybe I could grab on to their trunks and get a real view of this vast hollow with its hidden lake, or whatever lay waiting. Heavy trampling echoed from the woods again, back near the road I'd followed up from the bridge. It stopped when I spun round and looked.

I noticed a white sign. And then a heavy bronze pipe sticking out of the crumbly earth. I peered along its dark throat and smelled rusty water. I read the flaky signpost:

DANGER. STEEP, UNFENCED ROCKFACES. VERY DEEP CRATER.
ROOFING SLATE WAS QUARRIED HERE FOR 200 YEARS.

So that was it. The rocky waste all around had been blasted from this colossal pit. Gritty grey slabs with dark blue veins.

I felt the wind surge and went round the quarry's top ridge, aware how the day was darkening. At the corner of the forest was a sturdy log hanging from thick blue ropes. As I set it moving, something shifted once more in the woodland.

I pushed on through fleshy bushes of pink leaves.

Carefully I clung to a thick beech tree, right near the edge. My arms wrapped strongly around it. I pressed my cheek tight on the dry bark.

Then the ancient slate mine opened up before me. A giddy spasm jolted my head. My guts released a hot flush, like I'd swallowed acid.

The dizzying drop was at least a hundred metres on all sides. It gave me vertigo and a weird sense that I'd throw myself over. Down at the very bottom lay a gloomy lake. A blue barrel floated at the centre. Maybe it marked the deepest point. The shores were a chaos of rocks. I could just make out an abandoned rucksack down there. Also a plastic chair, balanced on a thumping boulder.

Suddenly I had to look round: isolated places are full of phantoms, ready to push you from behind. I inched away from the tree, back to the overgrown path. The pit's highest point was ahead of me still: an outcrop above the furthest rockface. Way below it were hollowed caves and scraps of rail tracks. I threaded a way over to the top.

I wobbled across its uneven dips and thick tree roots. Again I had to swivel round. I could sense eyes drilling into me, but saw nothing. I started to sing a poppy New Order track from Dad's record collection to banish ghostly prowlers. I probably just sounded scared, but began warbling that I felt so extraordinary.

I shut up after wailing a chorus about the morning sun. Even the wind had been silenced. The sky was a darker blue. An urge to run burned my legs. But instead I edged forwards, watching the bumpy ground. Time to fling one final stone and watch its long fall.

I picked out a silver birch tree a few steps from the dreadful edge. It was level there — an earthy shelf over the precipice. I grabbed a shard of slate. The wind blew up quickly so I let its first wave pass. When the air was calmer, I curled my left hand round the silver trunk. It was gnarled and crumbly.

Twisting almost right round, I let fly. A full body swerve. I launched the sliver of slate. The wind whipped in behind. My left hand slipped. I stumbled. All the weight on my right leg. My arms flapped wildly. I couldn't balance. I felt blindly for the tree. The dark sky swam. The quarry swirled like a black hole. My legs crossed. A blowy blast from all sides. My arms over the very edge.

Then came a sudden surge backwards. I felt uplifted, like a rush of wings. Now I was twice my height. I was leaving earth. The grim quarry faded. My thumping head felt another's heartbeat. Blood pounding on blood. I was dropped a level and lowered to my feet.

I spun round, hands up in defence. My legs buckled, leaving my forehead cushioned on a strong stomach.

My fingers rested there, then moved up in wonder. I arched my neck back, then further back. My gooseberry eyes must have ballooned.

Finally I found the face of my rescuer. It wore such crazy features that my breath rattled. My chin scraped on a thick leather belt. My head skewed back again, to see right up. A peaceful smile shone down at me.

I believed the top of this great being to be almost among the clouds.

TWELVE

His weird brown hat caught my gaze first. It was large with a wide, round rim. It looked warm and woolly and was made of soft felt. The sides and top were a bit punched in. From under it poked strands of bright hair, like stalks of corn.

His narrow face had the look of a strange puppet's. Red stuff was rubbed roughly into the cheeks. Dark lines were inked around the eyes. The same black marks were over the golden eyebrows. And also above the red lips, like a mock moustache. It was hard to guess his age under all that colouring, but his fair skin was firm and young. Late teens, probably, but most late teens I knew didn't grow to this size.

His right shoulder jutted up as if lifted onto a peg. He wore brown overalls cut at the knees. Below these were leggings of black and white hoops. Then came thick socks in heavy black boots.

As I knelt there, he backed away slowly and spoke

up. His voice was gentle, northern and slow.

'Saved . . . you. Aye? Did . . . save your life?'

I nodded, breathing deeply to try and settle. His eyes were bright blue even in the dusty dullness. Then he turned his great back on me, one shoulder sticking higher. His big brown overalls faded off into the wasteland. I just caught his voice again.

'Saved summat . . . one time. Tell 'em. Tell 'em . . . when they come.'

I didn't know if he was talking to me, or himself. From a distance I could now guess his height. My dad stood just under six feet. That made this guy somewhere around seven and a half feet. And slender with it, but I'd no doubt his limbs were strong. I'd felt the easy way he'd lifted me like a toddler.

My knees wobbled as I stood. I cast a look at the gusty void behind. I felt it sucking at me like a swamp. A chill wind whispered across its empty distance. The faintest of moons hung frostily over the far forest. It was quarter to five.

I stepped away, down onto firmer ground. The skyline was hazy red above smoky ridges. My lanky lifesaver sat on a fat rock, a stone's throw away. He was facing the far-off hills. His voice echoed in the twilight as he pointed at the stunning horizon.

'Look!' he said in awe. 'Just look . . . *look*!'

Then he turned and stared with his painted face. I smiled weakly and held up a hand. As I walked closer he took off his broad hat. He laid it in his lap. I sat shyly on the edge of his boulder, knowing this gangly strongman could crush me to dust. The two of us were alone in the dusky wilderness.

Then he spoke like a demanding child. 'Ain't scared of thee,' he said. 'Saved you back there.'

I looked at his brown felt hat. Little mushrooms were growing in the deep, wide rim. A few scraps of leaf and seed were also trapped.

'Yeah,' I breathed out. 'You did. Cheers for that.'

He laughed in loud gulps. I thought he was choking.

'Cheers!' he cried loudly. 'Get pissed, yeah?'

He grunted with laughter and waved his blond head around. I stared at the crazy disguise marks on his narrow face. Those rough red cheeks and thick black lines.

'Sure,' I said. 'And . . . by the way, I'm Glenn.'

'Glenn what?' he said quickly. 'Glenn, Glenn. Glenn what?'

'Glenn Jackson. Who're you?'

He grabbed his hat and placed it over his face. He held the battered top tightly and spoke softly into it.

'What?' I said, leaning over. 'Didn't get that.'

He slid the hat down until his rosy lips were free.

He mumbled something, then hid his face again. A high humming buzzed in his throat.

'Harlequin?' I said. 'Did you say Harlequin? Or Harly something?'

The buzzy hum stopped. He nodded, snorted and shook his yellow hair.

'Yeah?' I asked. 'I wasn't sure if you said two names. Or just one.'

He shook his fair straggly hair again. He sneezed enormously into the brown hat, then laid it aside.

'Har-le-quin,' he said, as if trying out the name. 'Harrr-lequin.' He giggled like a kid.

'Right,' I said, scratching my spiky scalp. 'Is that all? Just Harlequin?'

He gazed at the ramshackle rocks all around. Then he looked hard at me with wild blue eyes. They were never still, as if in some awful panic.

'Got cheese,' he said. 'Cheese 'n' bread for tea. Nowt else.' He flicked at the mushrooms growing around his hat.

'Oh,' I said. 'So, like, do you live nearby?'

He raised a hefty arm and pointed a long finger. 'There,' he said. 'In that one.'

I followed his line over the flinty landscape. Now I could make out a tumbling house of slate, about fifty metres off. I hadn't spotted it before. It blended in with all those other foggy chunks. Its four walls were standing, but the nearest side was crumbling. Timber beams poked out of the roof.

Harlequin stood up, letting me marvel at his loftiness. He stretched out his arms, gazing at fiery clouds of red and gold.

'Look!' he said. 'Oh look, Glenn Jackson. Just look!'

But then his body went stiff. He stood stock-still. His head went right back, his eyes racing over the orange-black sky. He made a pitiful moan. He lunged across to a boulder and clung on like a giant leech. His baggy body trembled.

He whined feebly. He waved at me to get down. I frowned back as if to ask why. An instant later and I knew.

I saw the fighter plane the second I heard it. A sleek brown blur. A shock of wings. A scudding rip-roar of jet. I stared up as if in a dream.

Then came the steely screaming. Then the howling thunder. All the heavens were left quaking. This metal monster scorched over like a rocket. Its pelting engines rattled the earth. I crouched quickly, hands over my ears. I heard Harlequin shriek, even in such a racket.

The fighter was nearly out of sight. A sonic echo

burst from the clattered clouds. The jet zoomed into the distance to swoop and swerve above dark hills.

The din faded to a drone. I got up and ran over to Harlequin. His grubby face was pressed onto the big rock. He pulled the brown felt hat over his ears.

I touched his right shoulder bone, sticking up like a stump.

'Harlequin?' I said softly. 'You OK? It's gone.'

He breathed a quiet reply: 'They see me?'

'It's gone,' I said again. 'I doubt anyone saw you. Why?'

He put a hand round his crotch and grabbed himself.

'I should go,' I said, edging away.

Harlequin peeled his body off the slate crag. He stretched back to his grand height and gazed up. I trod quickly over the quarry's debris. I heard Harlequin following a few steps behind. I felt a lurch of panic. I ran to the tree-swing and turned round. He was beside me in four strides.

'Thanks, Harlequin,' I said nervously, 'for saving me. Reckon I was a goner.'

His blue eyes flicked about, under inky black lines.

'Heard you sing,' he said. 'Sing again, you, when y'come back.'

I nodded and went hurriedly down the rugged

road. Harly's boyish northern voice came with me.

'Saved . . . your life,' he called. 'Tell 'em . . . if they come. If they find me.'

I didn't look back. My mind and guts were churning with delayed shock. My legs gave way as I tried to run.

I went by a row of dark old stone cottages. These would have housed the tough quarry workers in times past. Now they shine from tourist brochures as holiday homes.

Then came the grim rumble of that fighter jet returning. Not so close this time, but its full throttle still rattled my ribs. I watched it dart over. A skimming brown arrowhead. War in the heavens.

I turned to check on Harlequin, who squatted by a stout tree. Then his body began to fold in on itself. He ducked his head way down below his middle. The arc of his back looked all springy. His legs and knees tucked up tight. His left arm folded everything in. With his right hand he pawed the earth, spinning himself around like a ball.

He waited for the uproar to fade. Then he slowly untwisted and bounced up like some nifty acrobat. His long legs lolloped off, back into the drabness beyond.

THIRTEEN

A quick recce in Torbeck village, down a sloping road, found my new school. It wasn't much bigger than the science blocks at my old Burnley comp. A green sports pitch lay beside it.

Back up the lane, by a quiet crossroads, was a wooden bench with arms of white stone. A group about my age were crammed around it. They went silent as I passed. I smelled fag smoke and felt several gazes follow me.

And near the rows of council houses I saw the lad from yesterday who'd cycled by looking scowly. Streetlights picked him out clearly. He came towards me in the dusk on his bike again. His knees were still pointed out wide. His rusty head bobbed as he chewed hard on gum. He gave me an eyeball stare. Then he picked up speed and tried a wheelie. He was almost past me when he tried again. This time the back tyre skidded. The front one reared and the prat went crashing off.

Before I could call out he'd got up. He looked at me

and gave a dark mutter. Shoving his burly body back on the seat, he rode off slowly. He shot a hard glance back at me. Then he raised his arms like a trophy winner, his black T-shirt flexing with muscles.

I gave him a nickname on the spot. Beefwits. It seemed to fit. Beefwits — thick and bullish. I grinned and went indoors.

Dad was at the bottom of the stairs, his right hand over the phone. 'They rung off,' he said. 'Number withheld.' He gave a sleepy smile and slogged upstairs.

'Dad,' I said. He stopped, one hand on the banister, his back to me. 'So when's Mum turning up? I start school tomorrow. She was gonna iron my new uniform and check my stuff and . . . and . . .' I flung my arms wide in despair.

What else could I say? She was going to calm me down before my new life began. She was going to make everything happen on time and in order. Everything Dad could hardly do for himself right now, let alone for me.

'She'll be gone a while, Glenn,' Dad said. The claw of panic inside me bunched into a pounding fist. 'Blame her if you're feeling scared. I'm scared too.' And he went on up to his room.

The house felt cold. The heating hadn't been sorted properly yet. As I lay on the saggy sofa, two pencils bent in my back pocket. I must've left my little sketch-book at the quarry's edge when I flirted with near-death.

I did what I always did when I was upset, and got a large pad from my room. On one page I drew Harlequin's freakish face. The narrow cheeks, rubbed with red and inky dark marks. A golden shock of hair. That big felt hat with little things growing around it. And then his crumbling stone house. He had to be kidding about living there. Most likely he was just a weirdo travelling around.

I stroked my drawings of him. Such a big lump and yet he'd looked so full of doubt and fear. If Mum was here I'd have told her about it and we'd have gone to talk gently with him. It crossed my mind that he was on the run from something. An escaped crook, even. I checked on Dad's road map of the area and finally found a prison in a place called Haverigg, about twenty miles off. I'd ask around at school and see if anyone knew of a breakout.

This was a choice I could hardly take by myself. Did I risk wasting police time on a freaky stranger just passing through, or make a call and stop someone getting nobbled? I was about to run upstairs and let Dad choose when the ceiling banged, giving me a right start. Dad was throwing stuff around in a fit. I left it alone and got drawing again to think things through.

I doodled a sketch of Beefwits. His chubby cheeks and chin dotted with ginger stubble. The short hair and rubbery lips. I gave him a pair of horns, and a ring through the nose. A bull on a bike.

I leafed back through some old work. Burnley pictures mainly, of burned-out shops after the riots. I'd sat on the kerb across from a ruined pub, using charcoals to get the smoky effect of scorched walls. Then a baldy old copper had moved me along.

'It's not a bloody campfire,' he'd said. 'You're on a crime scene. Bog off and spray some graffiti.'

I didn't need to spray any. The smashed Burnley bus shelters had plenty from all social sides. PAKI POX . . . WHITE DYNAMITE . . . WHITEY SCUM . . . BLACK POWER . . .

I remember the first night of rioting. Some skinheads had bricked the home of a pregnant Asian woman. In response, local gangs turned their patch into a 'white no-go zone'. In the city centre an Indian taxi driver was badly mauled. As night fell, petrol bombs were hurled like primitive grenades. The sky turned a violent orange. Cars exploded; the police were pelted. Pub and shop windows were shattered.

Tension still smouldered the next evening. Sooty smoke drifted about like dirty fog. And on Bedlam Street something happened that would change my life.

Bedlam Street looks like it sounds. A narrow road with shabby houses built a century ago. The front doors open into the street. There are no scraps of garden, front or back. Black bin bags squat on the pavement like beggars. All day those plastic sacks are slashed open. Thieves rake through the rubbish for stray credit cards. Rats pick over the rotten remains of leaking takeaway cartons.

This was where a white gang had kicked off the havoc. Now it was the heart of the 'no-go zone'. But one man didn't know this: a man from the council. He strolled along Bedlam Street, strumming an air guitar, singing softly. He sang that catchy Asian fusion thing, *Brimful of Asha*, about movie scenes, movie screens and the magic of old vinyl.

He was going to report on a family's rotting walls. But he didn't reach their front door. He never got to check on dry rot. All he got was a kicking. He stumbled home and bled in the kitchen sink. His tough teddy-boy face had got cut up.

He was my dad, Nick Jackson; didn't care about skin colour as long as the music was good. He was a bruised and bloody mess. But his tidy quiff had stayed well gelled. Hardly a hair out of place.

Dad was in tears and wanted Mum, but she'd been working late shifts back then. We seemed to see less of her. She used to cuddle up with Dad on the sofa.

Now she mostly sat on her own, staring at the drawn curtains.

I looked back at my sketches of her. There was one I'd done two weeks before we moved. Mum had hardly known I was around. She'd sat at the kitchen table, left hand under her chin. A CD was playing by the cooker. Marc Almond crooning, 'Say Hello, Wave Goodbye', his voice all camp and heart-broken. Mum's curvy blonde hair was drab and pale. I could see her from the living room and worked quietly. I drew what I saw, but seeing it again now made me shudder. The face and slumped body of someone in pain. Someone toying with leaving their family? Maybe she'd been thinking of Ray. Maybe that night at the cinema had been when they finalized plans for leaving.

Dad heated some dull soup for tea. I made cheese toasties. I caught my reflection in a mirror, looking very white.

'You worried about new school?' Dad asked. 'Wanna talk things through?'

I slurped lukewarm tomato broth and shrugged. 'Be fine,' I said, with a confidence I hardly felt. 'Looks dead small compared to the Burnley comp.'

Dad snapped a toastie and yellow cheese drooped out.

'You be all right, Glenn?' he asked. 'Going there on your own? I could come with you.'

I nodded. 'No . . . I'll be fine. What can go wrong in a puny place like this?'

I was woken in the night by a thin shriek. It wasn't a dream. It kept coming in shrill squawks. There was a window on the right of my bed and I pulled the curtains apart. A screech owl sat perched on the sill. I jumped as it flew away, silver-brown and ghostly. It landed on next-door's fence, giving a mournful wail. Beyond it the black hills made bumpy shadows.

I got into bed and lay listening. I thought of Harlequin, screaming below that fighter jet, hugging a grey boulder like a crying child. I closed my eyes, but his painted face filled the darkness. Then came that gentle stumbling voice.

'Saved . . . your life. Tell 'em . . . if they come. If they find me.'

FOURTEEN

Dad was hogging the bathroom next morning. I saw him trim his neat sideburns. He got shaved, splashed on something pongy, then brushed back his quiff.

I looked at myself in the mirror, in my new uniform of black and blue. I left the glinting studs in my ears and moussed up my light hair. I had an official letter to hand in. I'd looked up the school's website back in Burnley. There were 350 pupils. My Burnley comp had 1500.

Dad was driving to visit a job centre in the nearby town. He wore a red denim jacket, blue jeans and cherry Doc Marts. He looked better now, apart from a sadness in his brown eyes. The fresh air made them water as we stepped outside.

Woodsmoke and mountain mist curled up cosily. My nose tingled. I followed small groups of kids past the bus shelter, Henderson's shop and the garage, then down the sloping road. Farmland stretched out green and brown for miles, beyond the school playing field.

A new housing estate stood across the way. A long bus pulled up, letting out a sullen straggle of children.

Then came Rembrandt bear's friendly saviour. My heart pattered. She was walking down towards me, black hair all wild in the sunny breeze. She nudged her old granny glasses up. Her blue blouse looked crumpled. Linking arms with her was Lavinia again. Lavinia's long brown hair was glossy and sleek. Her narrow face was really pretty, but with no flick of warmth. She stared coldly ahead, dragging the other girl just behind.

They couldn't be sisters, I thought. Friends maybe, though Lavinia looked well in charge.

I waited at the school gates as they passed. I smiled at Rembrandt's helper. She smiled back quickly, then stumbled. Lavinia pulled her along, speaking in a tired voice.

'Laura,' she said, 'you really shouldn't . . .'

I couldn't hear the rest. But I knew the girl's name now. Laura. Laura. I whispered it, watching her cross a tarmac area to the main school block.

Thump! Someone shoved me in the back. I jerked forwards with a gasp. Turning round, I saw Beefwits. The pavement was crowded with kids. A blur of jumpers and jackets.

Maybe it was a game: a sort of ritual welcome. Beefwits was bulky and untidy, his trouser legs rolled into odd socks. I wouldn't be a coward and just take this. I stepped up and shoved him back. A car crept by, the driver still belting up. Beefwits went heavily backwards, tripping off the kerb. He fell onto the car's boot, slid off and thumped into the road. His big backside took the weight. The car brakes groaned. So did Beefwits. The driver jumped out; a man with long black hair. Everyone gathered around. Beefwits reared up slowly, looking at his cut hands.

'Jesus, you thick lot,' said the man. He looked like a failed rock star. 'You all right, kidder?'

Beefwits nodded his rusty head. I heard intakes of breath behind me.

'What the hell . . . ?'

'What happened?'

'God . . . see that?'

'What *happened*?'

'Who's he? He new?'

The driver shook his long thatch of greasy hair. He caught my eye as he got back in and pulled away. Beefwits shambled off with some younger lads. He turned back at me for a long look, bumping into a dustbin.

My face was blazing. I spun round as if ready for the next challenge. No one came forwards; they just mooched off and looked at me like I was a freak. My heartbeat was up and running. I was isolated. I wanted to be Harlequin's height and go wild at everyone, hurling them over fields and mountains. Instead I trembled all the way to the school office. I handed in my letter and got a timetable. I looked blankly at its grid of names and numbers, my hands still shaking. Then I wished my dad had come with me, and felt the first flash of hate at my mum.

Every class I went to had one empty double desk.

'You'd better sit there,' each teacher said. 'Next to Barry Crookes. Except he's not here today. Where is Baz, by the way?'

'Off.'

'Gone to get new ears fitted.'

'Leave it. He's seeing a specialist.'

'Special case.'

'Special head case.'

Whoever this Baz was, it sounded like he didn't belong either. Seems I'd be lumbered with a misfit from the start.

I was mostly in Laura's classes and Lavinia was always beside her. Then I realized they had the same surname: Delaney. So they were sisters. I stared in surprise, 'cos they could hardly be twins. Lavinia was all posh and pushy with silky bronze hair. Laura looked sweet and scruffy, with holes in her dark blue tights, and hair that hadn't seen scissors in ages. Lavinia stared back, her narrow freckled face like stone. She whispered to Laura, who looked right and caught my eye.

Mr Brewin was watching all this. Trouble Brewin. He had the build of a retired boxer, and sharp grey hair. I heard he'd been fearsome twenty years ago, back when teachers got away with anything. Trouble Brewin had once held some lad out of a top-floor window by his ankles. Someone who never made V-signs at Brewin from the bus again.

Now the once-tough teacher was flabby and wheezy. He drove to the next village each lunch time for cigars and brandy. But his globby eyes could still become fire-balls. They burned into Lavinia as she hissed something at Laura.

'Words for the wise, Miss Delaney?' sneered Brewin. 'Or just more tittle-tattle?'

Lavinia gave him the hardest look she dared, then dropped her eyes. Trouble Brewin flicked at his brown tweed jacket. His voice was rigid as a clenched fist.

'You don't look a happy girl,' he rumbled, circling Lavinia. 'Bound fast in misery and iron! Isn't that what the prayer book says?'

The room grew hushed. Heads bowed low. Trouble Brewin was up for it, but there were no takers.

'Where's Baz Crookes today?' he growled, prowling

around. Obviously this Baz bloke was rarely away if his absence caused such comment.

'Not in, sir.'

'Needs new radars fitting.'

Brewin kicked someone's chair. 'Shut it, Gilbert. Your own ears don't work too well, judging by that last homework.'

I kept my head down, studying the general misery of maths. The room went very quiet for ten minutes, until a gradual snuffling noise took up. It became a murmur of stifled sniggers. The sound was menacing when you were the new boy. Then came a girl's low moan of disgust from the back. I felt sure this was all directed at me. I raised my head to risk a look round, but all sneaky eyes were on Trouble Brewin. He stood with his back to us, looking through glass windows into the next room. It's where Miss Mellors taught history. She was fresh out of teacher training college. She was all chirpy and chubby like a rosy-cheeked dairymaid. Her golden brown hair was neatly layered and short.

Brewin stood watching her like a man possessed. Both hands were fiddling in his tight trouser pockets. He rolled his podgy hips like an old stud. I wondered how drunk he could be at this hour. Behind him, twenty kids were stuffing fingers down their throats or shaking heads in despair. The same girl groaned again, turning it quickly into a choky cough. My head stayed well down, doing battle with a jumble of figures.

Lunch time found me in the noisy canteen. I ended up sitting with bratty Year Sevens, having nobody to guide me. Beefwits was being loud at a corner table, eating like a cement mixer. He swaggered past, nudging my chair.

In class it was hard to take anything in. I sat alone by the ghost of this absent Baz. There were more jokes behind me about his new ears. Lavinia sat nearby, always nagging whispers at Laura. Beefwits romped in every corridor, his bull neck thrusting on broad shoulders. His gloomy gaggle of mates gossiped like fishwives.

Then it was half past three at last. A load of buses turned up to lug children back to the outlying areas. The nearest town of any size was twenty miles away. In between were acres of ploughed farmland and scenic villages. Babbling brooks running by old white houses. Herds of cows blocking roads in the morning rush hour. Sheep along the white lines, scarpering in panic at car horns. Dreamy green hills with their heads in white clouds. Purple-brown mountains.

I sat on my bed at home, feeling shattered. As the phone rang below, Dad picked it up that second. He tried taking it into the living room but the wire was too short. I heard his low voice and could feel the tension in it.

'No . . . of course I haven't said anything . . . Like what . . . huh? . . . What is there to say?'

A moment later he called me down. 'It's your mum,' he said, passing the receiver.

I grabbed it. The line was crackly. 'Mum! Where are you?'

'Hiya, love. How was your first day?'

'Oh, um, a bit crazy. So, where are you?'

'I'm just away for a short while. A bit of breathing space, you know? I just wanted to check how today went.'

'*Breathing* space? Right. Well, are you joining us this week?'

I heard some sniffling.

'No, not really, Glenn. I'll see you as soon as I can. There's, like, stuff to sort out . . .'

'Stuff? What stuff? Is it Booths being funny?'

Mum sighed. 'No . . . no one's being funny. Just promise me you're all right.'

'No, I can't. What's the problem? Look, Dad's here still.'

'It's OK,' Mum said quickly. 'It was really you I wanted, Glenn. I'll phone in a couple of days, love. OK? And I'll put something in the post for you.'

'What sort of thing?'

'Something nice. Love you, Glenn. Bye for now.'

I shoved the phone back and marched into the living room for some answers.

But Dad had put a record on really loud. Something dark and moody, with a doomy drumbeat. Then a hunted, haunting voice that sang of walking away in silence. Of confusion, illusion and masks of self-hate. I shivered at those heartbroken words, knowing the singer had hanged himself, aged twenty-three.

Dad scraped about in the kitchen. When he kicked the closed oven door I got changed and went out.

A knot of teenage girls hung around the wooden bus shelter. They watched me draw near, all in uniform still. A dumpy redhead muttered into the ear of a matchstick blonde. Whispering eyes were on me as I passed.

Val in the shop had been right. News didn't hang around long in this place. And I guessed they weren't dead fussy about the facts either.

FIFTEEN

I still owed Val the change from yesterday and took it into the shop.

'Hiya, Glenn,' she said, knowing my name now. 'I met your dad earlier when he came by. Told me all about you. Bit of an artist, I hear?'

'Oh, nowt much. I doodle.'

'That's nice. We get arty types on holiday here. Writers, photographers, telly people.'

I bought some chocolate. The bright shop lights gleamed on Val's blonde hair, all tousled like she'd just got up. I wondered how long Dad had spent in here. He must've noticed how much Val was like my mum, all shapely and welcoming. They even wore the same pale blue eyeshadow.

'Bye, Glenn,' she said. 'See you soon.'

I waved, biting a gobful of Twix.

In minutes I was back on the white pebbly path, heading away from the top of the village through woodland. October sunlight striped the hillsides with gold.

Rocks on the drystone walls wore mossy green wigs. Somewhere high above, a fighter plane bombed over. A rumbling rustle stirred the red-orange trees.

At the crossroads, where the trail ended, I met an old man with a gun. He wore rough brown working clothes. The rifle, with its long black barrel, dangled from a stiff hand.

He nodded at me. 'Howdo, lad,' he said. 'Are you just enjoying a bonny day?'

'I am that,' I said. 'Do you live near here?'

'Raight down theer,' he said. He pointed at a farm-house over the road. I'd seen it from the paths yesterday.

'On holiday, are you?' he said.

'No. Just moved up here from Lancashire.'

'Oh, I see. What road you on?'

'Err, can't remember. The council-house bit.'

'Right. So you'll know the Higsons?'

'Well, not yet. Only just got here.'

'What's your dad's name?'

'My dad? Oh, Nick Jackson.'

'Farmer, is he?'

'No. He is . . . was . . . a council worker. Helps people with housing problems.'

'Hmm. And what do they call you?'

'I'm Glenn.'

'How old are you?'

'Nearly fourteen,' I said, rubbing the back of my neck. How many more questions?

'Hmm. You'll maybe know my granddaughter. At the second school, are you?'

'Just started. Bit late in the term but that's how it goes.'

'Hmm. Spot of rain coming, I think.'

I looked up at the blue-grey sky. Light and dark clouds were shifting over each other like wrestlers.

'They call me Father Charlie,' the man said. His long purple nose was dinted and whiskery. 'Used to be a priest in me youth. Took up the Lord's work in farming.'

'Oh. Amazing,' I said. 'Can't believe it's raining — it's been so sunny.'

'Aye, well, if you don't like the weather round here, just wait a minute. It can change in a tick. Be seeing you now.'

'Bye.'

He strode off towards his brown and white farmhouse, down a rocky lane over the crossroads. As rain fell in spits I gave up on visiting Harlequin. If he was on the run he'd be gone, and no longer Torbeck's problem. I stared up the rising pathway that led to the bridge, the waterfalls and the distant slate quarry. I felt a pang of regret that I mightn't see Harlequin again, with his twisty body and weird way of talking. And he'd probably saved my life. That's some debt to owe a person, no matter if they're a bit screwy.

I headed back on the stony white trail through the woods. When it ended above the village, I didn't head straight down past the Co-op and off home. This time I trod over the cattle grid and slogged up another rough route. A rambling V-shaped valley lay before me. A mountain range blocked the horizon like the final frontier. Dwarfed by those great peaks above them was a little white youth hostel. I wandered up past marshy flatlands, and slopes that rose and dipped like a roller-coaster of bracken.

Then something caught my eye. A flashing flicker above the lumpy hills in front. I waited, and another flare flew up. It looked like a firework. Spatters of sparkling yellow melted away. Well, it was getting on for Bonfire Night and there was always talk of banning fireworks. Why not lug them into the mountains? I knew the big peak in the distance was called King's Cragg. It was over two thousand feet to the summit.

The drizzle turned heavier, so I turned and headed home. The rain eased off a bit back in the village. Some lads lounging in the bus shelter stared at me. Their faces were in shadow. One gave a low, dirty whistle. Someone sniggered like a smutty kid. An angry heat rushed over my heart. I picked up my pace and got home, slamming the door. I was ready to have things out with Dad about Mum. I needed her more than ever just then. Suddenly I was itching for a scrap, for someone to take everything out on.

But Val from the shop was at the kitchen table with Dad. They had mugs of tea. She'd popped in to show him how to get the heating system going. He hadn't a clue. He was telling her one of his mad stories from work. He had loads, about the crazy unhappy people he'd met in Burnley's council properties.

'There was one old couple, right, lived in an upstairs flat of this manky house. I went in one time to check on things. And they'd cut half a metre from the bottom of each door. You get it? Each door in the flat now had this great gap above the floor.

'I'm going, like, "What the hell . . . ?" But this mad couple just sat there, stuffed into saggy armchairs. Seems they'd been fighting over whose turn it was to let the dog in. Or out. It used to go mad, they said, scratching at the doors. Either when it was hungry or wanted letting out for a pee.

'So this bloke had hacked a quarter from each door with an axe. It made things dead draughty. But at least their dog was free to wander and this pair didn't have to get off their lazy arses. Honest, Val, you don't half get 'em. And the old woman even denied it all. She shrieked, "Can't you bloody council people sort the woodworm in our doors? Look how much they've eaten away!"'

Dad could do people's whining cranky voices well. He'd made a stab at stand-up comedy in pubs, but was crap. He was far better around the kitchen table, with mates and beers back in Burnley. That seemed an age ago already.

'You been out exploring, love?' Val said.

'Hey? Oh, just around. Found that old slate quarry yesterday. You been there?'

Val's blue eyes widened. 'You be careful,' she said. 'It's dead dangerous.'

'I know. I don't suppose . . . anyone lives up there, do they?'

'In that bleak place? God, they'd have to be desperate. Why, you seen someone?'

'What?' I was going red and thought quickly. 'No, I mean, I met someone on the way, called Father Charlie.'

'Oh, Charlie. Bet he had a gun on him. Brings it into the shop an' all.'

The phone rang. Dad jumped up and I followed casually, arms folded, in case Mum was calling. Dad only spoke briefly, then went back to Val.

'Job I enquired about,' he said. 'No luck.'

'Ah, never mind,' Val said. 'Something'll turn up. I'll keep me ears open.' She finished her drink and got ready. 'Best be off,' she said. 'Mike and the kids can't manage supper on their own. Thanks for the tea, Nick. Nice to meet you.'

'Cheers, Val,' Dad said. 'Call by any time.'

The front door shut after her.

'She's nice,' I said. 'Looks quite like Mum, don't she?'

'Does she?' Dad rubbed his nose. 'Wouldn't say so. You hungry?'

'Not really,' I said. 'Feel a bit churned up. Don't think I like this place much.'

'For God's sake,' Dad said heavily. 'Give it a chance. We've only been here five minutes.' He opened a local paper at the job section and sat down, hands over his ears. We hardly spoke all evening.

Dad had kept our mobile phone, meaning I'd no way of contacting Mum on the quiet. Later I left a blank envelope on the table for Dad, with a note by it saying: *Please put Mum's address on so I can write to her.*

It was still there the next morning, with no address.

On my way down the sloping school road, a tin can skidded by me. It had either been flung or kicked my way. I squashed it with a stamp, casting a warning look over my shoulder. Lavinia was hauling Laura off up ahead. Beefwits tagged along by them, his bull's arse wobbling.

In class I found that the mysterious Baz was back. The guy I'd be sitting next to now. And I saw where yesterday's naff jokes about him came from.

This Baz geezer had his brand-new ears on.

SIXTEEN

They were hearing aids, actually, not new tabs. Silver blobs in each ear, with a wisp of wire. He'd got the biggest lugs I'd ever seen. They really caught your eye, being wide open and well padded. He wore bright round glasses and was a bit on the skinny side. His brown hair was all tiny curls, pressed flat on his head.

'All right?' I said, slipping in beside him. 'I'm Glenn.'

'Yeah, I heard.'

'Oh? Who from?'

'Everyone. You're big news already.'

'Big news! Why? What've I done?'

'Pushed the village idiot onto a moving car. Annoyed the divine Lavinia by being new and not fawning all over her. *And* somehow got her in Trouble Brewin's bad books. And you've been seen drawing. Careful, mate, they still burn artists around these parts.'

Then Goofy Garner came in to take geography. Tall and awkward, with a sprig of dark hair and his big teeth sticking out. He was the butt of naff rabbit jokes. Baz told me that carrot bunches appeared on his desk at Christmas. His brown cotton tie was looped with a reminder to do something or other.

Goofy started banging on about Locality Studies. Then he got stuck into Northwest pollution. I heard something about the nuclear power stations near Morecambe.

'And they're known as . . . ?' Goofy finished. 'Eeerrgghh!' he gargled. 'Anyone?' He stared around in disbelief.

'Someone? Come on! Lavinia?'

She scratched her sparkling sweep of hair. Goofy tried elsewhere.

'Glynn? Glynn?'

I caught Goofy's eye. He was looking at me.

'It's Glenn,' I muttered. 'Erm . . . I think they're Heysham "A" and "B".' I only knew 'cos we'd been on a trip there from Burnley comp.

'Heysham "A" and "B",' agreed Goofy. 'Thank you, Glynn. Wake up, dozy people, we discussed this last week. Crikey me. Crikey! And, Lavinia, aren't you doing your project on nuclear power?'

A touch of scarlet hit Lavinia's face. She was at the table on my left with Laura, who sat the closer to me. Lavinia glanced across with something like hurt in her eyes, her mouth drooping. I tried smiling in sympathy, but I tried too hard and smiled too broadly. I guess it looked like I was laughing. Laura snuck a faint grin at me. Lavinia elbowed her in the ribs.

'Eerrgghh! Lavinia!' gurgled Goofy. 'Don't treat your sister like that.'

Lavinia looked up, her narrow face a glassy blank.

'*Half*-sister, sir,' she said clearly. 'My half-sister. Laura's adopted . . . though I'm quite normal.' She patted Laura's wild black hair with a book. 'Poor little orphan,' she said. 'But I'll keep you safe.' Her eyes darted my way again.

Goofy stared at her, gob opening slowly. A sliver of saliva dripped from his bucky top teeth.

'I think everyone knows Laura's history, thank you,' he said coldly.

But everyone didn't know. It was aimed at me. Maybe in Lavinia's mind I would now think less of Laura and more of her. But she was wrong there, as I felt orphaned myself with Mum suddenly gone to ground. I smiled at Laura's batty glasses, like she'd nicked them off some old dear. Her head was bowed but I saw how red her cheeks were. She looked ashamed and shy at what Lavinia had said. With a fist she smoothed a trace of wetness from her cheek.

*

In a corridor at break, someone whistled as I passed. A low warbling whistle. I turned and met a fog of blank faces. Heads went into a huddle as Trouble Brewin bulldozed by. I walked off, heart thumping, past wall posters giving advice on drug abuse and depression.

I hooked up with Baz out on the green sports pitch. It was warm enough to sit on the dry grass. Baz's voice was quite posh for so far north.

'So, has anyone offered to be your buddy?' he said.

'My what?'

'It's a system here. Say if I befriend you, like, be your mate 'cos you're new, then you can put me up for an award. A special "buddy" prize.'

'Oh. Well, no one's offered to buddy me, or even talk to me. Guess you get the job.'

'Tops,' said Baz. He fiddled with a silver hearing blob and slipped one out when he saw me looking. 'Totally deafo without 'em,' he said, popping it back.

I looked at the little groups of blue uniforms dotted around. Laura and Lavinia were lolling with a few others. They all gawped at me, then lowered their eyes. Only Laura held my gaze, until Lavinia tugged her chin.

A fighter jet's metallic rocketing rattled the air. I shaded my eyes to follow it, but in seconds it was over a distant valley.

'What's with all the war planes?' I asked.

'Oh, they practise mountain flying round here,' said Baz. 'They're military jets . . . Tornadoes or American Strike Eagles. Come bloody low.'

'They zip over that old slate quarry,' I said. 'I was there t'other day.'

'Right,' said Baz. 'Don't jump in the lake down at the very bottom. It's deadly. Divers have died of the bends coming back to the surface.'

'Jeez,' I said. 'That makes the whole pit about . . . three hundred metres deep.'

'At least,' said Baz. 'Come on, there's the bell. You're not with me next lesson, but I'll be a good buddy and show you around.'

There was no sign of Baz at lunch time. Perhaps your buddy got a lunch break. So I took a sketchpad and walked out, turning right at the school gates. I went by a splashing stream beside the empty road. I stood on a bridge, watching water gurgle and glitter; I followed its journey. The midday sun was lovely – a real warm Indian summer. Clogging leaves lay thickly in the stream.

There was a tarn, a small mountain lake, where the road and river ended. A pebbly shore ran around it, with yellowing trees on all sides; in the water's glassy reflection they stood upside down. Orange leaves, all puckered, slithered at my feet.

A few ducks came to nose around. One of the adults fixed a sideways beady eye on me. A black dot in a yellow socket. Goldeneye! Its back feathers were dark brown; the wing ones lighter. I spotted a patch of red among them. None of the others had this marking.

Goldeneye squatted in front of me, still as a clay model. I sketched it with sweeps of pencil and crayon. Ducklings nudged it, but Goldeneye sunbathed and never budged. Its few red feathers were like stripes of honour.

I lost all track of time and had to hurry back. I was late into my history class. A sneering whistle broke from the back of the room. Another echoed it near the front like a sinister bird song. I caught Laura's eye and she winked at me. I smiled big time at this. Miss Mellors looked in sympathy at the flustered new boy, her cheeky round face fringed with blonde highlights. Trouble Brewin ogled her from the next room like a peepshow nerd.

After school I saw Baz in the IT room. He was on some website, with stars and planets filling the screen. I stood behind him.

'See you,' I said.

'Bye,' said Baz, not looking round. My buddy had

clocked off. His glinting glasses fixed on the computer. His wide waggly ears twitched.

Dad wasn't at home and it felt horribly quiet indoors. The blank envelope I'd left out on the kitchen table still hadn't been touched. So I filled in the address myself. I wrote:

TO MY MUM,
MAYBE IN ENGLAND,
POSSIBLY EUROPE (WHO KNOWS?!),
THE EARTH,
THE END

I left it where Dad could see, then put on a red running top and tied my trainers tight. I was ready to try to find that boyish giant again. I needed any friendship just then. And if he wanted help then I owed him. I knew the way home well enough now in case I felt any threat.

I went out quickly, eyes down on the grotty pavement. The phone rang inside as I was at the garden gate. By the time I'd got my key in the lock it had stopped. I went in and jabbed 1471, but the number was withheld.

Going past Henderson's, I almost bumped into Laura and Lavinia coming out.

'Hi, Glenn,' said Laura, lugging two heavy shopping bags.

'Bye, Glenn,' said Lavinia, tugging her half-sister by the elbow.

SEVENTEEN

F ather Charlie touched his cap to me. He was in a
field over the crossroads, by a few caravans. A rifle
rested in the crook of his arm. He watched me all the
way up the rutted path.

Twenty minutes later I was back in that sombre
desert. The disused quarry was like a gaping hellhole.
Harlequin's hut looked a crumbling ruin. The tree-
swing log swayed in a sunny breeze. Silver slate and
stone lay everywhere. The land beyond finally dipped
into a valley, with King's Cragg's ridges on the skyline.

I trod carefully to the tumbledown shelter. A rotting
wooden door stood half open. I tapped on it.

'Harlequin? Harly? You there?'

The names of old visitors were carved scratchily on
slate walls: BIX FROM PRESTON. MERLIN. RICHMOND
IRREGULARS N. YORKS. DAN — BLACKPOOL.

I looked inside the dark dwelling. Faint daylight
shafted through the slanting roof and a square hole in

the far wall. Sheep droppings and brown apple cores littered the muddy ground. I found a few old blankets and a roll of kitchen towel. Stuffed into a high nook was a scrunched-up newspaper. The roof's beams were charred as if by fire.

I poked around for clues to Harly's life. I rummaged through the blankets and kicked the rubbish away. Nothing. No scraps of letters or crumpled photos. Maybe he'd already headed off in search of a better hideout. Cold shadows made me shudder, so I went outside and round the back. And here the mass of rubble had been strangely arranged. Mounds of grey were piled into odd forms.

I walked slowly around them, making a few sketches. They showed the shapes of animal limbs and bodies. Lumpy legs and blunt heads. All made with shreds and shards of slate. The figures were quite big: about the size of real sheep. Thickly built from chunks and slabs, they lay at stony rest.

I remembered my other sketchpad that I'd left above the quarry. I found it by the silver birch I'd slipped from, before Harly had grabbed me away.

Then I saw him, stalking up the rickety road that I'd come along. I ran into the dusty clearing and watched him loom large. He wore the same broad brown hat and mucky overalls. His black boots crunched. All around him shuffled a flock of sheep. Two in front, three on each side and several behind. Their dainty trots kept pace with Harlequin's heavy steps. They followed him meekly, like gentle guards. Whenever I'd gone near any of them they'd barged away.

I kept my distance until Harly saw me and smiled, pointing to his derelict hut. The sheep turned and dawdled back the way they'd come, as if discharged from duty.

Harly kicked open his creaky door, bending nearly double inside. When I got there he was kneeling on the tatty rugs.

'Been hunting,' he said. 'Saw some owd bugger with a gun. Got this from his house.'

With a grin, he pulled out a loaf in brown paper. Then a slab of cheese in white cloth.

'Didn't he see you?' I asked. 'I mean, you being quite big an' all.'

Harly shook his head rapidly. 'Can make myself small,' he said. 'Like this.' And he knelt on the floor. He arched himself backwards like a willow branch. Soon his spine was over the backs of his legs. His thighs were dead straight. He kept stretching and twisting until his head rested just above his ankles. He was all boxed up into a rough rectangle shape. I never once heard his bones creak or crack.

'Hellfire!' I said. 'Where did you learn that? You a circus type?'

Harlequin slowly released himself and sat straight. 'Never learned nothing,' he said. 'You do it.'

'No way,' I laughed. 'And be careful if you're . . . borrowing stuff from Father Charlie's house. He might take a shot at you.'

Harlequin covered his mouth at this and stooped back outside. I saw him rubbing soft mud on his forehead. He pulled his hat down low.

I stood in the broken doorway. 'It's OK,' I called out. 'I'll not tell anyone.'

Harly didn't answer. He walked slowly around those animal shapes of rough rocks. I heard him whisper but couldn't catch a word. He went on his knees, then put his head to the smoggy slates. He pressed an ear against them and lay very still. Shaggy straws of blond hair poked out from under his hat.

Flat on his tummy, he reached both arms forwards as if grasping for something. Then his legs went out wide, in perfect level angles, like doing the splits. It looked inhuman. It looked impossible. But he did it as easily as me stretching out my arms. He lay with spread-eagled legs, quite content, in a position that would've been agony for anyone else. His eyes were wide open as if he'd gone into a trance.

As I watched him in awe, something caught my eye. A firework again, fizzing red sparks into the dark blue twilight. Just like I'd seen last night — and from the same place. It came from the hills around King's Cragg, back above Torbeck village, two miles away. I kept watching as a yellow flash rose and fell in floating twinkles. A purple flare shot from the distant black ridges. It exploded with a faraway *phut!*

This was enough to stir Harlequin. He looked up to see the final flickers. With a heavy groan he clambered to his big feet. I let him dart past me into the shadowy shack. He stumbled out, holding something. I edged away, my guts all jittery. I made sure the road leading clear of the quarry was only a hundred metres off.

Harlequin stuck something to his right eye like a telescope. It was a thick tube of cardboard, maybe the inside of a tin-foil roll. He stood by a sheep-shaped mound of slate. He searched the smoky skies, tilting his head up and around. Then he jammed the cardboard roll to his left eye.

'Oh God . . . no,' he moaned. 'Bloody . . . Christ!'

I took two steps back, knocking a heavy stone with my heel. 'What is it?' I said nervously. 'Another fighter jet?'

He also moved slowly backwards, still scanning the heavens. His low voice had a despairing ache. 'They're here. Now they know. They'll have my guts.' He marched over to me with big strides, thrusting the brown tube my way.

'See!' said Harlequin loudly. 'You see, Glenn Jackson. Who's bloody there?'

I stared up at his muddy, marked face. His blue eyes were racing. He breathed a cloud of mist, his big body all shaky.

I slowly lifted his useless telescope to my right eye. Through the cardboard circle I had a dekko at the landscape beyond. I saw dusky outcrops of cold rock; banks of bushes turning crimson in the fading light. Closer by were two slender yew trees. Their foliage lay like orange tinsel on black branches. Bold autumn colours. But the fireworks display had stopped.

'There's nothing there,' I said gently, passing back the long roll. 'It was only a few fireworks. It's nearly Bonfire Night — people always let 'em off this time of year. Maybe they're banned in Torbeck.'

Harlequin sank to his knees, his head level with mine. He muttered into my face, his breath strong and stale. 'Did save your life, yeah? Glenn Jackson? Tell 'em if they come.'

He held my shoulders with immense hands. Glancing down, I saw scorch marks on them. I looked into his restless eyes. Dark pen lines made a second layer of eyebrows. Black above blond.

'Of – of course,' I stammered. 'I won't tell no one. But what's wrong? I mean, who wants you?'

Harlequin sprang up suddenly, giving me a start. I backed away but his face melted into a slow smile. His rosy lips parted, showing grubby teeth. His cheekbones lifted, moving red-brown blobs.

'Got supper,' he said, patting his overalls. 'Have some, yeah?' He reached out his hands as if I were to hold them.

Suddenly I was hurtling through the air. I came to rest on two hefty shoulders.

'Jesus!' I shouted, grabbing Harly's head as I swayed back. He gave a friendly squeeze on my thighs and held me tight. He was either gonna hike into the hills and cut me up, or just muck about like a mad kid. Whatever he did I couldn't do much about it. The nearest house, apart from empty tourist cottages, was Father Charlie's place about a mile off.

I felt how Harly's right shoulder jutted bonily, and moved my leg near his neck to avoid it. My limbs went loosely down his front.

'Hey, you wanna put me down now?' I said nervously.

Harly just clumped off over the rubble and then lifted me down beside a cold stream. I breathed out and watched him closely.

Harlequin rinsed his yellow hair in the running

water. Cupping his long hands, he drank deeply. He looked over at me, his narrow red face dripping.

'Ain't no flocks yonder,' he said. 'No sheep shit in river. Can drink.'

Wiping his hands, he took food from an overalls pocket. He broke the loaf and cheese in half and offered chunks to me.

'Oh, er, it's OK,' I said. 'I need to scoot home. Have my tea there.'

Harly stopped chewing and gazed at me with a creased brow. He stared sadly at the stream, his cheeks bulging.

'Perhaps . . .' I said. 'Just a bite then.'

He smiled and stuffed big hunks in my hands. He crunched an apple down in three gulps and slurped at the stream. I checked my watch.

'Soz, Harlequin,' I said. 'I've gotta run. Get home.'

'Got mum and dad?' he asked.

'Just my dad, at the moment. Mum's gone away.'

Harly gasped. 'She dead, Glenn Jackson?' he asked. He bit his fingers hard and chewed.

'No, not dead. Just away.'

'You go home. Find your mum, Glenn.'

I got up, blowing my chilly hands. 'I will,' I said. 'But what about you, mate? Tell me stuff about your family. You got a mum still alive? Your dad?'

He threw down his hat and put his head between his

pointed knees. His big hands went flat over his ears. 'Harly?' I said. 'Harlequin?'

He didn't move a muscle. My knees knocked with cold. I waited for two minutes then sloped away. Looking back, I saw Harly hurling stones into the stream. Each impact made a splashy explosion.

Near the quarry's menacing edge I turned again. Now Harlequin stood still, on a boulder, his back to me. A great gangly scarecrow in dark silhouette. The world was dusky and silent. Hunchbacked hills on the skyline were brown as old leaves.

Harly stood peering through the cardboard telescope like some ancient stargazer.

EIGHTEEN

Val was cashing up inside Henderson's, bathed in warm yellow light. In the foggy October evening the shop glowed like a lighthouse.

I walked on, past the wooden bus shelter. Its back wall was plastered with graffiti. Nothing like the racist muck in Burnley, just old messages about who fancies who, or what a tosser Benny is. A few shadowy figures were parked on the bench inside. Three orange fag tips glowed. Someone snorted like a snuffling pig as I went by. A snatch of twittery whistling followed. My fists tightened and my eyes watered. I picked up a lager can from the pavement and lobbed it back so it pinged off the shelter. That silenced the blabbers for a second.

Dad was crashed out on the sofa at home. His records were scattered about, some lying on their covers. He stared at the ceiling, hardly noticing me. I was all wound up, but hadn't the heart to pitch in with questions about Mum. It was well clear that something was wrong

between them and wasn't mending easily. Dad kicked
the couch's arm with steady thumps.

Slowly he pulled himself together and started making
a curry. Some yellow spice got brushed in his dark
brown quiff. I rubbed it with a tea towel.

'Hey, steady there, mate,' he said, smiling. 'This
hair's insured for millions.'

'Sticks out a bit round here,' I said. 'Don't reckon
Torbeck's ever seen the like.'

I went into the living room and sifted through the
albums. Some top music would perk Dad up and make
it easier to talk. I pulled out an album called *Blood &
Chocolate*. Elvis Costello. His mad speccy Scouse face
gaped on the back. Mum said it was one of the best
records ever. Rough romantic stuff, like punky cabaret.
I put it on loud to remind me of her. Dad came in
holding a big dripping spoon.

'Not that one,' he said firmly. 'Not just now. Maybe
summat else, yeah?'

I took it off and found one of our few classical things.
Vivaldi's *Four Seasons*. Some rebel violinist smirked on
the cover with a spiky haircut. The sparky melodies of
'Spring' gushed out. I got my smaller A4 sketchpad
and started drawing. This book was becoming a bit like
a diary. I began with Baz and his whopping tabs. I
ended with Harly and that crazy cardboard 'telescope'.

I drew a picture of me and him to scale, with my head tucked under his ribs.

Dad's curry was OK, if a bit hot. He ate quickly again as if wanting to avoid any chat, and played Radio One loudly in the background. I was too nervous of his moods now to start anything.

Later we watched a costume drama on TV. The phone buzzed once then stopped. When it rang again, Dad jerked awake and stumbled over to answer, but the caller hung up. They'd withheld their number again.

He curled back up in the comfy chair, eyes drooping. He wrapped both arms around himself. I turned off the TV and lights, then went for a bath. Dad slept and muttered by the gas fire's glow.

He didn't appear next morning until I was leaving. His quiff was flat, his cheeks bristly, and yellow flecks crusted his tired eyes. A long-sleeved shirt was creased and sweaty from where he'd slept in the armchair. There was no way on God's earth he'd be going out like that.

'Oh hell,' he muttered, yawning and shivering. 'Dozed off downstairs. You had breakfast?'

'Yeah,' I said, avoiding him. 'I better run. Tek it easy, Dad. Don't work too hard.' I slammed the door, feeling ashamed of everything about our family right then.

On the way to school I saw a poster pinned on a
telegraph pole. COUNTRY FAIR. I read the details below.
*Sheepdog Trials. Hounds Display. Ferret Racing. Cumberland
Wrestling.* It was being held on Sunday.

But this was Wednesday morning, with Goofy Garner
first thing. I got queasy with nerves in sight of the
school with all the ganging up against me. It felt like
every face on the buses pulling in was glaring. I got
into a mad muddle and went by the wrong classroom.
A Year Seven group cheered with laughter. I ran to the
next building and saw everything as a blind blank. It
all looked topsy-turvy. I pressed my face at glass doors
until I got the right one.

Goofy gurgled at me. 'Eeerrgghh . . . morning,
Glynn. Not too late to join us.'

'It's Glenn,' I muttered, hearing several sneers and
that stupid whistling again.

Goofy stared around. 'Eerrgghh, is there a
problem?' His buck-teeth chewed a lower lip. A yellow
Post-It dangled from his jacket pocket. He took it off
and read it.

'Aha. I've got to nip and see Mr Minor,' he said.
'Carry on from last time.' He gangled off, tripping on
a long lace.

'All right?' I breathed at Baz.

My buddy just nodded and got working. But voices

from behind soon kicked in at me. A girl's mocking tone first: Lavinia's.

'Why's he got a drawing pin in each ear?'

'Dunno.'

'What's wrong with his hair? Electric shock?'

'Must be. Seen his dad's Elvis wig?'

I looked round and saw Lavinia grinning gleefully. Her face snapped into sullen mode as I stared her out. She smouldered and couldn't hold my gaze. Laura sat silently, gnawing her thumbs nervily. Lavinia leaned back in her chair, whispering behind a hand. The room got noisy.

Then the door burst open. Trouble Brewin: grey and gruff as an old buffalo. He filled the frame, his eyes like chunks of melting ice. They homed in on Lavinia. She sat back straight, red-faced, with a small grin.

Brewin boomed slowly, like a funeral bell: 'Oh, don't smile, Lavinia. You might bite your tongue.'

He waited for the frightened giggles to pass.

'Where's Mr Garner?' he grunted.

'Back soon,' said Baz. 'He's meeting the head.'

Trouble Brewin eased out slowly, voice like a viper. 'I'll be right next door,' he said. 'I'm in with Miss Mellors.' No one dared choke a snigger at this and the room fell silent. I tried to work, but my hand went shaky and wrote a scribbly mess.

At lunch time I went looking for that Goldeneye

duck again. I found it nosing along Burnside Tarn's pebbly shore. Leafing back a few pages, I studied my first sketch. This time I coloured in the red feathers that shone from its grey plumage. I did a rough picture of brutish Brewin. I gave him a pair of long black jackboots. I had him stamping on Lavinia's head as she lay smiling up at him, her glossy hair splayed out.

At home later, the house was hot and stank of gas. I left the light switches well alone. Running into the kitchen, I felt a blast of heat. It came from the grill above the white cooker. A layer of silver foil crinkled on the toasting tray. The iron grill bars glowed boiling orange. They'd been on for hours, maybe since Dad had made breakfast. This meant he'd not been back down all day. I heard a dull shuffle from his room upstairs. I turned off the scalding grill and knocked open a stiff window.

Dad clumped about again. I hated him then, the useless, vain pillock. And my runaway mum. I pictured her all tarted up for smarmy Ray at the cinema that time, or maybe out now in some fancy restaurant. Or at a wine tasting for Ray's department at Booths, her nose stuck inside a posey glass, pretending to be expert. I kicked a table leg, knocking the local paper off the top. There was homework to be done, but this new house felt like a prison.

I didn't get changed, not caring if my uniform got filthy. Outside, I jogged up the pavement, past the staring school stragglers. Past Val in the shop, waving on the run. I didn't stop until those twin churning waterfalls were ahead. Sweating and panting, I stopped on the worn-out path high up. Treetops rose from the steep river valley, blazing blood-red and bright yellow. Orange leaves flamed, or fell to earth as burned brown.

Where the branches parted I could see the deafening water below. I heard someone trying to sing, like a child who knows a tune but no words. A vast naked figure stood on a ledge, way down under me. It waded into the wild stream like some ancient god calming the stormy seas.

NINETEEN

Harlequin's lofty pale body stood still, bashed by the noisy currents. He was up to his knees, letting a cold flood swash through his legs. His long bony back was facing me. His bum looked hairless and muscular.

I stood twenty metres above on the trampled path. If I kept going along it, I'd turn right onto the flat bridge built over an archway. The water burst through this tunnel, then crashed into free fall, split by solid rock.

Harly lunged out with splashing steps. Yellow hair fell down to his firm shoulders. A bone in the right one poked up, making him look lop-sided.

He went close to the freezing blast of the waterfalls. He raised his arms as if to challenge their power. Now the cascades looked a trickle of their normal torrents.

Harly bathed himself all over, giving squeals of joy. Then above the plunging din came a harsher sound. The metal screech and rumpus of a fighter jet. Harly must've heard it too. He flung himself at the soaking slab in front and hid under its downpour. He waited for two minutes before stumbling out, staring skywards. I saw him stagger as a heavy swell hit from behind. Then he lay floating on his back, happily drenched from all sides.

It made me shiver just watching. The wall of water came churning down from King's Cragg's peaks, where dusty snow settled all year round. To reach Harlequin it had flowed over miles of marbled rock. But he cared nothing for all this, flapping around in the raw river.

I stood like a silent guard above until he hauled himself out. Under his clothes was a grotty blanket from the shack. He dried himself briskly, rubbing his mop of hair. After dragging those old clothes on, he sat on a rounded rock. He took something from an overalls pocket. I leaned over the drystone wall to see better. Harly sat sideways on to me, down in the little gorge, but never looked up.

He held a pair of thick marker pens. With one he inked some lines over his eyebrows, then dotted his face. The other one coloured his red lips until they were deep scarlet. The same pen was used on his cheeks in rough circles.

He rose like some big machine starting up. As I leaned on the low wall, I dislodged a loose rock. It skipped off the edge then bounced sharply into the swirls below. I didn't wait for the splash but legged it away, ashamed of spying for so long. A quick scream of panic came from the surging valley.

I didn't stop running down the crumbling trail until I reached the crossroads. To my right was the woodland path back to Torbeck. Across the way was Charlie's farm, and the busy main road ran by it all. I put my hands on my knees and sucked heavy breaths.

'Howdo, lad. You had a scare?'

I stood up sharply. It was Father Charlie, pressed against the hedge. Behind him in a dipping field were some caravans and a small tent. He leaned forwards on a hooked shepherd's crook. A shotgun lay by his old boots. He tweaked his checked cap.

'Running away from summat?' he said. His eyes were cold and keen, either side of that purple nose with its hairy warts.

I sniffed back runny snot and breathed out. 'No, it's OK,' I said. 'Just, um, late for something.'

'Aha,' said Father Charlie. 'That's what the good Lord made clocks for, lad. To keep us on track and on time.'

'Right,' I said, forcing a smile. I tapped my wristwatch. 'Best get along then.'

'Thought you mighta seen summat,' said Father Charlie. 'Summat a bit scary, like.'

I tried holding his gaze but had to look away.

'No,' I said, feeling short of breath again. 'Just . . . choosing which mountains to sketch.'

'Hmm. Well, you be careful up yonder.'

'I will,' I said, hearing footsteps on the woodland trail.

'Now then,' said Charlie, looking past me, 'here comes my granddaughter. The light of my humble old life.'

Turning to the right, I saw Lavinia at the edge of the pebbly path. Her thin freckly face went red and stared at mine.

'Howdo, lass!' Charlie called.

'Hi, Grandad,' came a sweet reply. She wore a pink running top and clean white jeans. I backed away up the old road, towards the quarry again.

'Bye then,' I said to Charlie.

He nodded and bent to gather his gun. I walked rapidly uphill for a minute. Looking round, I saw the pair heading down to the farm, Lavinia clinging to Charlie's left elbow. His old shotgun lay half-cocked over the other. Lavinia glanced back at me from a safe distance, her face all pinched.

I waited until they were inside the farmhouse, then sneaked down there to edge past. Soft yellow lights were on in a front room. I saw Lavinia sitting by a coal fire.

In armchairs on either side were Father Charlie and
an old woman. Mrs Charlie, I guessed. She had long
silvery hair in a plait. They were both leaning forwards,
listening as Lavinia held court. No sign of Laura.

I wandered along Father Charlie's tractor trail,
gouged out by years of heavy wheels. A breeze got up
and blew a blizzard of leaves. I kicked big splashes of
them, like Harly wading in that wild stream.

Back home in Torbeck, Val stood by the kitchen sink
with Dad. Some tins of steamed pudding were on the
table: chocolate, raspberry, syrup.

'You like those, Glenn, don't you?' Dad said. 'Just
gone past their sell-by dates, but that means nowt. Val's
brought 'em from the shop for us.'

I picked one up, feeling my mouth water. I looked
at Val, who was like a warming sponge herself. 'Thanks,'
I said. 'I'm that hungry I could eat these now.'

'Been exploring again?' she said.

'Yeah,' I said, putting down the tin. 'Saw that Father
Charlie. Found out who his granddaughter is. Quite
a surprise.'

Val smiled slowly, as if knowing that I meant Lavinia.
From a few bits Baz had hinted at, and what I pressed
Val to tell me, I got something of Laura's history. She
was adopted, which Father Charlie never approved of.

Said it wasn't God's way to meddle with families. Charlie's daughter was called Janice Delaney and she was Lavinia's mother. It was her husband's decision to adopt Laura. His name was Ronnie but he'd passed away a few years ago.

He'd thought Laura would be a good playmate for Lavinia, who even at six had a stroppy streak. And their eldest daughter, Elaine, was at college by then.

Val dabbed a tear when she spoke about Ronnie Delaney. 'Ronnie never got on with Uncle Charlie, but he adored Laura,' she said. 'They got her when she was five or six. She's a bit of a lost soul really, now that Ronnie's gone. I'm not sure Janice took to the idea, but went along with it for Ronnie's sake. She'd never dream of sending her back though, and tries to do what's best.'

Upstairs later, I drew Laura the 'lost soul' again. I put her shy face inside a big purple heart shape. I added a twinkle on the glass of her old specs, then some red ribbons in her witchy dark hair. Then I drew myself: how I was feeling. The final portrait looked wild-eyed. It stared back angrily. My cheekbones were jutting. My top lip curled like a slow sneer. I coloured my light spiky hair in shadows.

Then I began some charcoal landscapes of the mountains around Torbeck, built up from rough sketches

I'd been doing. No matter if this village was mostly full of divs, it had some awesome scenery.

Finally, in my A4 diary pad, I did a picture of Harly under the waterfall. Naked with arms raised as if in prayer or sacrifice.

I shoved the sketchbooks into my school bag. It was Thursday tomorrow and I was down for an art class. Something to look forward to after all the recent shambles. I was due a break, right?

TWENTY

Baz followed me out at break, holding some raffle tickets. 'Can't believe Lavinia talked me into it again,' he said. 'I bought three strips for that MIND charity and three for this local youth club they're trying to build. She sold you some?'

'Not likely,' I said, stepping away to avoid Baz's clumsy walk. His big flat feet were like a kangaroo's. And he was taller than me, with pointy elbows. 'I gave her fifty pence on the first day we got here,' I said. 'We met by chance when I was looking round.'

'So I've heard,' said Baz. 'She reckons you came on to her.'

'What? She said that?'

'She did, though I know she ain't your type. Not right in the head since her old man died. Maybe mental nuttiness is inbred there. Sorry, shouldn't speak ill of the dead.'

We leaned on the school hall's red brick wall, munching crisps.

'What happened to Lavinia's dad?' I asked, searching the sports field for Laura.

'You don't know?' said Baz, licking salty fingers. 'Soz, I thought even you did by now. Ronnie Delaney hung himself just after his fiftieth birthday, three years back. Did it somewhere inside the house one night. Lavinia found him at breakfast time. Ever since then she's tried to be man about the house, I reckon.'

'God,' I said, dropping my crisps. 'God, I didn't know that. Poor Laura. It was the dad she was close to, wasn't it?' I felt a stupid lump wobbling in my throat.

'It was,' said Baz. 'Maybe Lavinia feels guilty over her old man's death. My mum says kids often do in such cases, even though they're not to blame. Rough on Laura too, as it was Ronnie who chose her for adoption. Sweet on that girl, aren't you?' said Baz. He picked up his little backpack.

'What?' I said, feeling a blush steal over me.

'I see everything,' said Baz. 'Crap ears, sharp eyes. Catch you later.'

He bundled off to the IT room, his big feet clomping and elbows thrusting. He looked like a twitchy old man.

Mrs Broughton took us for art. She was youngish with long, light brown hair. She wore yellow dungarees and red cloggy shoes. She was also heavily pregnant and kept dashing out to lie down, or drink mint tea.

We sat at easels and began sketching a still life. Mrs Broughton placed a bowl of apples on a table. Behind it was a vase of yellow flowers with purple hearts.

'Just draw what you see for starters,' she said. 'Look at the shapes and textures. Use colours if you want, or try in black and white.'

Lavinia wasn't with us but Laura was. She sat shyly on my left. I could sense her eyes flicking across to my work. I started on the wooden apple dish, sketching its wide rounded curves and grainy lines. Using my own charcoal crayons, I caught the lights and shadows of each wrinkly apple. Laura had stopped work by now and was watching me. I had to keep my hand steady then. I dabbed and smudged with my fingers to blend the shades. I only used colour once, to make a single flower appear bright violet. It really stood out from the rest. Maybe that's how I was feeling — separate and alone. A world of colour on the inside, surrounded by greyness.

Mrs Broughton waddled over broodingly. 'Wow, Glenn,' she said, hands on heavy hips. 'That's terrific. Your old school report said you're good at art. I read it this morning.'

I felt a warmth inside that glowed on my face. No one was whistling behind my back now, or making snidey comments.

'Laura's another promising artist,' said Mrs Broughton. She rubbed her huge tummy, wincing. 'Maybe you want to give her a few tips? I've . . . just got to . . . excuse me . . .' She lumbered from the room to a ripple of embarrassed laughter.

I looked at the artwork on Laura's white A3 sheet. She smiled at me with blood-red lips, her eyes all shiny under those funny old glasses. There was a blob of dried glue over one lens. Her face was pale and curved into a cutely dimpled chin. Her long black ruffle of hair had a green ribbon.

I edged off my chair and stood over Laura's right shoulder. Her drawing was pretty good but needed firming up.

'You could have stronger outlines,' I said. 'Really define your edges – make them strike the eye.' I lowered my voice here in case I made a prat of myself. 'You ever seen Van Gogh's early stuff, his drawings of Dutch peasants?'

Laura shook her head. The green ribbon slid a touch.

'Well, he used thick black strokes to make each image stand out. Then he'd put in the detail . . . folds of clothing or marks on a tree.'

Laura held up the heavy pencil she was using. 'Show me,' she said.

I reached out slowly until my fingers found hers. She didn't flinch or pull away. I guided her right hand around the page. Soon her wooden bowl had a stronger rim and each apple looked separate from the rest.

Laura's thumb locked against mine as I leaned forwards and worked. Her snaky hair had a wild hedgerow smell. It was like fresh blackberries from some fruity shampoo. I breathed it in quietly, feeling my mind close over. I wanted to bottle that blackberry scent and shake it on my pillows. She leaned her head an inch towards my cheek. A wisp of her hair tickled my nose. The sun was beating through wide windows, laying a warm gloss over us both.

Then came the first gawky sniggers behind. I realized the room was in silence. Everyone was watching. Someone murmured a snatch of that Robbie Williams thing, *Angels*.

Two others joined in on the soppy chorus, about a waterfall and where it takes you. Laura's cheeks got a crimson glow and she softly shook her head.

Mrs Broughton came plodding back with a cup of water. Laura pulled her hand away. I rubbed my face, leaving charcoal smears.

Laura whispered, 'Thanks. I get it now.'

'Any time,' I said, pulling my chair up to hers. 'It's half term next week. I'm going off drawing in the hills. If you wanna come . . .'

Laura nodded. 'I'd like to,' she said, her dimple wobbling. 'I just don't know. Are things OK with you? I guess it's been hard.'

'Not great,' I said. 'Think my mum's gone off somewhere, maybe with a new bloke. My dad's in a right state. But you'll have to come round some time and—'

'Glenn!' said Mrs Broughton behind us. 'Is that a sketchpad of yours down there?'

My blue sports bag was bulging on the floor.

'Yeah,' I said. 'I've got others at home.'

She smiled, and patted her long hippy hair.

'Could I have a look-see?' she asked. 'Maybe we can get you to draw something for the school.'

My brain was foggy with Laura's weird beauty, and now all this attention. I reached into my holdall and passed the pad to her.

'Thanks,' said Mrs Broughton, with her wide, eager smile. 'I'll have a browse over lunch.'

I looked at Laura, who sat quietly at my elbow.

'You OK?' I said. 'Things at home all right, or shouldn't I ask?'

'They're OK,' said Laura. She rubbed both eyes

under her glasses. 'I'm not neglected, if that's what you think. Just a natural scruff. Makes it easier if I look out for myself now. Things were a bit different when Ronnie—'

Mrs Broughton's mobile rang loudly in our ears. She took it from a dungarees pocket and went out. She brushed past someone in the doorway: Lavinia. Her slender waspish face was pink and freckly. She didn't say a word, but loitered in the corridor while Laura fumbled for her things and ran after her.

I was still buzzing at lunch time. I'd brought sandwiches and took them down to Burnside Tarn. The tarn was like a small lake you could easily swim across. I stood on the shore, admiring the trees on all sides. Yellow, pink, orange, green, crimson leaves. The colours flashed like fireworks.

I saw Goldeneye duck again, dawdling in the shallows. Those few peculiar red feathers marked it out. I'd used a scarlet crayon to catch their likeness. Mrs Broughton would dig that picture, I thought.

Then my heart gave a terrified lurch. I clutched my head, realizing what had shocked me. I flung my sandwich to the ducks and started haring back to school.

The sketchbook! Which one had I handed over? And what was inside it?

The A4 diary pad? No, that was in my bag still, right

there with me. Mrs Broughton had the larger one in her room. Filled with what? Drawings of Goldeneye . . . Mum . . . Dad . . . What else? Trouble Brewin stamping on Lavinia . . . Trouble Brewin stalking Miss Mellors up a mountain . . . Beefwits done like a snorting bull . . . Harlequin's puppet face . . . Lavinia on a broomstick . . . I'd even done Goofy Garner in a rabbit hutch. A balloon caption by his buck teeth, going 'Glynn! Glynn! Let me out!'

I pelted up the road, back into the main building. Up two flights of stairs to the art room. The door was locked.

TWENTY~ONE

I leaned my sweaty brow on the window, then bombed off to the staff room with an excuse ready about needing my pad back. But Mrs Broughton wasn't in that afternoon.

I kept nipping back upstairs between classes. The art room was in use and my sketchbook had gone. Head swimming, I sweated through a grim hour of Trouble Brewin. Miss Mellors had a free period, so he sat scowling at her empty room through the glass divide. He closed his eyes and fiddled in his pockets. He stank of cheap cigars.

After school I followed Baz to the IT room to lie low for a bit. Baz called up a website with a whirling planet on the homepage. He clocked around various images of comets and star charts.

I browsed the BBC *Artshow* stuff. There was a link to some big Van Gogh society. I filled the screen with his painting *The Harvest*. Lush green and yellow fields with big violet shadows, a bit like the landscape around

Torbeck. Van Gogh had painted this one in Arles, down in southern France. The intense sunlight there inspired him. But the people of Arles took the rise out of this genius among them. Children and adults jeered him in the streets. They stoned his little house, climbing up to the windows where Van Gogh screamed like hell. Soon he was locked up as a dangerous loony; eighty locals wrote to the mayor to demand it. So the artist became an outcast.

I glanced up as Baz left, barging off down the corridor. I hung around for another hour until a cleaner came in to bug me. With no one about I sneaked back up to the art room. But after searching every shelf and table for my big sketchpad, I gave up. Tomorrow was Friday, the last day before half term.

Trudging back into the village, I glanced up at King's Cragg on the horizon. Great shadows lay sleepily over the burnt-orange bracken. Then a familiar sight sparked up from the lower slopes. Another firework, only this one looked like a rocket. I watched its dazzling climb until it burst into a golden shower. Nothing else followed after.

I stopped at Henderson's for sweets. From the door I could see down to the bus shelter and phone box. Lavinia was there. She saw me and gave a loud gasp of horror, gob wide open. She covered her mouth before slowly sliding her hands away. Some others were in the wooden shelter. I heard their wild voices, like a mob geared up for a lynching.

My hands were all jumpy as I paid Val. 'By the way, Val, you seen anyone strange?' I asked. 'I mean, the past few days.' I kept my voice light and jokey, though it wobbled. 'Any . . . giant people or such like?'

Val's brow creased before she smiled. 'No, no giants, Glenn. No ogres either. Well, perhaps a few trolls round here. Why, you drawing cartoons now?'

I looked all over Val's cosy blonde features. Even her accent was like Mum's — broadly northern but bright and friendly. I wanted to stay there with her and not brave the waiting scumbags.

'There's a cartoon character in us all,' I said quietly. 'My old art teacher in Burnley told me that. You just gotta look for it. Bye.'

'Bye, Glenn. Say hello to your dad. I'll pop round soon.'

I stood outside, nibbling chocolate caramel. I'd have to pass the bus-stop crowd, though I could stick to the other side of the road. I shuffled on, feeling a nervous fury inside me.

Beefwits hissed by from behind on his muddy bike. His rusty bull's head wore a baseball cap and he thrust his ugly mug out. He stood on the pedals, wheels whirling slowly. His dumpy face looked back at me. His podgy eyes kept staring. His bicycle curved into the middle of the road. Still Beefwits tried glaring me out. His brawny white neck was twisted right round.

A tourist family was crossing the road. Two parents and a little blonde girl. They'd been looking at the bus timetables. Now they wanted tea in their guesthouse, just opposite.

Beefwits finally turned his thick head back. He kicked the pedals. At the last second he clocked the family but ploughed right into them. The back wheel skidded out and rammed the little girl's ankles. Beefwits went sprawling onto the hard road. Right in front of Lavinia. She gave a yappy laugh then covered her mouth.

The bearded man, in a blue anorak, held his ribs. 'Pillock!' he yelled.

The little blonde girl was crying. Beefwits got up and made a playful grab for Lavinia, who screamed and squirmed.

In all the fuss I hit the small village green, crossed over and jogged home. I slammed the door behind me, leaning on it with eyes closed.

Dad tumbled lazily downstairs. 'Didn't know you were staying late,' he said. 'Detention?'

'Don't be thick,' I snapped. 'I was with Baz. My one friend.'

'Yeah? Ask him round,' Dad said.

'Round to what?' I said, staring hard. 'What we got here? And has Mum phoned again? She finished her holiday yet?'

Dad stood on the bottom stair. There were stains on his maroon V-neck jumper. The collar of his flowery shirt was bent. His quiff looked on the point of collapse. No gel today.

He spoke softly. 'Don't push it, Glenn.'

'Push what?' I shouted. 'She's either on some strange unplanned holiday or she's left us. Can't be both. Or can it? She gone wine tasting with Ray?'

Dad looked puzzled. 'What? Ray? Ray who?'

I jabbered wildly. 'Ray . . . Ray . . . somebody from Booths. I met him at the cinema with Mum the week before we moved here. She gone off with him?'

Dad sat down on the staircase carpet. Rubbing his face, he said, 'Listen, Glenn, I'll say this once and only the once. Your mum's taken off with someone or something to some place. I don't know who or what or where. Things were falling apart between us back in Burnley, which is why we thought a move here and having a second kid might save us. I'm really sorry it's all gone tits up. I'm in the dark too. No job, no wife, no mates, no money. Though don't worry, we ain't starving. No need to start selling your drawings yet, or getting free school dinners. And anyway, what's the school like? Rough? Boring?'

'Just plain stupid,' I said harshly. 'Baz is OK, if a bit weird. And a nice girl . . . Laura. I told her about Mum, but she won't spread it around. So then, we're without Mum until she decides we're worth knowing again. Nice one. Nice work.'

Pushing past Dad, I shut myself away upstairs. In the diary sketchpad I scratched an outline of massive King's Cragg mountain. With quick dots of colour I added firework flickers gushing up.

I had another A3 sketchbook just like the missing one. I got it ready to take into school. A number of the sheets had come loose and flopped out. I paged through it, finding only sketches from Burnley: family portraits, burned buildings, the new football stadium. I'd give Mrs Broughton this one, as I was starting to guess where my other had gone. What if it ended up in front of Trouble Brewin's pervy eyes? What the frick would happen then?

TWENTY~TWO

Mrs Broughton smiled when I found her at ten to nine the next morning.

'Hi,' I said, trying to relax and not stare at her baby bulge. 'Did you, um, take my sketchpad home? Only there's private stuff in there I'd rather not show. I just realized.'

Mrs Broughton stood like a placid cow in yellow dungarees.

'Oh no, I didn't,' she said. 'I came looking for it yesterday lunch. Thought you must've nabbed it back. Can't you find it?'

My stomach tightened. My head swam.

'It's gone,' I said, sounding hollow. I felt faint. 'So someone has taken it.'

Mrs Broughton wobbled about, poking in various drawers. 'I'm sure it's not been stolen,' she said.

I knew it had. Cruel artwork gone missing equalled yesterday's extra-bad vibes from Beefwits and Lavinia.

Oh sugar . . . I heard a tap on the door. It was Laura. My chest fluttered. Her snow-white face turned red.

'Hiya, Laura,' said Mrs Broughton. 'You lost something too?'

Laura stared through her quaint old glasses. She swallowed heavily, her pale throat bulging. Her voice was croaky.

'No . . . I've . . . got a message,' she said. She wiped her eyes with gentle fingers but wouldn't look at me. She seemed lost for words and stood there open-mouthed.

I ended the awkward silence. 'Anyway, this is another of mine,' I said. As I held out the A3 book to Mrs Broughton a dozen sheets flopped onto the floor. I saw Dad's dark brown quiff, in charcoal, peeping from the pile. 'Oh hell,' I said. 'Sorry, it's not bound very tightly. If the other pad turns up can you tell me, asap?'

'Of course,' said Mrs Broughton. 'And I won't snoop! Not if it's private.'

I edged out, looking into Laura's chalky face. I was love-struck and panicky. Then in English, when tired old Miss Naylor sagged out to fetch more books, the voices began. From the back of the room, as always. Some lad this time, trying to sound scared and lonely.

'I want my mummy,' he squeaked. 'Mummy come home. Nobody loves me.'

My face burned up as I stopped writing. How had they found out about Mum leaving? Baz was on my left and turned sharply, a bony elbow jabbing me. He spoke dead loud. Maybe his hearing aids were playing up.

'How dramatic, George! What raw talent. You should try out for the school play. Oh sorry, you did, and *ahhh* . . . some little Year Seven kid got your part. *Ahhh.* Diddy diddums.'

Nobody laughed then. A few grunts. My buddy was well fired up.

Lavinia's voice cut in, somewhere behind me. 'Some people have *no* sense of humour,' she sighed.

Baz turned again, bashing me with knobbly knees.

'Some people have a sick sense of humour,' he said. 'Just so happens you're one of them.'

Miss Naylor slumped back in, her arms full of William Golding books. I sat up straight and cracked my knuckles on the desk. They rattled like gunfire in the sudden silence.

I didn't see Baz again until home time. I found him in the IT room, his face pressed to an online swarm of blue stars.

'Thanks for earlier,' I said. 'If I pitch in it'll just make things worse. But someone's got it coming. I swear.'

Baz moved the white mouse carefully. He clicked

once and the screen's image became cosmic dust. Hundreds of glowing purple dots against black outer space. If Baz had heard me he gave no sign. My buddy was on half-term holiday now.

I waited around until the crowds had gone. I walked home the long way, circling the village, by Burnside Tarn. My Goldeneye duck splashed in the shallows. Its red feathers flashed at me out of grey wings and blue water.

Back at home, Dad was all excited. He hopped around the kitchen, shoving tins on shelves. White bags with the red Henderson's shop logo crinkled on the table.

'Guess what?' he said happily. 'Got a job. Start tomorrow, though I've been helping out already. Good news, yeah?'

'Yeah,' I said. 'What's the job?'

It seems Dad had been going to Ulverston most days. The small town, ten miles off, had a job centre. He'd gone for lunch in the same café each time. Probably spent the afternoons there drinking tea and staring through windows. He'd heard the manager complain about being short-staffed. So Dad offered himself on the spot.

'Pay's lousy but better than nowt,' he said. 'And I've nabbed a few leftovers for tea.' He opened the fridge to point proudly at vanilla slices. 'How was your day?'

'The worst,' I said.

'Right. Teachers cutting rough, are they?'

I stared at Dad's back as he whistled and put the kettle on. I'm not sure he even heard me go upstairs. I felt shattered after a week that seemed like years, and soon crashed out. I think the phone rang and Dad kept shouting 'Hello?' but I couldn't keep awake. I dreamed I was back in school. Trouble Brewin had an arm round Laura. His fingers were groping inside her shirt. I carried a sketchpad and all its pages fell out. Each one had a naked drawing of Laura. She picked them up, dusting them down. Her dark hair was brushed back behind her ears. She wore big silver hearing aids, like Baz. She began to get undressed, peeling off holey blue tights—

'Glenn?' A tap at the door.

I sat up stiffly, trying to hide the excitement in my trousers.

Dad said, 'I've done some pasta. You want it now? I'm going out later.'

'Going where?' I asked, yawning.

He smiled broadly, his firm jawline rising. 'You'll see,' he grinned. 'Time I made some impact around here.'

I groaned as Dad bounced back downstairs. He'd talked about 'making an impact' back in Burnley. It hadn't got much further than his lame stand-up comedy attempts.

In the kitchen I heaped mushroom bolognese onto

sticky spaghetti. It was past seven o'clock. I'd slept a couple of hours. After eating, I put my arms on the table and rested my head there.

My brain buzzed. I had visions of Harlequin, who I'd been too drained and tired to hike up and see for two days. That lonely woodland path and mile of rough road to the quarry seemed eternal. Next time I'd have to ask him some hard questions if he hadn't moved on. He was always so evasive or just clammed up. I'd take some food and get his confidence. I'd seen no supplies in his rotten old shack, so he was either starving or stealing. Tomorrow. I'd go tomorrow, first thing.

I thought of my vanished mum and what Dad had said about saving their marriage.

What would it be like having Mum around, if she was carrying a child? I recalled an evening two weeks before we'd left Burnley. There'd been some neighbours over for supper. Dad had stood behind Mum, gently massaging her shoulders. He'd talked about having another kid, now we were off to the sticks. Mum hadn't said anything, just dragged a knife across her empty plate. Everyone had watched her, listening to the quiet screech of cutlery on china. She drank lots of wine that night and slept on the sofa. She was still there the next morning, under a spare duvet.

My daydreams were cut short. I heard a flopping

sound on the landing above. My full stomach heaved and sank. I sat straight and waited. Surely Dad wouldn't . . . not in a poky place like Torbeck. Even back in Burnley the joke hadn't come off.

Footsteps slowly flapped down the stairs. The kitchen door into the living room was closed. I leaped up to open it and took a desperate breath at the sight before me.

Dad stood there proudly. He wore a black rubber diving suit. His feet were covered in frogman's flippers. He held a snorkel in one hand, a face mask in the other.

TWENTY~THREE

I spoke weakly, pleading, 'No, Dad. No. Not here.'
His quiff was trapped bushily under the suit's tight hood. But the rest of his head was visible. He smiled and held out his hands.

'What?' he cried. 'Why not? They've got a James Bond theme night on at the Queen's Head. I'm going as 007 himself. Y'know, like in — what was it? *Thunderball*? Don't be such a spoilsport.'

'I'm not,' I said. 'But . . . Dad! Torbeck's not the sort of place for your humour. You'll just get laughed at.'

Dad dropped the snorkel and face mask. He put his hands on rubbery black hips. 'I don't get it,' he said. 'What you got against this place? We've only been here a week. I'm trying to make the best of it, whatever your mum does. James Bond theme night . . . wish I'd thought of it.'

I pulled my spiky hair tight. 'I'm going out then,' I

said. 'Give me the key 'cos I'll be back earlier. And please, Dad, don't overdo it. This isn't Burnley where you can melt into the crowd. And even there no one laughed when you wore this on stage.'

I took the key, and some bread for the ducks. Dad stared after me. I heard him flop clumsily into the kitchen. He'd be slapping up the street later in those foolish flippers.

I went round the back way, walking through two sheep fields to avoid the village. I wore a light red jacket and black jeans. My well-worn trainers kicked sandy dust on the tarn shores. A couple of small boys threw stones at the swimming swans. Their stocky dad was nearby, all pink slaphead and rubbery neck. He spoke in a thick Brummie accent.

'That's it, lads. You scare 'em away. Nasty snappy things.'

Tourists up for half term, I thought. Hellbent on wrecking something before they left. The three of them strutted away towards the village. They left a farm gate wide open, despite the big bold sign saying: PLEASE CLOSE!

I went back and shut the gate, then ambled to where the road leading from school came down by the tarn. Goldeneye and its ducklings mooched around. I tore white bread into bits and lobbed them out. This drew a crowd of other winged waddlers. Even the bombed swans began drifting back to dry land.

An excited quacking built as I chucked stale chunks. Then from behind me came another noise. I glanced back up the tree-lined road. A crowd was heading down on foot or on bikes. Their distant shouting and stamping mixed with the duck noises. I threw a last slice and stumbled towards the woods. They only made a fringe forest around the tarn but I had to hide. I'd no doubt who was in the approaching gang. I lay at the foot of a lofty chestnut tree, making a quick bed of yellow-brown leaves.

The sunset glowed on the dark water. But its warm light died among the trees. I waited in cold shadows.

Bike tyres crunched on the shingly shore. The ducks' quacking rose in alarm. I heard a flurry of wings. I smelled druggy smoke on the slow breeze. Peeking round the tree, I saw a dozen people from Torbeck. I only knew a few by name. Lavinia was there; so was Beefwits and his mates. They all clomped around in big expensive trainers. Mountain bikes were stashed on a fence. Some of the crowd were too old for our school. No Laura.

Beefwits was all over Lavinia. She ran away, shrieking as he tried grabbing her round the waist. Then someone shouted above the general jabber.

'Oi! There's that duck! Must be . . . Look, it's got red feathers.'

Other bleary voices joined in.

'They've all got red feathers, pillock.'

'No, they haven't. Look, thicky . . . that's the only one.'

'Oh yeah. Hey, Tony. Tony, come here.'

'Do what?'

'Over here. I found Mrs Ducky.'

Beefwits barged over in long brown shorts. A black baseball cap made his meaty face look dark. He knelt out of sight for a second. When he stood up he held Goldeneye by the neck. Its beady black eyes glared from yellow sockets.

Beefwits ran among the group, thrusting the duck out. 'Who's for a pretty red feather?' he yelled. 'Lavinia, look what I got!'

He plucked fiercely at Goldeneye's body. It kicked out with webbed feet. Beefwits held the terrified duck at arm's length. He dribbled and blubbered in mad excitement. His grip grew tighter on Goldeneye's damp neck. It flapped madly in mid-air. Beefwits crouched low. Shrubby bushes were now blocking my view. Someone was cheering. Another threw an empty can high, then headed it away. I heard a sudden snap. Then Beefwits got up with a mad grin of rusty freckles. He stumbled away like a drugged sleepwalker.

'Oh my God!' came Lavinia's voice. 'That's so gross.'

'Jesus . . . you nutter.'

'Not a pretty picture now.'

I squeezed against the tree. My feet scraped roughly over the leaves. I froze at the noise and closed both eyes tight. *Must be that one . . . look, it's got red feathers.* That was me being attacked out there, not just Goldeneye. Both of us betrayed by my sketch-pad.

Everyone gathered at a picnic table near the tarn. Someone had a portable CD player and put on something rappy. It's why that lot never heard an old man approaching. He crunched by only metres from me, having wandered in from the trees on the far side. He didn't notice me hiding, just plodded on down to the shore. He was tiny and plump with a hat and walking stick. I'd seen him around the village before, blobbing along and tutting at pavement litter.

On the shore was a hefty boulder. The old man lowered himself beside it, his back to me. He removed his hat. Then he sat watching swans glide on the moonlit waves. He leaned his head on the rock as if lost in memories.

Out of his vision the party carried on. The music got whacked up louder, making the old geezer cover his ears. Cans were lobbed onto the shingle. Then I saw Beefwits get up with a gun. It was only an air rifle but looked risky in his hands.

He began by firing into the tarn, making little plops on the surface. Then he turned the barrel on a clutch of waddling ducks. He shot into the shore. Puffs of dusty gravel made little clouds in the darkness. Someone stopped the music. I heard bike chains whirring. A slow slog began back up the road.

But Beefwits returned to the bench alone. He scoured the tarn through his gunsight like a soldier on night patrol. The air rifle was pointed at the boulder. Beefwits couldn't see the slouched figure on the other side. He pinged a pellet at the great rock. It roused the old man. He half stood with bent knees. A split second later came the second shot. The old fellow clutched his neck. He gave a gurgle and sank down. I heard his legs creak. I heard his moans of shock.

By then Beefwits was bowling back towards the school. There's no way he'd be fetching help though. No way he could know that I'd been watching. Then through the trees I saw a couple on the shore way over to my left, walking their dog. The old bloke must've seen them too. He clawed his way round the rock, then hobbled across, holding his throat. His hat and stick lay like forgotten stage props.

Fear wormed around my insides, taking slow bites. I stayed put for an hour. Only when the shore was dark and empty did I finally crawl out.

And there among the stony pebbles was Goldeneye. The duck lay tumbled onto one side. Its webbed feet were still. Its neck was all twisted. Some of my bread had gone down that throat earlier, with short gulps of life. One red feather had been yanked loose.

With gentle fingers I touched the crippled neck. It was warm still. I lifted the plump duck and hid its body under a pile of red-gold leaves. Evidence. Ducklings tried shoving after me into the shrubs, then followed me back to the moonlit shore. Orphans now. They quacked and flapped for their murdered mother.

I quickly tore back home across two fields. I nipped like a thief through someone's garden, then out the front at the bottom of our road.

And there on the doorstep sat the James Bond frogman. Head in his hands, and quiff gone flat. The snorkel and face mask lay at his flippered feet. I shut the garden gate and stood still.

'What?' I said. 'What?'

Dad sniffed loudly. He stared up at the moon's curved white ring.

'I got the wrong date,' he said. 'The Bond theme night's on tomorrow instead. Had to sit there for hours while everyone cracked up at me. I kept ringing to see if you were back. You've got the key. Where the hell you been?'

I stared at the chipped path leading from the front door. I handed Dad the key and followed him in. He slopped into the kitchen and sat sighing at the table.

I fled upstairs to my diary sketchpad. With savage strokes I drew Beefwits, tearing Goldeneye apart. And another, showing him with rifle in hand, aiming at an old man. I signed and dated the drawings. There was proof on paper now, even if they tore out my eyes and tongue.

TWENTY~FOUR

I woke early on Saturday morning with a furious heart. I couldn't lie still. Below last night's drawings I wrote down everything I'd seen. I made rough sketches of those faces I could recall.

Dad got up at eight, before going to Ulverston for his new café job. At least now he might pack that diving suit away for good. He'd once used it for a pub comedy night in Burnley. He'd worn the mask and stood on stage, gargling chart hits with beer from the snorkel. The audience was meant to guess the tunes. It'd gone down well for about a minute, then Dad was booed off.

After the front door slammed I went back to bed. I woke again at eleven o'clock, dead sure what to do. I'd go to the phone box and call the police. I'd give the names I knew and say what I'd seen. The police might trace the call to our home if I phoned from there. No one must know it was me. I'd just watch the cops turn up and cart them all off.

Another day of blue skies. I'd heard it always rained in Cumbria. The village road was busy as cars piled in for half term.

Where the council-house row ended lay that scraggy triangle of green. And sitting on its grubby bench was Laura. Traffic motored by behind her. She gazed ahead – past the houses and estates, the school and endless farm fields beyond. Her eyes were fixed on some far horizon. Warm round eyes magnified through old glasses. Thick rims of light plastic, curving at the corners.

She had on a dark blue jumper. The sleeves hardly came down to her wrists. Her white jeans were holed at the knees.

I stood there, taking in every detail. Laura snapped out of some deep trance and saw me.

'Hey, you OK?' I croaked nervously.

She shook her head, looking around. 'Come here,' she said. 'I got something for you.'

I walked over on floating clouds. For once there was no one spying from the bus shelter across the way. Laura dug something out of a pocket. A roll of shiny green ribbon, like the stuff she looped in her black hair.

Her voice was quick and anxious. 'It's for your other sketchpad,' she said. 'I saw how it fell apart on Friday.

The one you gave to Mrs Broughton. You can tie it with some ribbon. Oh, and your . . . Rembrandt teddy friend. He seemed a bit scruffy that day on the pavement. Maybe you can give him a nice green collar. My silly old Creepy Crawly thing's got one, to make him look less gross. They can be like soulmates, OK? Like us?'

She twisted her fingers in knots. I felt my heart flare. For a few moments last night's cruel darkness got washed away.

'Thanks,' I said, almost whispering. 'So I guess you know where my other pad went. Was it Lavinia?'

As Laura nodded, her scrawny body sagged. 'I took her back into the art room,' she said. 'I wanted to show her what you'd taught me that morning. But she found your book on the side. She just dug straight in and saw your portrait of her on a broomstick. And those ones you'd labelled "Beefwits".'

I put my head back, watching a plane scorch white lines over the sky. Laura giggled quietly. 'And that one of Goofy Garner in a rabbit hut.' She giggled again. I wanted to laugh with her, but last night had emptied me out.

I leaned my face close to Laura's. 'Listen,' I said, 'something happened. That duck I sketched got killed by Beefwits. And some pensioner got shot in the neck. I'm calling the cops.'

Laura turned white. 'No,' she breathed. 'You can't, Glenn. Then the school will get involved. They'll have to get your book back and see all those other drawings. The ones of Trouble Brewin . . . remember?'

I watched one of our neighbours go by; a middle-aged woman with a scrunched-up face. Her hair had a touch of blue rinse. She was chain-smoking, as always, and wore a vile fake-fur coat.

'And I've heard about last night,' said Laura. 'It's all around the village. If Lavinia gets done for being there she might think I was the one who grassed them up. And all those drawings you did got nicked off her and passed around the school. She's twigged that I like you. But she's like a laughing stock now, along with Tony Grant. Beefwits, you call him. They're out for your blood.'

I shivered. 'OK, I'll keep quiet, but only for your sake and not for ever. Look, you're trembling, Laura. Come back to ours for coffee. Hang with me for a bit.'

'I can't,' sighed Laura. 'Everyone went out earlier but they're back soon. I've been sat here since just after breakfast. I didn't want to miss you if you came by.'

'Stay, Laura,' I said, holding her arm. 'I'll show you a mad secret up in the quarry.'

Laura pulled away. 'I'll see you, Glenn. You're dead nice, but I can't be with you just now. Things at home are difficult again. And I'm sorry about something else. It was me who told Lavinia that your mum's gone away. She demanded to know everything we'd talked about. I thought she might sympathize, what with her dad not being around any more. But she spread it about like it's some great scandal. I'm sorry. Honest I am.'

She walked away quickly, over the green ground and off to her tall house. I put the shiny roll of ribbon in a jacket pocket. It rested against my aching heart.

TWENTY~FIVE

Val had a queue in the shop, so there wasn't time to chat. I wondered if she'd heard of Dad's disaster last night. But the outraged gossip was all about old Mr Guthrie, who'd been 'nearly murdered by the tarn'. I stood there guiltily, feeling somehow involved. I knew it had been a cowardly accident. From the way people yakked you'd think there was an assassin on the loose.

I made tracks along the woodland path, now thick with leafy decay. I crossed the bridge behind the waterfalls and carried on up Quarry Road. There were mushrooms the size of beer bottles on the verges. One had a scarlet stem and a fleshy cap. Dad went off with his mates once, including big Geoff, picking magic mushrooms. The sort you get spaced-out on. They went off to the gritty hills of Pendle, in Lancashire, where Alice Nutter and the other Pendle witches were hanged. Dad's pals were more used to eating magic mushrooms. They brought him home speechless and he got up very late the next day. He forgot to collect Mum from Booths. They had a row about it.

Spots of rain fell as I reached Harly's shabby shelter. He lay inside, quite still, on his stomach. He almost reached right across the glum room. Then he arched his legs and chest like someone doing wild yoga. His boot soles were nearly touching the back of his head. He formed a strange circle with his whole bending body. I spoke softly, going gingerly inside.

'Harly? You all right? I've brought some grub.'

Harlequin's great spiny back went flat. He fumbled about for his big hat, his face all smudgy and red. His cheeks had streaky marks of mixed colours. Maybe he'd been crying. I knelt gently, holding out food as if befriending a wild beast.

Harly fell on the nosh like a wolf. He had a hip flask of spring water and slurped loudly. He tore a hunk of cake. 'It my birthday?' he asked. 'This my cake?'

I raised my eyebrows. 'How'd I know? How old are you?'

'Thirteen,' said Harly, his mouth full.

'Don't be daft,' I said. 'I'm thirteen and a half. You must be, what . . . eighteen?'

'Dunno,' said Harly. 'Thirteen was last birthday I

had. Then got sent away some bad place. Had no birthday then. Not with presents or cake and stuff. Just a day like all others.'

This was the most he'd ever told me. He handed me the hip flask and I drank. I wanted to know more but reckoned I'd take it slow.

'So, what present would you like?' I asked. 'If it was your birthday?'

Harly scratched his blond bristles, which never grew beyond stubble.

'Got book once,' he said. 'Story 'bout a girl. I knew her. Wore this long red thing, yeah? Got scared of wolves.'

My mind ticked over. 'You mean *Little Red Riding Hood*?' I said. 'It's only a story. You didn't know her.'

Harly looked all shy. He stared at the floor, picking scraps of mud. He gave a slow smile. 'Reckon I knew her,' he said. 'You got that book, Glenn? Bring it, yeah? Read it for Harlequin?'

'Blimey,' I said. 'Not any more. The village library might.'

'You bring it, Glenn Jackson. Bring her back.' His blue eyes were racing brightly.

'I'll try,' I said. This was going OK. I'd ask him where he was born and stuff about his family.

But Harly suddenly stooped out of the gloomy shack.

'Hey, wait up,' I said. 'Tell me more about your birthdays.' I heard what sounded like slate being smashed outside.

I quickly cleared our leftovers into the bag. A long arm came round the door. Harly felt for his cardboard telescope. Outside I found him scanning the skies and hills.

'What is it?' I said.

An orange light flashed from distant King's Cragg, back above Torbeck. Harly moaned and sank to his knees. He dug at the earth with his cardboard tube. Pulling out a fat wriggly worm, he whispered to the tiny creature.

'Ask what they doing,' he hissed. 'Tell 'em stop. I goin' away. Far off.' He sent the blood-red worm sliming back into the soil. After flinging the mad telescope through his door, Harly bluntly strode off. 'Goin' hunting,' he called back at me.

'Don't go, Harly!' I shouted. 'I wanna ask you things. I wanna . . .'

But he kept going and yomped off to the woods leading down the valley. I wondered if he'd found some place else to thieve from, besides Charlie's farm. I remembered how he'd snuck up behind me that time he saved my life. He really could be stealthy.

I watched him barge away over the grey land, then

out of sight. As another firework rose I made a rough guess at its location. Maybe now I could sneak round King's Cragg and see which loon was obsessed with firing rockets from a mountain.

TWENTY~SIX

The slate quarry's drab acres dipped into a lowland of wild pastures. Here it was all chewed-up fields ponging of sheep droppings. The soles of my battered trainers got clogged with stinky stuff.

Through yellowing trees, way down on my left, ran the white woodland path. I strode through stiff heaps of brown bracken. The secret heights of the mighty mountain edged closer. I hiked on for about a mile before reaching the lower slopes round the back of King's Cragg.

The afternoon was now all crisp and golden. As I went higher the wind blew up and the climb got sterner. I passed a few climbers with backpacks and hand-stitched leather walking boots. They looked with concern at my threadbare footwear. I heard their tuts and sighs of despair, but slogged on.

King's Cragg had loads of false peaks. Just when I thought the top was finally in reach, then came another big ridge ahead. I stayed on the sheep trails, worn smooth by centuries of hooves. But I began to blunder about, having lost sight of my original target. It all seemed the same up there: one gasping crag after another; a maze of splashy streams and volcanic rock.

Torbeck's grey and white houses were like matchboxes from on high. I'd noticed that you never saw anyone from the village out in the woods, or up in the hills. It was all just tourists, with maps and flasks and backpacks. Most people in Torbeck went about with eyes down, never going further than the few shops or pubs. How could you live in such a place and have no connection with all this wildness? No wonder someone was getting away with zapping fireworks about and forever going unnoticed.

Something whizzed up high and wide overhead. A shower of red sparks in the sea-blue sky. To get near the likely launch site meant clambering up a gruesome slope ahead. I gave it a go. Its brown ridges booted my shins. Its cold fangs bit my fingers. Spiky crops of gorse needled me. At the top I squelched off into mossy turf, my trainers filling with freezing liquid. I tumbled with tiredness and got muddy hands.

Then I saw the first burned-out rocket. A blackened cardboard shell on a thin wooden stick. Further along the gusty ridge was a spent Catherine wheel. Finally a few squibs and Fizzbangs — little soggy tubes with peeling starry paper.

I stood on this great height, letting the wind bluster and batter. My red jacket billowed like a parachute.

The view was immense: a misty pink skyline, hazy humps of hills turning black in the distance, bright green meadows threading through everything. I stood alone, on top of the world.

Next I had to slither down a scree slope of rock fragments. Both my hands got dusty and bloody. Then it was away over rolling earth, all orange in the late afternoon. Giant rockfaces, like the quarry's walls, loomed ahead. Below one was a shallow dip. I walked quietly forwards over gentle bumps. For the first time I felt nervous and stopped. This had to be the place. Yet there wasn't a soul about. The great glowing landscape boomed around me. I'd come too far to go back. I forced myself down one last slope.

Then I was in sudden shadow, dwarfed by a rock formation. A flinty outcrop. It swept away on my right like some chunk of a giant comet. It guarded a shallow hollow. I tripped noisily on a toe-busting crag. I hopped around, mouth open in silent protest. Whatever was round the corner should've heard me by now.

Sneaking forwards, peeking round the rocky shelf, I saw a big brown boot. It shifted and showed a patch of white leg. The body was hidden round the bank. With three firm steps I was into a gully of daylight. I held up my arms as if in surrender. Now in full view was the mystery rocket launcher. He sat cross-legged with eyes closed, his young face full of sunshine. I shook my head.

It was Baz the buddy.

No wonder he hadn't heard me. His fat silver hearing blobs weren't in. Yet he somehow sensed me there. Behind crystal-clear specs his eyes opened, left then right. He spoke as if in a dream.

'Glenn?' he said. He shielded his eyes. 'That you . . . Glenn?'

'It sure is, Baz. Thought you knew nowt about fireworks being let off.'

He scratched his flat brown curls, getting up with a grin. His voice was quite slow and strange. 'Did . . . I say that? Maybe I've got . . . secrets to . . . protect. Haven't we all?'

I frowned. 'How come you know what I just said?' I patted my own lugs. 'Your hearing things aren't in.'

Baz watched me closely, then waved a carefree hand. 'Oh that,' he said thoughtfully. 'It's OK . . . I can lip-read. Have done for . . . years. Comes in handy, don't you know.'

I laughed. 'I bet it does. Especially round here.'

We stood and smiled secretly for a second. Baz fished his lug aids out of a blue anorak pocket. 'That's better,' he said, putting them in. 'Damn things nearly explode when rockets go off. The loud bangs get a bit boring.'

A chill wind blew down the narrow gully. It slammed off the precipice towering above.

'So then, dude,' I said, 'what's all this in aid of?'

Baz crouched on his walking-boot heels. 'Well, I'm working under orders,' he began. 'And you better keep this quiet, city boy. It's all been worked out. Our autumnal Earth season is the best time for it. So, anyway, I collect fireworks each year and keep enough to get started around September. Sometimes, if I've got enough, I mark out a landing strip. Right on the top of King's Cragg. Best at night though, so the bright colours really show.'

'But why, Baz? What the hell's it for?'

Baz sprang up, pointing at the dark blue heavens. 'For them!' he cried. 'For when they come! This mountain has the power to attract alien life. It's one of a few special sites around the world that has this vibe. I read about it in *Psychic Babble*, a mag I've been getting for years. They've got a private website and everything. I'm their King's Cragg watcher of the skies.

The fireworks highlight the exact spot, if any alien craft is attracted.'

Baz casually took out a packet of toffees. I stared at him as the wind spiked my hair. He had to be kidding.

'What's more,' Baz went on, 'a group first came here in 1950. A human group, that is, called the Atherians. They said that friendly aliens were circling Torbeck. Then a UFO got sighted nearby. There's nineteen mountains worldwide storing the right spiritual energy. King's Cragg is number five on the list. It's a *great* honour.'

He wasn't kidding.

Baz offered a toffee, which I took with numb fingers. He covered his ears two seconds before me. We both yelled as a low fighter jet raged over the rockface above. My bones crumbled.

'Phew!' said Baz, a minute later. 'Imagine being in a war with those buggers flying at you. The Atherians thought friendly aliens would bring world peace. Guess we're still waiting.'

I sucked sweet sticky toffee. 'You're a right weird git,' I said, grinning.

Baz laughed, his anorak flapping. 'Spot on. But maybe I'm the best mate you've got round here. Anyway, you've found me out now, so keep it quiet,

yeah? And we'd best head back down soon. But first
. . . follow me.'

He bumbled over to the base of a thumping cliff. I
could see how its top ridges seemed to sway under
passing clouds. Baz laid his palms and forehead on
dark rock. He stroked it lovingly, his voice charged with
wonder.

'It's like the whole universe is holding its breath. The
cosmos is half living and half dying at all times. That's
why it's a vital system. Human beings are desperate to
belong to something greater than themselves.
Otherwise they feel like part of them is empty.'

'Wow,' I breathed, rubbing my hands on stone. 'How
d'you know all that?'

'Read it last week,' said Baz. 'In *Psychic Babble*. Come
and lie down a minute.'

We lay on the hard autumn hillside. The crag's great
stormy bulk stood guard. The dipping sun made our
shadows long.

'Feel your spine,' said Baz, wriggling about. 'Feel it
connect with the mountain's vibe. I know I can. Maybe
it's 'cos I don't hear so well that I get it.'

I joggled about, though my back just got colder.

'Wow,' I breathed again. 'What amazing ideas.'

'You just have to connect,' said Baz. 'I've been a
believer since I first came up here. But don't you try

and find our special website. Its password is known only to a few of us. I had to prove I lived in Torbeck first, right near King's Cragg. Site number five on the global list.' He sprang up and grabbed a rucksack. 'OK, lecture over. Let's make tracks.'

We thumped back down the golden slopes together. Dusk was crawling in.

'Baz,' I said, 'if you can lip-read, d'you know what people say about me?'

'I do know,' said Baz, tripping over his big boots. 'And I know it's all crap, as usual. They say yours is a — what's it called? — a problem family. One that got moved from Burnley and dumped on Torbeck's doorstep. And that your dad beat your mum, so she left.'

I stopped still in shock.

'Come on,' shouted Baz, 'keep moving! It's further back than you think. I thought you knew all that gossip stuff.'

My face was burning. 'No,' I said. 'How the hell would I? No one has the guts to speak to your face. Did Lavinia start it?'

'Lavinia and that youth you call Beefwits. He got mad when you made him look a tosspot that first morning. He ain't used to being shoved onto moving cars.'

'And Lavinia?' I said. 'Apart from not fancying her like the other lads, what's my crime?'

'Lavinia loved her dad,' said Baz, walking at a fair lick. 'Ronnie Delaney. I remember how him and Lavinia and Laura went everywhere together. You hardly saw the mum. Even though Laura was only adopted, Ronnie really made her one of the family. After he died, Lavinia got all jealous about anyone being near Laura. Boys especially, or any male friend. She was only taking on Ronnie's role, I reckon. Seeing your old man swinging from a beam can't do much for your sanity. Not when you're only ten.'

I stared at the sleepy village below, with all its drama and trauma. Then I glanced back up at King's Cragg's angry jowls.

'Guess not,' I said. 'Suppose I should sympathize, but I can't.'

'She don't want sympathy,' said Baz. 'Or she wouldn't admit to it. She's fragile really. Must be to put on such a show of strength. And your clever piccies of her and Beefwits got quite widely seen. Told you to be careful with your drawing. Told you on that first morning.'

He had warned me, but I still felt I wasn't to blame for all this. At least now I'd solved the fireworks mystery and could stop Harly fretting about strange sightings. I also had Laura and Baz on my side. Maybe

Mum would come home soon and make herself a force in the village.

Baz left me to take a route across the marshy valley at the foot of King's Cragg. 'You'll find a way to fit in,' he said as we parted. 'And tell your dad not to try so hard. I lip-read something about his fancy-dress get-up. A diehard local might've pulled that off, but never a stranger. Not in Torbeck.'

I went back into the village alone, down the road past the Co-op. Lavinia stepped out of the tourist-tat shop with collecting tins and empty raffle books. She looked nervy, put her head down and didn't bother staring at me. I overheard a group of adults in Henderson's doorway talking about the events I'd witnessed last night.

'They want a bloody youth centre. Somewhere proper to hang out. At least Lavinia's trying to get summat sorted.'

'They want a bloody whipping! Never mind a cosy playroom.'

'Poor Mr Guthrie. Goes down there every evening, in all weathers, to remember his wife. It's where they first met.'

'No news on who shot him?'

'Not yet. Some piece of chicken shit.'

'Could be any of 'em. Could be him over there . . .'

By 'him' I knew they meant me. I was under suspicion too, for being new and unknown. In a place like Torbeck, as I was quickly learning, that's the worst crime of all.

TWENTY~SEVEN

D ad lay low over the weekend. Friday's frogman disaster had wounded him somewhere deep. Val popped round on Saturday evening to borrow some of his records, and they talked about memories of growing up in Blackburn, where they were both from. Dad got out a cheap bottle of plonk.

'Great,' said Val. 'Mike's got the kids — I need a breather.' She slumped back on the sofa as Dad tussled with the corkscrew. They sat close together, legs touching, and sang along to *24-Hour Party People*, a funky Happy Mondays album from the Mad-chester scene in the late eighties.

Upstairs, I took out the green ribbon roll Laura gave me. Charities often made loops out of such stuff to pin on your coats. Red ones to support AIDS victims, or pink ones for breast-cancer care. I cut a length of green and twisted it into a similar figure. But mine was a badge to support first love. That was my big issue.

I made several, sticking one on my jacket with a safety pin. I'd wear it with pride but only me and Laura would know why.

Sunday morning dragged by. Thinking I might find Laura, I decided to go to the country fair I'd seen advertised. Along the woodland path I followed a din of dogs and loudspeakers. One of Father Charlie's fields had been cleared for the event. He strode about, gun half-cocked over one arm like a squire. A silver crucifix dangled from his open shirt. He pretended not to see me.

There were loads of stalls around the field, displaying various banners. WE WANT BRITISH MEAT. SAVE THE COUNTRYSIDE. NO TO WIND-POWER FARMS. SUPPORT WIND-POWER FARMS. CHRISTIAN AID.

Everyone there seemed to have a dog: terriers, lurchers, poodles, sheepdogs. They pulled on choking chains to sniff each other. Some guy did a falconry display, with birds of prey landing on his gloved arm. In a big humid tent you could watch Cumberland wrestling. Two muscular guys grappled in a roped-off ring. A great cheer went up as the sweaty fight ended. The winner came forward — a geeky bloke in thick glasses, wearing turquoise woolly pants and a white flowery top.

I went back out and saw Lavinia nearby. She sat behind a desk selling raffle tickets, urging people to take an extra strip. She noticed me, then my green ribbon, and went purple. Her mother, Janice Delaney, stood by with a warm red face. She was laughing away at a story some farmer was telling. There was a touch of hysteria in that laugh, the way it went on and on at a high pitch. She didn't sound in control. She was still shrieking with mirth after the guy had wandered off. Lavinia nudged her mother on the hips to quiet her. A fat-arsed huntsman in a red cape slotted coins into the collecting tin. Lavinia pouted politely, tearing off lines of tickets. She joggled the tin loudly, attracting more custom. Her mother stood swaying, eyes closed, in a pink dress.

At the top end of the field was a makeshift bar with handpumps and barrels under a canvas roof. And that's where I saw Harlequin. I stopped stone-dead in surprise. What the hell did he want down here among strangers? He towered over the other folk, a plastic pint in his great fist. He gulped down a jar of cider and ordered another, fumbling with piles of loose change. It was clear he couldn't count them.

His face looked absurd. Thick black blocks over his eyes, and both cheeks rubbed with red. He'd inked a dark moustache on in squiggly lines. He looked like some drunk sideshow clown. His yellow hair straggled out from that broad brown hat. His overalls were clean but crinkly where he'd washed them in a stream. Thick hoopy socks rose from his work boots.

A few little lads hovered shyly behind him. They lifted their right shoulders the way Harly's jutted up oddly. Harly turned and grinned at them through his messy disguise. They ran off in giggly terror over the sheep-nibbled grass. Harly sank another golden pint of cider. I kept my distance, not sure how he'd react if I went across. Part of me didn't want to be seen with Harly, what with him looking so freaky, and I felt ashamed. He wobbled and belched with a big red smile. I'd catch him later somewhere. For all I knew some of these people might even know him. Maybe he was just a village idiot type who no one could tame.

By now a crowd had gathered around Lavinia's booth. It seemed a popular cause to throw money at. Lavinia's beaming mother drew raffle tickets from a Henderson's bag. Her grin looked wild, her eyes almost glaring. She shook the bag with vigour like some hyper child. Father Charlie, her dad, read the winning numbers through a loud hailer.

'Pink eighty-six! The winner gets this ginormous teddy bear! Step forwards . . . pink eighty-six!'

A man about my dad's age trundled out. His face was an embarrassed red under blond curls. He took the massive brown bear with a daft smile.

'Now then, David!' rasped Father Charlie. 'I know you've no kids of your own. Looks like you've got yer hands full now, lad.'

It happened to my dad once, in the days before he met Mum. He reckons it's one of the worst things that can happen to childless adults. Winning a cuddly toy in public, at a raffle or a fair. He says you curse that the wine and cheap chocs went to someone else. You give a false grin, then cringe and blush. You see the envious eyes of scornful kids. Then comes the real problem. Which of the waiting brats to give the unwanted prize to? The nearest one? The grubbiest? The youngest?

A little girl from Torbeck solved poor David's crisis. Her face was painted all stripy like a tiger's. She edged forwards and stroked one of the teddy's giant paws.

'Ahh . . . ahhh,' she cooed. 'Lovely thing. No children to play with. Aaahhhh.'

David eagerly took his chance. He thrust the bear into the girl's open arms. It was way bigger than her, but she staggered off happily. Her thanks were muffled by a huge furry head. David looked on, hands in pockets, as the next winner bagged a bottle of organic champagne.

Beefwits and his pack of cycling mates rode by. They all gawped back at me, giggling like infants. Beefwits pedalled ahead, arms raised in fisty triumph. His wheels went right through a sludgy cowpat. The crusted thing broke open, sliming his tyres in stinking yellow.

He obviously thought he'd got away with his crime at the tarn. The police had scooted around the village but no confessions had been prised out. The gang was staying schtumm. By now the blame was being pointed at city kids, up on half-term hiking and camping trips. They came and went by the minibus-load, so it was reckoned the culprit had long gone.

I touched my green looped ribbons. Still no sign of Laura, but I felt ready to try searching out Harlequin. If he was necking back cider on an empty stomach, I could persuade him to shoot off home and I'd meet up later with some food.

Back at the outdoor bar a large crowd was milling. Everyone was looking at Harly and muttering as he stood stiffly by some empty barrels. He kept giving rapid head shakes under that brimming hat.

Then he lurched about, gripping his hat right down. People stepped out of his way. I strode closer, hearing their curious comments.

'Where's that thing from? A freakshow?'

'Looks half-cut. Hope he's not entertaining the kids.'

'Who did his make-up? A real botch job.'

'Funny right shoulder. Perhaps he fell off a trapeze.'

'Is he on stilts?'

'Must be. What time's the show start?'

'Dunno. Is he a clown or a juggler?'

'He's never on stilts. Look, his legs are bending.'

'Course he is. How else d'you stand over seven feet high? Watch, I'll prove it.'

A chunky bald farmer stepped up, holding a hefty walking stick. He thwacked Harly across the backs of his legs. I heard hard wood on solid flesh. Harly screamed with shock.

The farmer sprang back. 'Bugger me,' he said. 'What the hell . . . ?'

Someone laughed aloud. 'Don't sound like stilts to me, Arthur.'

Harly whirled round, blue eyes narrow and burning. The farmer backed off but more people pressed forwards. They were sure this was outdoor theatre, or at least a fight brewing. Harly clutched his long tummy. He began to twitch and shake, giving little shrieks. His odd shoulders jerked and hunched. Grabbing the sides of his hat, he started spinning around, faster and faster with quick steps. People were laughing and teasing. A rough circle of bodies formed around Harlequin. Kids' heads pushed through adult legs to watch.

Harly's face ducked from sight. Then his big dirty

boots came thrusting up. He was doing a handstand. He walked on his palms, trying to get through the throng. But everyone pushed him back, his legs wobbling in mid-air. I knew he was trying to hide. This was no performance. His hooped leggings hovered above hats and haircuts. The walking handstand came to a halt. I heard Harly shrieking and pushed through to the front. His upside-down face, just above the earth, was the colour of dark blood. His tongue lolled out.

Then he flipped back onto his feet. Harly spun in a big blur. He jumped with loud thumps on the spot. His head was bowed; his hat down. Someone threw orange peel at him. It struck Harly's chest. He stopped bouncing and looked up, his wild eyes visible. His red-black face was all soaked with tears. They were streaming down.

The crowd gave a huge 'AAAHHH!'

'Go on, mate!' someone yelled. 'Do your stuff. Ain't got all day.'

Harlequin began pacing rapidly around the circle. He looked caged in, searching for an escape. He stared down into each face as if to frighten them away, or find an ally. I backed off into the clearing before he reached me, scared proper now. Harly stomped around ever more quickly and roughly. His great frame brushed those on the inside of the throng. The circle grew tighter. More and more people shoved and barged in. Harly stormed about. His nose bubbled frightened snot over his lips.

A handclap started up, getting faster and louder. Then a rapid chant, 'HEY! HEY! HEY! HEY!' Over and over it went, in time to the claps. '*HEY! HEY! HEY! HEY!*' It sounded tribal.

Harly pressed bony hands to his ears. Still he raged around the ring. His mad, wet face was grimy red. He was chest, head and shoulders over everyone. A giant puppet being swirled on stage. Then he went sprawling to earth with a thud. Someone had stuck out a foot. The crowd roared, all thrilled by this bizarre spectacle.

I ran at the horde of people and tried shoving through. But they were packed solid, and an elbow under my chin sent me sprawling.

Harly sprang up like an acrobat. He'd no idea who'd legged him over. But with fists held high he dived into the mob. Still taking it for a show, they stayed put. Harly dragged some nearby bloke out. It was David again. Pink ticket eighty-six. Lifted by his crown of blond curls, he screamed and flapped in mid-air. The children gave a chorus of squeals, with groans from the adults. Empty plastic pint jars were hurled.

'*Harly!*' I yelled, cupping hands to my mouth.

'Harlequin! I'm here!' I moved clear of everyone, waving arms across as if stopping a train.

Those flicking blue eyes gazed out towards me. Harly let David drop like a useless toy. He barged through the gasping onlookers, reaching me in seconds. I was lifted up, my insides lurching, and came to rest on broad shoulders. Harly plunged away past the stalls and food stands. I arched my head back to see everyone watching. Lavinia, with gob open; her mad mum laughing; Charlie shaking his gun; Beefwits and his prats gawping.

I looked right down on them all. Strolling couples and kids jumped out of the way. I clung to Harly's neck as he charged through Charlie's field, my bones juddering. Barbecue smoke wafted in a blast of greasy grills. Car-boot stalls rattled with useless tat as Harly crashed by. He dodged through parked cars on Charlie's farm tracks, then over the busy road, up onto the quiet woodland path.

He wandered into a shade of browny bronze trees, with me lodged over his head. Harly fumbled with a zip on his overalls, then did a loud spurting wee like a horse passing water. It stank of hot apples from all that cider. I thought of a similar scene from a book that Mum used to love reading aloud. Then it came back to me. It was like the giant Gulliver, pissing over the Queen's castle in Paris.

TWENTY~EIGHT

W hen he was finally done, we moved off and I got lowered onto mossy rocks. Harly sat on a thistly bank beside me, rubbing grubby sleeves over his face. His red smudges were like warpaint.

He was calmer away from all those people. He took off his hat and listened to the chirping birds. We watched cars fly by on the road below. Glum kids pressing noses at the windows, dying to get out. Parents with red faces arguing in the front.

Crimson and copper leaves floated down. Harly grabbed one as it scurried by. Holding it to the sunlight, he rubbed its thick dark veins. He stroked the blushing leaf over his nose.

'Look,' he said, so very calm now. 'Just look . . . look!'

I studied the leaf carefully, stuck it in a pocket, then gazed anxiously over at the bustle in Charlie's fields. A crowd still buzzed and blethered by the bar. The gossip would be raging about both of us. *Scaring the children like that! Attacking poor David! Who the hell were they?*

Then a rattle at my left ear. Harly was shaking a small brown plastic bottle. It had a screw cap and some pills inside.

He gave a wide grin, lifting his inky moustache. 'Got drugs,' he said, joggling the jar again. 'Dr Fuller gimme them.'

'Who's he?'

'Doctor at school I come from. Ain't going back. Can't make me.'

I took the bottle. It had a long name printed on the white label, ending in '-oxide'. I read out the other details. 'Avoid alcohol and using machinery. One a day. Do not exceed stated dose.'

'God . . . Harly, you shouldn't drink cider with these. What they for?'

Harly took the jar back, stuffing it in his overalls. 'Took three last night,' he said. 'Couldn't sleep. Got cold. Got lonely. You found Riding Hood yet?'

I chewed my fingers, feeling way out of my depth. 'I'll try the local library. Look, Harlequin, I wanna help if I can. But you've really gotta trust me. And if you're hiding from something, why come to the fair today? There's hundreds here from all over. You don't half stand out in a crowd. It's not your looks that'll give you away, it's your height. You can't disguise that.'

He jammed the big hat down over his ears. I looked at its deep rim, a garden of its own, with little mushrooms and windblown shoots growing. The moist woolly brown felt it was made of allowed trapped seeds to sprout.

I stroked his right elbow. 'Come on, Harly, at least tell us where you're from. What about this school you were at? Where was it, somewhere round here?'

He put a finger to his red lips and whispered, 'Done bad, Glenn Jackson. I done bad stuff. Now they comin' for me and I got nowhere.'

'Who's coming?' I said urgently. I thought of Baz yesterday. 'Is it because of those fireworks you keep seeing? They're not gonna harm you. It's only . . .'

Only what? Someone trying to attract alien life with Catherine wheels? Try telling Harly that, Glenn Jackson. I breathed long and slow through my nose. I'd best go slow here. He was cracked up with cider, pills and that country fair mob.

'Gotta sleep,' Harly said wearily. 'Tired now. You bring Riding Hood and sing songs again, yeah?'

He got up creakily and shambled away, his hat brushing low branches.

'Be careful, Harly,' I called after him. 'If anyone sees

you they might follow. And stay away from Charlie's place. I'll bring you some food.'

He waved the back of a huge hand. I went off moodily in the other direction. I'd bet Mum would've known how to handle this. At work she dealt with loads of difficult people, from awkward customers to staff with personal problems.

It was over a week since I'd seen Mum, the longest I'd ever been without her. Slouching along the path, I had to imagine what I really knew of her. The warm snug face, chunky build and bright hair. Fond of Manchester music and Italian cooking. A teenage punk who once had her hair in pink stalks. The evening course at a local tech where she'd studied basic accounts. Then the long hours working in Booths. The simple happiness at getting promoted, and celebrating in Pizza Hut. The endless clearing up around the house of Dad's records and my paint stains. I felt tears pricking. That squeaky, mocking voice from Friday at school seared through me.

'Mummy come home . . . Nobody loves me.'

And then . . . there she was. My mum! Not far away at all. I could see her face, her crumpled floating face. Why was Mum drowning in the shallow river, the one that came splashing down over the woodland's white stones?

It was my A3 sketchpad, stolen from school, thrown in the stream. It lay open at a sheet with a painting of Mum I'd once taken days over. Now the heavy colours were blotched and runny. I pulled the ruined, soaking thing out and rested it on bracken.

Every portrait was a blurry mess. There were pictures of red-brick factories back in Burnley, or of the few old school friends who'd been patient enough to pose. Their features were dissolved and grotesque, as if seen through glass. Thick dribbles of coloured paint ran around the edges.

Without going berserk I carefully tore out every big page. I found a thin branch on each of the next eleven trees that I passed. I thrust an A3 sheet through their woody fingers to dangle in the breeze. Looking back when I'd hung the last one, the forest was like a gallery of bizarre modern art. Great white pages flapped among the greenery and yellow, with big murky images.

I wanted everyone who strolled by to wonder at such twisted brushwork.

TWENTY~NINE

With Dad away at work on Monday morning, I went through his jacket and trouser pockets. Finding several quid in loose change, I went out into the first blast of cold for days. My legs felt wobbly after yesterday's upshots and I dreaded seeing anyone who knew me. The sky was blue-grey with a frisky breeze. Golden leaves flew about like nimble wings. The first day of half term.

I spent the cash in Henderson's on food for Harly. More bread, some tomatoes, orange juice and strong Cheddar.

Torbeck's library was in a long slate building. An old redheaded woman worked there with a big red setter dog. They looked well-matched. I found a copy of *Little Red Riding Hood* in the picture books. I also took a Van Gogh biog and a dog-eared copy of *Kes*. The library woman never asked for any ID. I just filled in an address card and went on my way.

Huffing up the quarry's road, I passed those dark stone cottages. There was a crumbling outdoor toilet on the edge of the woods nearby. The door's bolt had been busted, so maybe Harly had been using the bog there. He had to go somewhere.

A bunch of Geordie tourists were taking photos of the quarry. They stood at one edge, clutching each other as the deserted pit whined in the wind. Its inky black lake rippled in a kingdom far below. Trees on the crater's rim sighed like sleepy giants. An excited Newcastle woman shouted in her husband's ear.

'It's amazing, pet! Like summat from *Lord of the Rings*! Y'half expect to see that whatsit . . . Dildo Baggins?'

The group ignored me as I stole up to Harly's shack, a hundred metres away over the slatey wasteland. He was crouched in a corner, hat on his face. Checking no one was watching, I tapped the door quietly. He took the hat away.

'They gone?' he asked.

I shook my head and lifted the bag. 'Breakfast?' I said.

Harly nodded eagerly, pulling a dirty blanket around him. Cold autumn air flowed through a square hole that might once have been a window. Now it just blew in earthy outdoor smells.

Harly glugged juice from the carton. His teeth chattered as tomato seeds dribbled on his chin. He bit the cheese packet open and stuffed bread down. Then the dirty shack got shaken under the ricochet of a fighter plane. The singed beams above us trembled. As the jet's echo faded, Harly whispered through a mouthful of blanket.

'All morning . . . They been out all day . . . Never stop searching.'

I knelt on a sharp slab. 'It's all right, Harlequin,' I said. 'It's only military stuff. They practise mountain flying, for when there's a war on.'

I knew that made no sense to him. He wasn't listening anyway, just whimpering under that foul blanket. It was ages before he came out and two other planes howled over in that time.

The sun broke its cloud cover, sending a warm shaft into the dingy hut. Peering round the door, I saw the Geordies had gone, and left three McDonald's cartons.

'Safe now,' I said to Harly. 'Let's go outside. Oh, and I nearly forgot.' I emptied the books from a Henderson's bag.

Harly seized one with Red Riding Hood on its cover. He smiled through his mad scarlet blotches and black lines.

'Read it later, Glenn Jackson,' he said. 'You tell it.'

He bent like an old man to crouch out. On the way he jabbed an old newspaper deeper into a top ledge. Its grimy paper poked from cracked slate.

'Need shithouse,' Harly said, grabbing a roll of kitchen towel. He let rip with a fart that would've ruptured a smaller person. He hulked over the rubble towards those old cottages and their outside bog.

Waiting in the sunny stillness, I poked around the weird rocky heaps Harly had made. Rough shapes of animal bodies in three lines of three.

Harly ran back soon after, looking over his jutting shoulder. Then he bounded down to the stream for a splash.

'Seen some bloke with a gun,' he said, his red face dripping. 'Coming this way mebbe.'

'Father Charlie,' I decided. 'We'll make tracks.' I'd had the idea of hiking over to King's Cragg with Harly, to see if Baz was making ETI contact. It might ease Harly's weird worries, and Baz was mad enough to take Harly at face value. Maybe between us we could prise more info out of Harly. He was dodging my questions too easily.

Harly ran back and kicked open the shack's door. He came out clutching the cardboard roll.

'Need this,' he said. 'Can see for ever.'

I was about to smile, or agree that his useless telescope

gave great views, but then a low-flying jet zapped in from the hills behind the quarry. Harly hit the deck, face down, sprawling long and wide. He arched into a ball, chest and head curving up and backwards. Both hands were locked together along his spine. His legs bent like rubber. His boot soles were up on his shoulders. The space his body made was a rough circle.

The jet's bladed wings veered right. A screaming dart swung away over King's Cragg.

Now Harly changed shape. He curled up dead still, like an embryo, his face between jack-knifed thighs. Another bolt thundered from the blue sky. This one from the west. It scorched over King's Cragg towards the quarry at three hundred miles per hour. A brown blur, arrow-like from nose to tail. I imagined being under fire in a war zone. And then I was.

When the bomb dropped, it fell at an angle from the jet. It looked like someone had thrown a barrel out. Then came an explosion which shattered the earth. A mile away, but still loud and shocking. I flinched and fell back. Smoke swept up in the deep valley between hills and quarry. The jet zipped on, out of sight in seconds. The boom from its lost bomb echoed around the mountains.

I lay stunned, but Harly scrambled up, grabbing his hat. He screamed and ran to the hills, over the stream with one leap, then sprawling through heaps of high bracken. I crouched by the shack, scanning the sky in panic.

The fighter returned minutes later, but slower this time, dipping its wings. It swung left over Torbeck with a rumble. I went running after Harly. I heard his freaky, frightened wailing. But he was out of my reach in minutes on his whacking long limbs.

THIRTY

I legged it down the half mile of crumbling track — Quarry Road. Another explosion could be looming. I passed a startled Father Charlie. My head was full of crazy images — American planes being hijacked to bomb the Northwest. My clothes were sopping with sweat. I stood on the bridge behind the waterfalls, gulping air. Farm trucks went thumping up the road right by me. A whining siren echoed through the valley.

The blast must have been heard back in Torbeck. People from the shops were out on the pavements, their eyes to the hills for once.

The lunchtime news came too soon to give any details. I hung around our garden gate for a bit in case more planes came soaring over. TV crews passed through in the afternoon. When it all seemed calmer I made a stab at some homework. Dad was back by six and we put the telly on.

The Northwest news round-up had a full report. An

F15 Strike Eagle, a US military jet, had been on a routine training mission. Due to mechanical failure it had dropped a ten-kilo bomb onto a remote site near Torbeck. The planes normally just carried dummy bombs. A sizeable hole had been blasted in an empty field. A US Air Force spokesman said an inquiry was underway. The Shadow Home Secretary was asking the government for a quick response.

I saw film footage of the old quarry, King's Cragg and the charred field. The local MP was on, 'expecting answers to the questions this awful event raises'. Some locals were shown too, moaning about the constant low flying.

'We can't sleep safely in our beds . . .'

'Next time we might not be so lucky . . .'

'Left me speechless . . . Didn't believe it at first . . .'

My dad was amazed. 'Strewth! It's like that — whatsit? Friendly fire. And we thought Burnley got violent, Glenn.'

I sat quiet. I daren't mention what I'd seen, or I'd have to give a reason for lurking around the quarry. And if Dad could hardly talk about Mum, he'd be hacked off to hear about Harlequin's mad mysteries.

He was chuffed with himself though, now he'd got a job. He whistled in the bedroom, tidying his hair. And there was decent grub for tea, brought back from the café: leftover veggie sausages, ciabatta bread, apple slices.

'Geoff's coming tomorrow,' he said. 'He'll be here sixish, so let him in if I ain't back.'

I hadn't seen big Geoff since the day he'd helped us move.

'And I'm popping out later,' Dad went on. 'Not the Queen's Head this time. Thought I'd check out The Ploughman; it's meant to have good beer. You wanna come? They let kids in these pubs, being all touristy.'

'No, thanks. And you're not off to . . . make an impact, are you? Just a quiet drink?'

Dad smiled. 'Just a quiet drink,' he said. I watched him leave at half past eight. But something about what he was wearing bothered me. Not the shiny Doc Marts, or the leather jacket and red jeans. Then as I sat watching telly it hit me. His T-shirt. Oh hell . . . not that one. Not in that pub of all places.

It was an old Smiths tour shirt. It showed a soldier in a tin helmet, and the slogan 'MEAT IS MURDER' in big letters. Dad had gone to The Ploughman – a pub where huntsmen, cattle farmers and local butchers met. That's the carnivorous crowd he'd be mixing with in his 'MEAT IS MURDER' T-shirt.

*

He'd sat at the bar where the regulars gather. There were plenty of people in after the bombing drama. Everyone wanted to have their say and yak about who'd been interviewed on the news. The village was buzzing with snotty anger. That air-rifle attack on old Mr Guthrie still hadn't been solved either. Blokes much older than Dad stood sucking pints and spinning tall stories. After a while, when things were quieter, they noticed him enough to start firing questions.

'New round here, aren't you?'

'Where you from?'

'Why'd you leave there?'

'Where's the wife . . . she not come?'

'Funny time for her to go away. What with you moving and all.'

'What's that on yer shirt? *Meat . . . is . . . murder.*'

'Meat's murder, is it? Ah right. What d'you eat then?'

'What y'reckon shoes are made of, lad? It's a cow's hide on yer feet, not plastic wrap.'

Dad tried to humour them, but his old stand-up jokes hardly raised a laugh. This wasn't his crowd and he knew it. He told them about his mate Geoff, coming to stay tomorrow night. And how big Geoff had once got so drunk he'd eaten a pub's Christmas decorations. He'd scoffed paper streamers and a few burst balloons.

Even a shiny Christmas cracker, and later puked up its naff keyring.

Dad rocked back on a bar stool, laughing. No one joined in; they just sipped brown pints or rolled cigarettes.

'Tek a while to put up, y'know,' one said. 'Them decorations.'

'Aye, bad luck to bring 'em down early.'

'That's raight. Not afore Twelfth Night.'

'Can't be good.'

Dad finished his pint and left with a perky 'Cheers!' He limped back home, having got it badly wrong again. The phone rang as he came through the front door.

'For you, Glenn!' he shouted, then drooped upstairs.

Thinking it must be Mum, I spoke sulkily. 'Yeah?'

'Glenn? It's Baz. Your buddy.'

'Baz! Which planet you been taken to? Can they fetch me?'

'Still on this one, worst luck. You busy tomorrow? I've got a little project you might enjoy. Now that you're in on my secret other life.'

'What project?'

'Tell you tomorrow, if you're on.'

'OK, I've no other invites. What time?'

'About eleven. Have a packed lunch ready. See ya.'

I went off to bed, still wondering where Harly had ended up. I drew his handstands and other recent acrobatics. He did it without thinking — his own bizarre genius. Tomorrow, after what Baz had planned, I'd search for Harly in the hills. Some instinct told me he'd not gone far. Either he coughed up some truths or I'd threaten to stop feeding him. If I didn't find him then TV crews might, or tourists, or whoever Harly felt was tracking him. And that country fair crowd would be after his blood. Someone must have seen Harly hiding out by now, no matter how careful he was. I knew Father Charlie was hunting. It felt like the net was closing in.

THIRTY~ONE

B az came round as the church clock struck eleven.
It was always nine minutes fast before noon, and
seven slow afterwards.

'Bit warm out there,' he said, putting down a heavy
rucksack. He was sweating, yet wore an old duffel
coat and black woolly hat. He cleaned his glasses
with bog roll. With his hearing aids and shabby coat
he looked like a boy aged sixty. My very uncool
buddy.

'Heard you found a new friend on Sunday,' he said.
'Some great beanpole who whisked you off. What's
happening, Jacko? You got a secret life too?'

'Did have,' I said, slicing a tomato. 'Calls himself
Harlequin. Been living rough up near the quarry. He's
a bit sort of backward, but friendly, and he saved my
life once. Then that bomb dropped yesterday and he
just took off.'

'Wowzer,' said Baz. 'We're a scary pair. Might see

your giant later if he's hanging around still. We'll be quite high up.'

I licked marge off my fingers. 'To do what exactly?'

He threw a new copy of *Psychic Babble* at me, the journal for alien-friendly mountain watchers. 'Turn to page twenty,' Baz ordered.

I flicked through to a photo-feature. There were three pictures taken from the air showing the same image. Carved into a hillside somewhere was a huge smiling face. It looked the size of a great crop circle, but with a beaming mouth and eyes.

'It's a sign of greeting,' said Baz. 'People living near the special mountain sites are being asked to take part. So if an alien craft hovers over King's Cragg they'll read the face as friendly. The mountain vibes attract them first, then the breezy expression calms their nerves. You get it?'

Like hell I did. 'How we ever gonna make one like that? We're bound to get seen. It's asking for trouble.'

Baz shook his flat curls. 'Not a bit. And, anyway, it's your chance to stick two fingers up at everyone here. Make a great big smile in the hills to show they can't get you down.'

I wrapped some sarnies in foil. 'Couldn't we do a great big V-sign instead?'

'What?' cried Baz. 'I'm trying to attract them from

beyond, not repel. And no one from Torbeck's gonna see us. You could launch the next Mars mission up there and no sod down here would notice. So what d'you say?'

'I'd say we're both cuckoo, but what the heck! How do we go about it?'

Baz picked up his bulging rucksack. 'Follow me, city boy, and I'll show you. After that bomb yesterday we've gotta restore some good karma round King's Cragg. Double-quick.'

Striding up the village road like men on a mission, we saw Laura and Lavinia. I thrust out my chest, showing off the green loop. Lavinia tugged Laura, crossing the road well before us.

'Charming,' said Baz. 'Know what your biggest mistake was, Jacko?'

'No. So tell me, Captain Kirk.'

'Your biggest mistake,' said Baz, tripping over his long feet, 'was liking Laura and making it so obvious. Not that you'd have got close to Lavinia either. If I was a shrink I'd say she's got some possessive disorder since Ronnie topped himself. Y'know that stuff she put round about yours being a problem family? She's only trying to hide the problems in her own. Face it, mate, you're onto a loser. Laura's under wraps.'

'We'll see,' I said as Baz trod on my toes. We took

the rising road past the Co-op, with dreamy green pastures on the right. 'I ain't quitting.'

'Fair dos,' said Baz, clomping over the cattle grid. 'Long as you know what you're dealing with.'

Baz led me up into the spacious valley, where water lapped lazily in marshy beds. King's Cragg's peaks lay ahead in rising triangles. The youth hostel below glowed white under the sun.

But Baz pushed me onto a path going up the lower slopes. 'Wrendale Bank,' he said. 'It's not dead high but it lies on a smooth slant. You can see it for miles, from above, below or to the sides.'

We had a steep climb as the day grew hazy and warm. My sweaty face drew a glut of black midges. Baz panted under his bulging blue rucksack. At last he stopped and threw it down. He took out a fat tape measure, a rusty can, a thick pole and some sharp shears. From his duffel pocket came a tin of white spray. I watched as he drove the pole into soft earth. The bracken there was up to our knees.

'Ready?' said Baz, handing me the tape measure. 'Right, you stay here, holding this end. Press it firmly on top of the pole and hold real steady.'

He plunged through crackling ferns for about forty metres. The tape just kept feeding out and out for ever, until Baz halted.

'Keep it tight!' he shouted. 'No wobbling.' He began to lunge around in a perfect circle, holding his end firmly. He sprayed a white ring of bracken as he went.

All this time he stayed the same distance from where I stood at the centre. I kept the tape nice and taut, watching him all the way around.

In ten minutes he was back at his own starting point. He fed the tape out another two metres beyond the first circle and did the same circuit again. Another huge loop of sprayed bracken.

I looked on amazed, beginning to guess his method now. Clever stuff, I thought. This design is gonna be immense.

And I was right. The bracken growing between the two sprayed rings, two metres apart, was to be cut away. When the space was hacked clear there'd be the huge, round outline of a face.

'You've twigged,' said Baz, looking at my smile.

'Who does the cutting?' I asked.

'Me,' said Baz. 'You follow behind with this can of weedkiller. Splash it in the gaps I make and the plants won't grow back for some time. You ready?'

Baz got busy with his big shears. He snipped and snapped at rusty stems. We both lobbed the cuttings out of the way. I dribbled some horrid chemical into the round clearing, telling myself it was in the cause of cosmic bonding.

Over an hour later Baz had his magic circle. We ran around it like sprinters on an athletics track, but the job was nowhere near done.

'Peepholes first,' said Baz. So we went through the process again, on a smaller scale, hacking out a pair of eyes. I had to take Baz's word for it that they were level. The mouth was a bit easier — a long slice of slashed bracken.

I flung myself down after that, knackered out. Baz got sarnies from his rucksack and I downed a tin of warm shandy. We ate in the afternoon sunshine, looking down over Torbeck and Burnside Tarn. I told Baz about Friday night and the death of Goldeneye duck. I didn't mention old Mr Guthrie. There'd be a time and place for that. When Mum came back, *if* she came back, she'd support me through any local vendettas.

'Don't surprise me,' said Baz. 'If it wasn't you under attack they'd find someone else. But they know you're a fighter and that scares their sort. And you've got a talent like they can only dream of.'

Baz passed me a cigarette. 'My nan's,' he said. 'She tries not to leave 'em lying around, but I found a pack in her spare slippers.'

We lit up and smoked chokily. I lay back in the crackly ferns, watching the sky clear to a brilliant blue.

'Tell me some more psychic babble stuff,' I said. 'What's up there waiting, Baz?'

Baz relit his burned fag end. His wide ears waggled like a signal was coming in. He was deep in thought.

I rolled onto an elbow. 'And why are you sure these visitors would be friendly?' I asked. 'They might be lethal sods. You could invite mass murder onto King's Cragg.'

Baz offered me another ciggie. I shook my head, feeling the last one scarring my throat.

'Some experts would agree,' said Baz. He stroked his flat brown curls reflectively. 'Stephen Hawking says we should just keep our heads down and that anything heading here would be hostile. But we've already been sending billions of signals out for seventy years, since radio and TV began. Something out there is just now getting hold of our early cartoons, or a wireless broadcast from pre-war Texas. They know about our culture, all right. Either they're too weak from laughing to invade, or they're pretty peaceful. I can't see them killing each other like we do.'

I lay thinking about this as a fighter jet screeched over.

Baz looked up too. He said, 'Some poor pilot's in the squelch after yesterday. There're crowds heading near the quarry to see the famous bombed field.'

I felt anxious then to finish, and sat up. 'Have we done here?' I asked.

Baz grinned. 'Just the ears,' he said. 'Let's make 'em big and ugly like mine. My unique universal signature.'

It was late afternoon by the time we were through. Baz had also insisted we mark out a cigarette shape, dangling defiantly from the long mouth slit. I wanted to fling my bruised bones on a bed of bracken to rest. But the thought of crowds poking around the slate quarry had me worried. Suppose Harly was taking those pills, with a mob gawping at him in his rotting room. It could all send him haywire again.

I skipped after Baz down Wrendale Bank.

'Don't look back,' he said. 'I know you're dying to, but wait until we've got the full view below.'

It was worth waiting for. I felt a nervous jolt when I turned and saw the scale of it. This enormous wheel of a cheeky face cut into the hillside. The eyes were nearly level. The mouth was a bit crooked, but so what? A twisted smile fitted my mood. Baz was dead proud of the great big jug lugs. And of the fag, jutting from the lower lip like a rebel poet's.

'Hellfire!' I breathed. 'There'll be a right row about this.'

'Tough,' said Baz. 'Just keep quiet. And thanks, by

the way, Glenn. From me and whatever might be attracted by it.'

I stared some more at our day's grafting. A slow satisfied grin curled onto my lips. That beaming broadside up there was better than any V-sign. It was a ballsy 'up yours' to the cruel world below.

I left Baz at the woodland path, his rucksack jangling away downhill. Despite the moaning muscles in my legs I jogged along. Going upwards past the rampant waterfalls was harder, then tougher still up the hilly half-mile of Quarry Road. Small groups of sightseers came straggling by. It was colder now and chilly sweat was caking my skin.

At the top of Quarry Road I suddenly ducked into the woods. Father Charlie was prowling around. I watched across the wasteland as he peered through the shack's ruined window. Harly had hinted at stealing stuff from Charlie's farm. Food for sure, and maybe even money. At last Charlie trudged away down Quarry Road, right past my hideout, gun cocked and ready.

In the slummy dwelling were the crumbs of our last meal, and the library books I'd left after that explosion. Baz's matches rattled in my pocket. I must've nabbed them earlier. I rustled up some stray wood among the rubble for a little fire in the shack. I'd let the smoke drift through that window gap and alert

Harly I was here if he was slinking by. I could wait a couple of hours, reading books by the firelight.

But the cold flaky timber wouldn't light. Then I saw that newspaper I'd seen Harly ram under the low ceiling. On tiptoes I jabbed an old copy of the *Daily Record* until it fell. It was dated December, five years back. I crouched by the cold sticks, my back to the half-open door. The paper's cover featured a sex scandal, and I stuffed the front sheets among the twigs. I scraped three matches alight. A Celtic striker on the back page began burning.

As the flames took hold, the shack's door slammed open. Harlequin raged in, his back bent. His violent screaming blew me down, his big hat falling onto me. He kicked the smoky woodpile. He stamped on the matchbox. Doubled up like someone punched in the guts, he snatched the grimy sheets. Still screaming in long bursts, he slung them aside.

I sprawled on a foul blanket. My gooseberry eyes goggled at Harlequin. He grabbed me by my jacket, dragging me over the grubby ground. His blotchy face was a blur of howling mouth and red cheekbones. A second later I was outside, the door slammed behind me.

It groaned back open a touch. Just before I fled I saw Harly kneeling. He banged his bare head on the sharp slate walls. I heard each sickening crack of skull. The torment of his loud wailing chased after me.

It still stung my ears back in Torbeck. Clammy with freezing sweat, I made it home at last. I stood against our front door, my red nose running, my cold eyes streaming.

THIRTY~TWO

Geoff's blue car was outside. Dad's best mate had arrived and I should have been here at six to let him in.

They were sitting at the kitchen table, the smell of a burned fry-up clouding the air. Geoff wore his XL claret Burnley football top. His thumping big fists cradled a bottle of bitter. His dark hair was cut even shorter on his plump scalp. Dad's quiff was well slicked back.

'Where've you been?' he called. 'Poor Geoff were sat outside for an hour.'

'Sorry, Geoff,' I said, feeling my heart slowly settle. 'You all right?'

'All right, mate. You?'

I held out my palms, nodding back bluntly. Geoff reddened as if he could sense my problems. He slurped his bitter and ran a slice of bread around a greasy plate.

I spent that Tuesday night getting cleaned up and

letting my muscles unclench in the bath. Later I cut some of Laura's green ribbon and looped it on Rembrandt bear's paws.

Dad and Geoff had gone out drinking. There were still some other pubs Dad hadn't made an arse of himself in. But a night with Geoff would be testing. Dad couldn't be sensible after three pints, whereas Geoff only got going after six.

I woke in the night with my bedroom floor throbbing. The stereo was on full in the living room below. A moody bass riff pulsed over acoustic guitars. A lonely ache trembled in the singer's voice. Something dreamy and melancholy, about half-dying when the one you love passes by.

Finally the sound of rainfall under sweet closing chords. I crept downstairs in blue pyjamas. The room was heavy with smoke and one dimmed light. Dad sat sprawled in the armchair, eyes closed, breathing harshly. He held a roll-up fag, its ashy tip on the verge of breaking. Geoff had his bulky claret back to me as he lay sifting through CDs and vinyl. He lifted the record-player stylus, killing the sound.

'Geoff?' I said softly, startling him. He rolled over, spilling a bottle of Hawkshead Bitter. It frothed on the carpet like burning acid. I put it upright, my bare feet getting cold. Dad snored and gasped.

Geoff's face was a drunken pink, like a piggy mask. He scratched his receding dark hair. 'Yeah, mate?' he said. 'What's cooking?'

The sitting room was quiet now apart from Dad's grunts. 'Where's my mum, Geoff?' I asked. 'Isn't she coming back? Have you seen her?'

Geoff sat up heavily, crossing his legs. He looked at my crashed-out dad. He looked at his gold watch. It was half past midnight.

'She'll tell you herself,' he said. 'I'm sure of it. She misses you, Glenn. She's bound to.'

I shivered a little. 'Geoff? Is she . . . staying with Ray? Is my mum with Ray now?'

'Who?' said Geoff, thrusting his chubby chin.

'Ray. Some tosser from Booths' wine section. I met him once at the cinema with Mum.'

Geoff began to frown then relaxed into a smile. 'No, Glenn. She ain't gone off with Ray. She'll phone you soon, I'm sure. Maybe get to meet up this half term.'

'Right,' I said, gnawing a thumbnail. I got up stiffly. 'Oh . . . and Geoff?'

'Yes, mate?'

'Can you, erm, keep the noise down? It's just the neighbours . . . We don't really know them.'

'Yeah right. Someone's already been round to complain.'

'Who?' I said, in a panic. 'Not Val, was it, our friend from the shop?'

'No, I met Val earlier. Nah, just some sour old crow banging on the window. Face like the back end of a dinted bin. Don't reckon much to this Torbeck place. I nearly punched some tosspot's lights out earlier. These blokes were taking the piss out of your dad. Not to his face or anything, just sniping in a pub corner. Ain't very subtle round here, are they? Or brave.'

'Not very,' I said. 'A few nice ones though. G'night then, Geoff. Give my love to Mum if you see her.'

'Right. Cheers, Glenn. Keep your pecker up.'

Next thing I knew it was quarter past ten. Wednesday morning. Dad must have struggled to work somehow. Geoff's car was gone. The phone rang as I watched some bread under the grill.

'Glenn? It's Baz. Thought I better tell you this. I went up near Wrendale Bank earlier. Wanted to take some photos of our work and get them off to *Psychic Babble*. Coming back, I saw someone crouching against the drystone wall. You know, the one running by that woodland path? It could only have been your massive mate, 'cos even kneeling down he could be seen a mile off. Seemed scared of going down to the village.'

'Go on,' I said quickly.

'Well, I goes over to see if he wants owt. You said he was friendly. Then he begins ranting at me. "Tell Glenn Jackson. Tell him to bring breakfast. Got money, got drugs. Tell him from Harlequin." Anyway, he said this a few times, then sort of stood on his hands and walked away. You sure about all this, mate? You want some help?'

I could smell burning toast. 'Not yet, Baz,' I said. 'Keep quiet though, yeah? I guess he saw us together yesterday so he trusts you. I've gotta go, my breakfast's in flames.'

'OK. Well you just be careful, Glenn. 'Cos from where I'm standing your crazy mate sounds pretty desperate.'

THIRTY~THREE

I had enough pocket money to go shopping but raided the fridge first. In Henderson's I caught the smirky glances of two blokes. They wore building-site clobber with dusty boots and were waiting near Val's till. It was dead obvious they'd been talking about Dad, or me. They couldn't meet my steely green gaze though.

At the cheese counter I grabbed some crumbly Lancashire. But I thought Harly might fancy a change, so went for soft French brie and pongy Italian blue.

It was just after midday when I reached the quarry site. Harly's slender red face filled the shack's hollow window. He'd been waiting for me. His bloodshot blue eyes peered under a crumpled hat. Going inside I saw the remains of that old newspaper stuffed back up in a crevice. Harly spread out a squalid blanket.

'You sit, Glenn,' he said gently.

I sat down, feeling my uneasy nerves relax. Harly bit open the packet of brie.

'Stinks!' he said. 'Bloody stinker!' But he ate it anyway, even the rind that I always cut.

'The blue one's even stronger,' I said.

Harly sniffed the Italian chunk. He dabbed some onto a chocolate éclair and gorged. A carton of grapefruit juice went down in one quaff, some of it trickling over his bristly chin. He sat back against the flinty wall, gasping, his bright hair brushing a cobweb.

'Seen summat,' he said, reaching over to clutch my wrist. 'Came in the night and sits there spying.'

I chewed a cold veggie sausage from Dad's café. 'What came in the night?' I asked, thinking of Father Charlie. 'Spying from where?'

Harly crawled on hands and knees to the door. He put his hatful of head through the gap, with me peering out above him.

Harlequin whispered, 'Up there in them hills. Look . . . look at bloody size of 'im!'

I squeaked the door open further. You could see Wrendale Bank a good mile to the west from here. Like Baz had said, it was visible from almost anywhere. Our alien-friendly face, hacked into the bracken slopes, beamed back. It had the kind of staring eyes you get in paintings that seem to look at you from every angle.

'Come back in, Harly,' I said. 'It's OK, it's not been

put there to watch you. It was just two lads messing about yesterday. I saw them.'

Harly crept back to his cold corner. Tucked up to the wall, he shook his head violently. 'Wasn't there before,' he said. 'It watches and watches and only since I come here. Only since they dropped a bomb, Glenn Jackson.'

He squeezed his tired pink eyes shut and snuggled into a blanket. I saw two of the library books under a jumble of smashed wood.

'Harly?' I said, wriggling over to him. 'You got that other book? The Red Riding Hood one? Only it's not mine, mate.'

His eyes opened and fluttered, staring around the dull den. Some other soiled blankets were piled on the far wall. He pitched forwards and yanked the book from under them.

'Been looking,' he said, wheezing through a heavy chest. 'Can't read it all.' He caressed the cover picture. It showed a dreamy girl with a basket on her arm. She had long black hair and a bright red cape. Harly rubbed a stubbly blond cheek against it, then lobbed the book at me.

'You sit here, Glenn. You read. Want some drugs, yeah?' He rummaged under the blanket and shook the jar of pills.

'No. And you just be careful. You hear?'

He pulled the rug over his knees like a granny. I sat on the patch he spread alongside. My head rested back on his big bicep. I read out the book's inside-cover details.

'Original title was *Little Red-Cap*. Collected by the Brothers Grimm around 1812 from Jeanette Hassenpflug. Also influenced by *Le Petit Chaperon Rouge*, from 1697.'

I cleared my throat and began. Harly kept stopping me to grab the book and fondle the girl's pictures. There was one of the wolf in a top hat and fancy jacket, licking his lips. Harly bashed it roughly, denting several pages. I finished the last lines and let Harly nick the book back.

'Found your mum yet?' he asked, coughing up dark phlegm. 'She home yet?'

I shook my head, feeling it rub on Harly's overalls. 'Not yet. What about yours, Harly — have you still got one? She waiting for you somewhere?'

He lifted the blanket off, stepped over my legs and hunched away. I sighed heavily, tidied our lunch litter, and followed. I found him gazing up at that face on Wrendale Bank. Its crooked smile and jutting cigarette looked sinister. Harly pulled his hat lower to shield his eyes. He tapped at the slate mounds with beefy boots, kicking pieces back into the blunt animal shapes.

'Did have mum once,' he murmured. 'Did save her life like I done yours. She in heaven now with Badger. All dead and buried . . . like this . . .'

Harly got down and laid himself out flat and long. Face down, he dug a little hole in the earth, putting an ear to the cavity.

'What do you listen for?' I asked.

'Sssshh. Them voices.'

'*What* voices?' I urged. '*Whose?*'

'Them dead ones. Waiting for me. I gonna pay for what I done.'

I knelt beside him, lightly touching his endless spine.

'Listen, Harlequin, I don't know what's ever happened to you. But you're starving and freezing to death like this. It's winter soon — you can't go on living here. Let me help you, mate, if I can. You saved my life, remember? And someone's bound to find you up here, after what happened at the country fair.'

Harly sat up slowly, his back rising like a drawbridge. He pulled me to him, his bicep tight round my Adam's apple. I threaded my fingers under his muscles to ease the pressure. His voice was all subdued and scared.

'Ain't going back no more,' he whispered. 'Stay here with you, Glenn. But I gotta sleep now . . . taken drugs. Come back soon, yeah, with stinky cheese?'

He lifted me up under the arms, making my stomach swirl. 'I'll be back,' I said, stranded in midair. 'You rest. I'll come back soon with some proper help.'

Harly's blue eyes narrowed. He shook me like a shabby puppet. 'Who you told?' he whispered. 'What you done, Glenn Jackson?' The muscles in his neck tightened. His grip dug into my armpits.

'N-nothing,' I said, dangling and shaking. He shook me again, making my jaw rattle. I bit my tongue's tip, tasting wet blood. 'Harly, stop! Leave it!'

His red and black painted mouth dropped open. He rested me onto the rocky ground and began whimpering. His back stooped and he tucked both elbows around his face.

'It's OK, Harly,' I said. I touched his crooked shoulder. 'It's OK, I've said nothing. But my dad's a good bloke. He could help you.'

Harly clutched his hat's corners. He jumped on the spot. 'Tell no one else?' he said.

'No one,' I agreed. 'Not ever.'

Harly stumbled into the grotty den, his muddy laces trailing. I trudged home, tasting a chill in the air's hazy smoke. Now it felt right to tell my dad about this, him being some sort of grown-up. In his job for Burnley council he'd met all types. I remembered another of his many mad stories. On my thirteenth birthday, six months back, he'd told it to my former schoolmates who'd come round for pizzas . . .

Dad had been inspecting a ground-floor council flat. The old couple living there had complained of an odd smell. They'd also heard peculiar noises from above and pointed out a spreading stain on their ceiling. Dad went off to inspect, his guts turning over in dread. He'd always feared finding some victim of a gruesome murder.

There were two more flats up the dusty dark stairs. One was occupied; the other had been empty for ages. The tenant was a known dope dealer from Blackburn. A pale thin guy with dreadlocks. He'd battered the door through into the unused flat.

Dad went in, flashing a torch. Its beam picked out smashed glass, empty cartons, a syringe, a white rocking horse. Dad heard strange scufflings. The stench was awful. He crept into the dismal kitchen and yelled in shock. A flock of young sheep was huddled there. They baa-ed in terror and barged about. It seems this drug pusher had been driving around Lancashire farms at night in his van, nicking lambs. He'd smuggled them back to his place to fatten them up in secret. They'd be sold to a dodgy butcher for cash in hand. Hence the smell, the stains, the noise.

'The floor all covered in sheep shit,' Dad finished.

'Then this dreadlocked druggie appeared on the landing, dancing all trance-like . . . spaced out on ecstasy.'

My mates had lapped it up. They thought Dad was cool with his loud music, teddy-boy quiff and crazy tales. And he was funny given the right audience; he could be cool.

But that Wednesday in Torbeck, when he got home, he was neither.

THIRTY~FOUR

He hunched on the sofa, hands clasped.

'The café ain't keeping me on,' he growled. 'The manager says he can't afford my wages, but I reckon he just don't like me. Thinks I spend too much time chatting to customers. They dig me though. Hope his bloody business goes arse up.'

I sat beside him, smelling the café's chip fat on his jacket. 'What we gonna do, Dad? It's like we're just hanging on for the ride.'

He slumped back, pulling cushions into his lap. 'I dunno, kidder. We may have to chuck in the towel. Maybe it's better here in summer, but not out of the tourist season. All the pubs and hotels I've tried are on winter staffing now. I never counted on your mum leaving for good.'

'For *good*?' I cried, standing up. 'She said that? She's got a job waiting with Booths in Ulverston. Won't that sort things out? What the frig's going on?'

'We'll soon see, mate,' Dad sighed, flicking on the TV. 'But something's gotta give, and fairly quick.'

I grabbed the remote and turned off the TV. 'You're splitting up?' I shouted. 'Is that it? And all you can say is that something's gotta give! I want my mum back.'

Dad stood up sharply. He yelled, 'And I want my wife back! And yes, something has gotta give. Just don't ask me what or when. Don't ask it again!' He tore the remote out of my hand and zapped BBC1 on. The dopey *Neighbours* theme tune floated out.

Then the phone rang. Dad lunged into the hallway and grabbed it.

'Hello!' he bellowed. 'Hello!' A few seconds later he returned, looking indignant. 'That keeps happening,' he said, 'about this time each day. When I answer, it goes dead and the number's withheld. Could be some local jerk ragging us, I suppose. You upset anyone?'

I stared him out, feeling a red mist coming down. 'How about asking if someone's upset *me*,' I cried, jabbing my chest.

Dad stared back. 'Why? Have they?' he asked.

'Oh forget it,' I said, running upstairs. 'Forget everything. Loser.'

*

I hid away in the kitchen later, making jacket spuds and beans. Dad grumpily grated some cheese on his, but I couldn't face any more of the stuff. We called a truce, played Scrabble and listened to a Stone Roses album with its awesome guitar chords. It was like we had to fill the silence.

Later, the local TV news had more details of the recent bombing incident. An American military spokesman came on, dead sombre in dark blue. The weapon had been dropped, he explained, without the flying crew's knowledge. An urgent review of training procedures was under way. However, bombs used on training runs were not meant to carry live explosives. He regretted very much . . . Failure in the system . . . No such previous occurrences . . .

None of which would've meant a sod to Harlequin. With Dad job-hunting in Kendal on Thursday morning, I made Harly some sarnies and a flask of hot coffee. He needed it, when I found him shivering under his manky blankets. His mouth got burned as he slurped too fast. His overalls and thick socks smelled badly of rough living. Grease and mud caked his yellow yarns of hair.

Stuck on the jagged wall was a picture. It hung limply, glued with Harly's wet phlegm. Red Riding Hood strolling sweetly through a green field.

'Harly! You can't *do* that. It's not my book to rip up.'

He knelt in the dark earth, looking at it with his head on one side. 'She all different now — all bigger,' he said. 'Not like when Mum did read it.'

'A different version,' I said. 'That's all it was — there've been hundreds published.'

Harly's face began to redden. He was blushing like a kid on his first date.

'If I could have . . .' he began, swallowing nervously. 'If only . . .'

'If only what?' I asked, crouching on my heels.

'You know,' he giggled, rubbing his eyes like a big cat. Then he went serious and shoved both hands under his chin.

'No, I don't know,' I said. 'What is it?'

Harly picked up the hat and hid his face. 'If only I coulda . . .' he mumbled.

I lifted the hat away. 'Could've what, mate?'

He loomed forwards, his face close to mine. His blue eyes were flitting and flashing. 'If I could have . . . married . . . her. Yeah? Red Riding Hood. Things might be all right then, yeah? Be safer then and nothing ever gone wrong.'

I stood up, feeling the blood leave my head. From somewhere I found a small voice. 'Yeah, that would've been fine. Both of you safe with no wolves about.'

Harly burned bright pink again, smiling to himself. His painted face looked madly happy as he hugged his chest. 'And Badger,' he whispered. 'Badger kept safe and not—'

We both flinched. Something had smacked hard on the rotting roof. Then a second sharper crack hit the side wall. Harly moaned and found his telescope to peer out of the window gap.

'Bastards come back!' he spat. 'Kill 'em this time. Snap little necks.'

I pressed my head against his. A gang of lads hung around on bikes a short way off. They saw us peeping out. The quarry loomed blackly behind them. It was Beefwits and four other goons. One held a catapult. He loaded it with a lump of stone and fired at the shack. The tattered roof got banged again.

Harly shrieked in my ear and bungled his way out. A sudden fighter jet screamed its dark thunder above. A squealing Harly flung a rock up at it. Beefwits and the others fell about laughing in a huddle. Someone rolled on the earth, legs kicking the air. Then they all got down and did the 'dead fly'. But not for long.

Harly ran at his mounds of animal shapes. He kicked one apart, finding a thick wedge. Taking three great strides, he hurled it like a missile. It cleared the sprawling group but he was ready with another. He slung this one with venom. One lad got struck on the back. He grunted, too winded to cry out. He fell face down on a bike wheel, his black curls on the spokes. Harly fixed on him like a wounded prey. He whammed a second slate at him, and a third, striking stomach and head. Blood ran down a boyish white neck.

Now there was wild-eyed panic. Harly lumbered here and there with fistfuls of rock. He pelted the gang as they scrambled onto bikes. Beefwits got a blow, full on his raised arse. He jerked and slipped, his balls crunching on the crossbar. Everyone sped off towards Quarry Road.

Harly galloped after them, flinging anything he could pick up. He veered out of sight, down the road past the tree-swing. It was three minutes before he stumbled back, wiping dusty hands.

I backed away to the stream, frightened of the sheer bloodlust I'd seen.

'Got buggers,' he said, grinning, towering towards me. He laid friendly hands on my trembling head. 'Ain't scared, Glenn. They not hurt you.' He pulled me close and soothed my shaking. I daren't edge away and offend him. His vast hands gripped my shoulders and took the tension.

Then he marched over to the slatey animal shapes

and mended the messed-up one. Soon it was a squat body again, with stumpy legs.

'Glenn Jackson,' he said, calling me over. He was quite calm now, though he stank of sweaty fear. He pointed at the piles arranged all around. 'I done thirty?' he asked.

'God . . . no way,' I said, still a bag of nerves. I was expecting half the village to appear soon with guns and pitchforks. 'There's one, two, three . . . eleven, I think. Why thirty?'

'Ten sheep,' said Harly. 'Ten pigs, ten cows. Gonna build 'em all day. Ready for Bonfire Night.' He rushed about, gathering shards like he'd forgotten the violence of minutes before.

But I was in turmoil. I had visions of our house being bricked in revenge. News of the incident would be all over Torbeck by nightfall.

'Gotta run,' I said, feeling a need to safeguard my home. 'I'll come back later or tomorrow. You OK for now?'

But his big body was bustling everywhere. He strode swiftly through the rubble, searching and grabbing.

I ran off past the quarry's abysmal edge. Down at the crossroads I stopped for breath, then crossed over, taking the shorter way home through Charlie's fields.

My feet quickened as my head told me to just get home. But I felt a sudden strong urge to protect someone, or be protected myself. I had to see Laura right then, no matter what her cruddy family said.

THIRTY~FIVE

Burnside Tarn glinted on my left, across the main road, through yellow tree cover. Mulchy leaves filled the roadside paths. I went weak with wild nerves as I thought about calling on Laura. I sniffed the autumn air with stubborn snorts. A bull bellowed back at me like a revved-up chainsaw.

Without breaking stride I stalked up to the Delaneys' front gate, catching shaky fingers in the lock. Laura must have seen me coming from inside. The front door opened as I banged on its green wood. For a second I looked past her into the dim house. This was where Ronnie Delaney hanged himself. A white staircase led to the first floor. Laura's witchy hair was wet like she'd been in the shower. She wore a yellow shirt and old jeans and stood there in bare feet. Her cheap glasses had spots of water on the lenses.

'Glenn!' she whispered. 'What . . . ?'

'Hi,' I said, knowing how fast my words would spill.

'Get your shoes on, you're coming with me. I don't care where, I just think we should, so let's go.' I felt faint. I was leaving earth in slow motion.

'I *can't*,' Laura hissed, clutching the door. 'I'm walking on eggshells all the time here. Janice, that's my . . . mum . . . she's not thinking straight. She believes what people tell her. Some are saying you shot Mr Guthrie. You were seen running home from the tarn that night. Janice goes to any length to keep up appearances since Ronnie died. I can't just come out . . .'

Something filled me with blind madness: some desire or pent-up anger. I grabbed her arms and pulled.

'You can!' I shouted. 'Sod your false family. Come on, let's go!' I had both hands tightly on her thin bare arms.

Then her mum stomped in from behind. Janice's cheeks had more rouge than Harly's. She yanked Laura's T-shirt and hooked her back inside. As the door slammed I kicked it repeatedly, scarring the paintwork.

From inside the house came a thin shriek. Then another and another in short bursts. I knelt and pulled open the bronze letterbox. Peeping through, I saw Mrs Delaney in the hallway, fists grinding at her temples, making that noise. Laura wasn't there. I got up, let the lid fall and faced the village.

The wooden bus shelter, on the other side of the green, was full of school kids. Amazing how so many could cram onto a dull old bench. Everyone had been watching across the way. I stared them all out but no one held my gaze. I crossed the scrap of grass, turned left and was home in a blur. I'd noticed the alarm on a woman's face who passed me. In the mirror I saw myself red with sweat and all mad-eyed.

There was a slim parcel jammed in the letterbox, addressed to me, in Mum's writing. I tore it open and found some chocolate, two ten-quid notes and a set of expensive crayons. No letter or note.

The phone rang and I snatched it with unsteady hands. 'Hello?'

'Glenn? Hiya, love. It's Mum.'

'Mum!'

'At last! You been out making new friends?'

I gave a short, hateful laugh. 'Yeah, that's right, Mum. You been doing the same?'

A puzzled silence. 'What d'you mean? Has your dad said something?'

I paced a tiny circle, sniffing deeply. 'Dad? No, he's got nothing to say. Nothing useful. Nothing . . . intelligent.'

A longer silence. 'Hello!' I rapped out.

'Hmm. Well listen, Glenn, I'm coming over next

week. There's things to discuss and sort out. You'll be around, won't you, one evening?'

'Oh, I've no great plans so I'll be here. That's if the house ain't been burned down in revenge by then. Or this giant I've met hasn't killed us both in a mad pact. Or I've not been done for harassment. Otherwise, okey-doke, Mum. I'll be waiting.'

A nasal sigh. 'Look, Glenn, I'm sorry about things. I don't know what all that was about, but I'll try and make things better. I love you and always will. I'll talk to your dad later. You take good care, darling. Did you get my parcel?'

'Just now. Your letter must've dropped out.'

'Well, OK, there wasn't one. I didn't know what to say. There will be.'

'All right, Mum, bye then.' I dropped the receiver with a perfect slam and sat on the bottom stair, gripping my aching head. Two minutes later the phone rang again. I jumped up and looked hard at it, then reached over more calmly.

'Yes, Mum, what else? Hello? Mum?'

There was a silence where I felt a queasy fear.

'It's . . . Laura.'

'Laura! God . . . when . . . Where are you?'

'At home. Janice has just popped out. Your number's in the phone book, from the last family at your address.'

I pressed my free hand on the wallpaper to steady myself. 'Laura, I'm so sorry I grabbed you. I'd never hurt you, never.'

'I know. This place can quickly send anyone mad.'

'It's creepy,' I said. 'Village of the bloody Year.'

'Tell me about it. And I'm sorry if you heard Janice wailing earlier. Any little trauma sends her off these days. Listen, Glenn, before someone comes in, on Sunday I'm going to Uncle Charlie's. It's his three-hundredth birthday or something. Even I'm allowed to make an appearance for once. I can meet you somewhere. Lavinia says you go up near the quarry. I'll find you somehow.'

'Brilliant!' I cried. 'Let's say on that bridge by the waterfalls.'

'OK. It'll be the afternoon some time — about three? Sorry to be vague. Oh, and you know what you said once about Van Gogh . . . being your favourite artist?'

'Yeah.'

'Well, you're mine. You and . . . um, somebody Heaton-Cooper. He was a Cumbrian landscape artist. When Ronnie was alive he took me to a Heaton-Cooper exhibition in Grasmere. He led me round each portrait and our arms were linked. Lavinia hung about, looking bored. I asked how come the pictures said more about nature than I ever could. And Ronnie said something like, "If you could say it in words there'd be no need to paint it." And then he went and killed himself. And nothing's been the same for me since.'

I smiled sadly and said, 'Well, you're *my* favourite.'

'Favourite what?'

'Favourite of all time.'

Laura giggled, her voice sounding close. It curled inside my ear.

'I've got some special new paintbrushes,' she said. 'They cost five quid from Ulverston, but Lavinia paid for them. In a way.'

'Yeah?' I laughed. 'In what way?'

'Well, you know those raffles and collections she's always doing? Well, one's for a fund that's going towards getting the village a new youth centre. People are always moaning that there's nothing to do here. But she will leave that money tin out where fingers are tempted to stray. If you . . . know what I mean?'

I was bowled over. 'What . . . you . . . you take . . . ?'

'Borrow's a nicer word,' said Laura. 'Let's call it fair dibs for the way she orders me around. D'you think I'm evil?'

'God, no, of course not. I'm just—'

'Surprised? Good, I like to surprise people. Back to favourites,' she said. 'What's your, erm, favourite colour?'

'Purple. Yours?'

'Oh, purple always. Favourite food?'

'Lasagne,' I said, thinking of Mum's cooking. 'Yours?'

'Strawberries and ice cream.'

'Sounds good,' I said. 'Favourite music?'

'The Rolling Stones. They were Ronnie's favourites.'

'The Stones!' I said, sounding impressed. 'God, I thought I was retro with all my dad's Manchester stuff. Your go.'

I heard a chair squeak down the line. 'OK,' she said. 'When's your birthday?'

'April eighteenth,' I said, 'making me thirteen and a half now.'

'Wow, I'm April twenty-second, making me four days younger. The Delaneys adopted me when I was six.'

'Where were you born?'

'Glenn, gotta go.' Click. Hmmm.

The line was dead. But I wasn't — I was far from it. I jumped into the living room, scrabbling through Dad's vinyl and CDs. Out it came, The Smiths album with *that* song. Dad's all-time fave, and mine, and everyone's who's ever heard it. *There Is A Light That Never Goes Out.* The sweeping violins tugging your heart open. That urgent rhythm, heavy with strummed guitar strings. Those aching words, mad with love and longing, and love and death. I bounced onto our scraggy sofa then off again. I used an empty beer bottle like a mic. I spun around as if the cold living room were a gilded stage. Then I played the song six times over, louder each time. I ran upstairs for Laura's green ribbon and wrapped it around me like a binding. I looked a right sight in the mirror, but at least my soul had some fire again. I rubbed some of Dad's best hair gel in my blond spikes.

At last I lay on the couch, heart thumping. I fantasized about Laura's wet hair, bare feet and pink arms. The fantasy grew more intense. I felt hot with new urges. I was growing up fast.

THIRTY~SIX

I shut myself away upstairs later. The daft joy of Laura's phone call still buzzed me. But I was calmer now and ready to turn this passion into some drawing. I'd not done much since my sketchpad got stolen, and I had moments of sick dread about how I'd be treated at school next week.

By my bed was a Van Gogh calendar that Mum got me last Christmas. Over the October sheet was his *Bedroom at Arles* picture, from 1888. It showed a sparse room with a single bed and brown-green floorboards. Then you look closer and everything else is in pairs: two yellow paintings, two chairs, two pillows, two jugs, two bottles, two portraits, two jackets. That was how friendless and full of longing he'd been. He couldn't even stand his coats to look lonely. It always made my eyes well up to study this portrait, and even more so after the calls from Laura and Mum.

With swift strokes I updated my diary pad. I did

Harlequin raging after a crowd, slinging stones like Goliath in reverse. Then I spent an age over a study of Laura, with her favourite strawberries floating around like love hearts. I thought of her nabbing off with Lavinia's money, and gave the picture a guilty secret smile. Mona Laura.

On Friday morning, next day, I had to steel myself to go outside. No one had bricked our windows in the night; nothing was daubed in paint on the door. Maybe having a huge crazed friend counted for something, or Beefwits' tribe had been shamed into silence.

I bought cheese and chocolate in Henderson's. Val smiled at me, all wavy blonde hair and cosy cheeks. I tried smiling back but couldn't quite manage it.

'Val,' I said, knowing I sounded awkward. 'Has anyone said stuff about our family? Sorry to ask, only things might be getting a bit dangerous.'

She packed my shopping into a white bag. 'If they have,' she said, 'I know better than to listen. It's easy to be paranoid in these places. Most of what people say is just nosiness. Yeah, there's a nastier element here, always will be. But you'll be fine if you stick to the right friends. Laura tells me you're quite an artist.'

I couldn't help the proud smile that broke out. It was the sound of Laura's name that did it. I thanked

Val and was about to leave when I saw a familiar collecting tin. It stood on the counter with MIND stamped on. I picked it up.

'One of Lavinia's,' said Val. 'She's been collecting for mental-health charities ever since her father took his own life. Poor Ronnie. You'd have liked him, Glenn, with all his interest in the arts. Lavinia raised over five hundred pounds for MIND last year. That's some going in a place like this.'

I put my change in the tin, but only in Ronnie's memory as he'd been so good to Laura.

The sky was overcast but it still felt dead mild for autumn. A storm had to be brewing. This was the driest October for decades, though it got bloody cold at night in Torbeck. Something to do with mountains and high altitude, Dad said.

I hiked on up to find Harlequin, taking half an hour, and found Baz. He was snapping photos of the quarry's great gloomy pit. There was a rusty iron rail across a rim of gorse bushes. Baz rested on this, camera in hand, then faced towards distant Wrendale Bank, far beyond Harly's dwelling. That's when he saw me.

'Glenn! You little earthling, creeping up like that. You looking for your giant who half killed Beefwits?'

'You've heard?'

'I lip-read it, actually, through the Co-op's window.

Beefy was griping to a mate who works there. Word's gonna start spreading. He'll not call the cops though in case they question him over old Mr Guthrie. But someone else might. In the meantime, we've caused quite a stir with Mr Smiley over yonder.'

Baz kept zooming the lens about, his wide ears wobbling. Two silver hearing aids glinted under the leaden sky.

'Yeah, I'm here for Harlequin,' I said. I held up the white bag. 'If I don't feed him no one else will. You wanna meet him?'

Baz shrugged his anorak shoulders. 'Sure. Maybe he's been watching the night sky. You think he'd let you know if something appeared?'

'Don't ask him anything clever,' I said. 'He's not . . . you know, like us. Bit hard to predict his moods, an' all.'

'He said something odd,' Baz pondered. 'That time I came across him asking for you. I forgot to mention it. He went, "Seen you up yonder, mate, lookin' with telescope. Got one too. Can see for ever." So, what's all that about? He been spying on my star-gazing?'

'He might've,' I said. 'He can move dead quiet for a big bloke. And he's got himself a telescope, only not one you'd recognize.'

I trod carefully over the drab wasteland. Baz kept

kicking into bruising boulders with his flat feet. Harly's weather-beaten door was open slightly. Then a tormented scream erupted followed by violent slapping. I inched closer to the rotting den. Harly hunched around his cramped space, blond head scraping the ceiling. He struck his palms on each wall with loud smacks.

Baz could just make out the frantic scenes. He backed off, touching my shoulder, and whispered, 'On second thoughts . . .'

I whispered too. 'It's OK, it'll pass.'

Baz retreated further, stumbling on a slate heap. 'Maybe when he's better . . .' He kicked hastily off towards Quarry Road, camera in hand.

'See you, good buddy,' I muttered.

Harly yanked the dangling door wide open. Screwing his eyes up, he looked out.

'Been waiting,' he said calmly, straightening to well over seven feet. He pointed out a large slate in the wall near his door. Two spidery words had been scratched with a sharp stone: *Harlkwin Grim*.

'Been writing,' he said proudly, all torments quickly gone. 'Done my name like them brothers. Them who wrote *Riding Hood*. Is right, yeah?'

I didn't like pointing out there was a double 'm' in Grimm. I hadn't realized Harly could write, let alone hazard a guess at his own bizarre name. I nodded.

'You wanna swing?' said Harly, pointing over to the woods. 'Got swing there, made it for playing.'

'OK,' I said, putting down the carrier bag.

Harly loped over towards the amber forest. The swing was a hefty log, bound and hung from a tree with strong blue rope. There was loads of similar debris lying around.

He lifted me under the arms and sat me on the thick wood. I clung to the creaky rope, feeling its tug on the branch above. Harly pushed me forwards, gently at first, then with stronger strokes. The rope held firm as I swung about like a kid, my guts lurching. I swayed high enough to snatch a leaf. It was darkly green at the edges. The main body was yellow, ringed with black spots.

The leaves were like butterfly swarms resting on dark tree arms. I let mine go from on high, where it fluttered into Harly's hat.

At last I shouted for him to stop. He rocked me more slowly then grabbed my shoulders as I swung back his way. I was like a little cub in his great bear-like embrace.

'Gonna look after you, Glenn,' he said softly. 'Now we both got no mum.'

I sat awkwardly on the lumpy log. 'Mine's coming to see me next week,' I said, twisting to face Harlequin.

He whispered with ticklish bad breath in my ear. 'I know them who did finish my mum. But I never meant bad, Glenn Jackson.'

I slipped off the swing and clumped to earth. 'What d'you mean?' I asked, trying to sound casual. 'Who finished your mum?'

Harly tugged his hat down so his ears were well covered. His voice was a harsh whisper. 'Never told no one,' he said. 'But Riding Hood knows. She killed them wolves with big stones. Stuck 'em in their guts. They never come back then. She clever and brave, like me.'

THIRTY~SEVEN

We ate outside, under coal-black clouds. Harly washed his filthy fingers in the stream first, then held them out for me to inspect. We sat on a smelly blanket among the spooky animal shapes made of slate.

Half a mile away you could hear the waterfalls, like the far-off boom of a motorway. Harly dipped a finger in the rim of his battered hat. A ladybird sat on his wide grubby nail. Harly mouthed something to it, then watched its black wings buzz off.

'Walk on your hands again,' I said later. 'It's dead ace.'

Harly's face went creased and puzzled like he hardly understood. Then something clicked and he sprang upwards from his palms until his feet were sky high. He made a perfect vertical figure with no wobbles. He scampered about, using his fingers like toes. He pattered across to me. A packet of biscuits lay open. Harly nabbed this with his upended teeth and carried it away.

Next, he eased his arms apart with very slow slithers. Then his legs went wide too, making a huge human star. I clapped and cheered. Harly's face was growing ever darker. I could see the tension in his thick thighs.

'Stop!' I called out. 'Don't make yourself ill. Doesn't it hurt your right shoulder?'

He shook his upside-down head. 'Is mended,' he gasped.

As a car came up Quarry Road to park, Harly fell and bounded back to the shack. I followed casually, watching the Fiat crunch to a halt. Peeping through a crack in the shelter, I saw Harly huddled in the corner, his twiggy fingers tracing Red Riding Hood's face on the library book.

I was getting jumpy in case Laura phoned again and I wasn't there. I whispered through the draughty door. 'See you, Harly, gotta run. But I'll ask my dad to help us. Keep out of sight. Other people know you're here now.'

The hat was down over Harly's nose and eyes. His jagged knees were tucked in a big triangle. Maybe he muttered back, or he'd taken pills earlier and crashed out already.

A family of four stepped from the car. Mum, Dad and two little lads in sky-blue Manchester City shirts. 'Don't go near that old shack,' I called over to them.

'My dad's a local farmer and they're pulling it down soon. Could crumble any minute.'

They took my lies at face value, waved and rambled off towards the quarry's far edge.

I mooched around at home, glaring at the silent phone. I was gagging to natter with Laura again. I kept picking it up to check the dial tone hadn't cut. But it never rang and Sunday afternoon seemed an age away. Then from the bathroom I heard something slip through the front door onto the mat. I had a panic vision of burning fireworks being posted and leaped downstairs.

There was a slim envelope with my name on. I ripped it open to find an elegant new paintbrush. A scrap of paper was twisted around the slim stem. It read: *To Glenn, with love from Lavinia and half of Torbeck. Oh, and me (Laura). Big hug and kiss till Sunday xxxxx.*

I yanked open the door, hoping to find her waiting. But the little garden and pavement beyond were empty. A lacy curtain across the way flopped back into place. I stuck out my tongue at the house opposite and went back to my gift. I brushed its delicate bristles over my lips. I tickled myself behind the ears with it, and along the neck, imagining Laura's fingertips doing the same.

Dad came back later and filled in some forms at the

kitchen table. 'Couple of possible jobs,' he sighed. He didn't look well. His firm jawline had gone bristly and slack. There were flecks of dandruff in his curly quiff — a thing previously undreamed of. Both eyes had groggy red rings. He yawned heavily, printing his name in neat blue capitals.

'Oh balls-up,' he growled. 'It says fill this one out in black.' He screwed up the form and lobbed it onto the greasy oven. I sat down opposite, tracing mug stains on the unwashed table. Something needed saying.

'Dad . . . Mum said she's coming over next week. She tell you that?'

He yawned again, rubbing his creased brow. 'She did. After that we'll know how things are and can maybe make proper plans. I didn't know . . . or didn't see that she wasn't happy. Thought we were all plodding along just fine. I told you we'd got this idea of having another kid, what with you being old enough to look after yourself. Then the night before we moved she left a scrappy letter, saying she needed some time alone. Though I doubt she's really alone. So roll on next week and we're all in the know.'

'Right then,' I said. 'And . . . what if—?'

Dad held up his hands and half blocked his ears. 'What if, what if? It'll all be sorted whatever, Glenn. I'm sorry it's been a rough ride for you, really I am.

You've been brilliant. You made any friends or anything? Or don't the kids take to strangers any more than their parents?'

'It's about the same,' I said. 'But there's Baz, who's unusual, and Laura's a top girl who likes art.'

'Oh aye?' Dad said, cheering up. 'Bit of a dazzler?'

'Very. Not dead glam or anything. Just different. Can't explain it really.'

Dad smiled slowly, like he'd almost forgotten how. 'That sounds for real,' he said. 'When you can't explain those feelings it normally means they're genuine. Believe me, I know, or did once.'

I felt awkward hearing this and got up. 'God, we've been here two weeks tomorrow,' I said. 'Don't it feel like a long time?'

Dad nodded with grim certainty and flung down his pen. 'Long time?' he said. 'Feels like a bloody life sentence for summat you ain't even done.'

THIRTY~EIGHT

D ad didn't go to work the next morning. 'Let 'em cope on a busy Saturday,' he said. 'I'm paid up to date, so sod it.'

Later we went out together into Torbeck. It was the first time we'd done that. Val tapped on Henderson's window as we passed, and mouthed something to Dad, who gave a thumbs-up.

'What's that about?' I asked.

Dad sniffed and turned up his leather-jacket collar. 'Private,' he said. 'We need any shopping? Val says you're keen on their bread 'n' cheese.'

I took Dad up past the Co-op, over the cattle grid, which he trod daintily across, then up the shambling sheep track towards King's Cragg. He kept his eyes on the rundown path, to stop his Doc Martens getting roughed in the ruts. A four-wheel-drive swerved round us, heading for the mountainside hostel. At the foot of Wrendale Bank I halted and pointed up.

'See that massive smiley face?' I said with pride. 'I did that.'

Dad's face lit up and he punched my shoulder. 'No way!' he cried. 'What a monster!'

I told him about Baz and his cosmic plans as we hiked up the brown bracken slope. Dad was ecstatic.

'Hey, soft lad,' he said, 'it can't be all bad here if you're pulling stunts like this. You reckon those jets might think it's a target for bombing practice?'

'I'll just blame Baz,' I said as Dad went jogging round the beaming circle.

'Fantastic scam,' Dad said when he came back, dusting his shoes. 'Let's go for lunch and celebrate. There's a pub I ain't been in yet. Wassit called . . . The Moon? Sounds about right after visiting an alien arena.'

I felt a nervy twitch. 'You sure you want to?' I said. Dad and pubs had been a tragic mix recently.

'Why?' he said. 'There someone you want to avoid?'

'Loads.'

Dad sat beside me in the rustling ferns. 'What they been doing to you?' he asked. 'What they been saying?'

'Some load of old shite,' I said. 'And there's this whistling thing going on. Whenever I go by anywhere, or in a classroom – it's like some dirty little signal they've got.'

Dad looked up at the grungy sky. The air felt close

and you could taste the rain to come. '*Whistling?*' he said. 'You got some lads whistling at you?' He gave a snigger. 'Perhaps it's a strange local mating call,' he went on. 'Y'know, like animals make when they're randy. Maybe they all fancy you and can't show it another way. Or it could just be they're total tosspots. Whistle back and flutter your eyelids. They'll probably run a mile screaming for their mammies. *Whistling!* Jesus wept!'

This was the dad I'd been missing this past fortnight — sarky and blunt, making things feel better. He snapped a stem of rusty bracken. 'Life looks a bit aimless round here to me,' he said. 'Spend your whole life in a titchy place and you're gonna get bored of the same old, same old. Then someone new comes in and it's a bundle of fun to make 'em a scapegoat. Come on, mate, let's try The Moon and put a brave smile on.'

I stood up, feeling more hopeful. Over a shandy and chips I'd tell Dad all about Harlequin. No matter that the great lump had saved my life, I couldn't manage his weirdness by myself. For his own sake Harlequin needed someone to make sense of those frightened ramblings.

Dad and me went skipping down Wrendale Bank under ominous clouds. 'You ain't gonna tell jokes at the bar,

Dad,' I said. 'That's not a question, it's an order.'

'I'll behave,' Dad promised. 'Might try a few old stories from work though. Even you laugh at those, misery guts. So how's your great artwork doing?'

'It's grand moody scenery round here,' I said. 'There's a quarry nearby I wanna draw properly. Tell you about it over lunch.'

We crossed the scraggy valley to softer green pastures on the far side. A slippy old truck trail took us down to the top of Torbeck, past barns and farm buildings. As we came nearer The Moon pub, Dad got busy with a comb on his quiff.

The Moon was an old coaching inn, where travellers used to rest up on long journeys. Now it had a land-scaped beer garden and a play area for kids. Raucous laughter spilled from a crowd around some benches by the door. The blokes all had black jackets and ties on. It sounded like a party was kicking off.

I'm sure the noise level went down as we appeared. Everyone held pints or wine glasses, the women wearing dark skirts. The small paved area near the entrance was crammed. Little children sat on wooden tables, eating and throwing crisps.

Dad must've recognized someone. He bowled up to the noisy throng, clapping his hands loudly.

'Don't tell me!' he called heartily. 'Some poor devil's

gone and got married. Who is it then? Come on, who's just signed their life away? Own up, y'daft bugger, and I'll buy yer a drink.'

A hush fell quickly. Glasses were rested on the concrete or slid onto tables. The tidily dressed nippers went quiet. Some cocky blond youth spoke up.

'It's old Mrs Monkton's funeral reception,' he said. 'Show some respect for the family.'

'D'you wanna leave us to it, mate?' called another.

'Aye, go and polish your snorkel,' came a third voice from the dark doorway.

I stood there shrivelling with shame. My face was flaming. Dad held out his hands, saying, 'Sorry, folks, sorry. No dramas. Sounded like a party from a distance. No offence.'

He backed off with a rueful smile and I followed him downhill to the village. Dad grumbled all the way. 'Easy mistake to make,' he muttered. '*They* weren't showing much respect . . . Couldn't see any grieving going on . . .'

We'd run out of pubs he could show his face in. So it was beans on cheese on toast at home, watching *Grandstand*. Dad snapped off the TV when horse racing came on. We sat in empty silence, hearing birds twitter in the quiet road outside. It sounded like they were laughing at us.

After our latest pub disaster, Harly never got a mention that lunch time. Again, I hadn't the heart to burden Dad with it all. Maybe if we'd taken some action that day, things could've turned out different. But we never did. And so the final drama of events became almost inevitable.

THIRTY~NINE

'D ad,' I began, watching his eyes droop, 'I need
to tell you summat. It's important, like.'

It was late that Saturday night and we were watching
football highlights. Dad sat up straighter when I spoke,
and muted the TV. He seemed a bit more himself now
after the lunch-time nightmare. He'd had his three
bottles of Hawkshead Bitter, all he could take, and we'd
indulged in the local Cartmel Sticky Toffee Pudding
from Henderson's. Now the living room was nearly
dark.

'Sorry, mate,' he said. 'Nodding off there. What's
up?'

I played with my hair, feeling tiny grains of slate grit.
'There's this . . . strange sort of friend I've met, who's
living rough up in those quarries. I was mucking about
near the edge one day and he saved me from tipping
over. He needs help though, Dad, proper help. He's
a bit simple . . . Oh, and he's well over seven feet tall.'

'Christ,' Dad said, sitting upright. 'You don't half pick 'em round here. So where's this guy from? What's he do?'

'No idea,' I said. 'Can't make much sense of him. Don't reckon he's an escaped con, though he tries to disguise himself. You not heard owt? He's been seen around.'

'Heard nothing,' Dad said. 'I'm excluded, haven't you noticed?'

'Not by Val,' I said. 'She came round when she heard about your job going.'

'Val's no cheap gossip. So, what d'you want me to do?'

'Can you meet him?' I asked. 'Tomorrow night? You're good with strange people.'

Dad watched a goalscorer's silent celebrations and sighed through his nose. 'All right,' he said. 'But if I think he's not safe it's gotta be a police matter. And you keep away from up there till we go together. Hear?'

'He'll just run off if any cops come,' I said.

'So be it. You're my priority, not him, even if he saved you. So, no promises.'

It rained heavily in the night. The warm, dry October ended in thunderclaps and lightning lashes. Great savage drops clobbered my window for hours. I lay anxiously thinking of Laura and if my date with her would be washed out. I sent vicious thoughts up to heaven to quell the downpour. The quiet roads beyond sounded sloshed with puddles.

By the early hours the storm had gusted away and I dozed off. I woke about half past ten. Sunday morning. I got the nervy buzz of a strange day ahead.

Dad wasn't in, but he'd left a note saying Val's husband needed help with a job somewhere. *Cash in hand! See you later to go meet King Kong!*

The sky was bright blue and white, like the storm had rinsed everything clean. The roads were damp and splashy but the drying wind felt fresh. I set off into an empty village, carrying a bag of grub, and a sketchpad to pass the time with later.

The gales had ripped more yellow leaves from woodland trees. The stony path was ankle deep in gold. At the crossroads I looked slyly down to Father Charlie's. Several posh cars were parked around his farm buildings. Extended family, probably, along for the big birthday bash.

Going upwards, I heard how the deluge had swollen the furious river. The two waterfalls were on full fountain display. Split by the thumping rockface between them, they bucketed in white waves. I crossed the flat bridge onto Quarry Road. The tarmac's ruts and mud holes were filled with water. My socks felt soggy where my naff trainers were leaking.

I found Harly sitting in his dark doorway. He looked shivery on a sodden blanket.

'Here,' I said, offering a carton of orange. 'Vitamin C. Were you drenched last night?'

Harly nodded, his yellow teeth trembling. 'Bloody froz,' he said. He sniffed some gunge into his throat, spat it and coughed heavily. 'Going soon,' he said. 'Gotta walk to Skelwith soon. Five miles there, five back. That Charlie come here last night with his gun. "Aha," he sez. "Got job for big lad like you."'

'Oh yeah?' I said, sitting on a rock beside the door. I split a cheese baguette, giving half to Harly. 'What job?'

Harly slugged on the orange carton. 'Friend of Charlie's wants heavy stuff shifting,' he said between gulps. 'Getting money for it. Charlie come here last night, says to go for three o'clock. When's that?'

I looked at my watch. Quarter to one. 'Hang on,' I said. 'You say Charlie came up here last night? I don't like the sound of this job he's suddenly lined up. Don't go. Stay put and later we're gonna meet my dad. It's OK, he's friendly. We just wanna help.'

Harly nodded, but said, 'Gotta work, need money. Buy new home. What's time?'

'You can make it for three at the speed you walk.

But be dead careful of Charlie. I heard him kicking and screaming at the sheep in his barn t'other day. Made me shiver hearing all that rage. Have a good look round when you reach this workplace. Mind your back.'

I checked my watch nervously, sure it was gonna pack up on me. 'I'm meeting my friend Laura later, so I'm hanging around.'

'She good to you?' said Harly. 'She nice, Glenn?' He got up now and wrapped the blanket around him like a cape.

I yawned and ambled to another boulder, sitting with my back to Harly. 'Yeah,' I said, feeling warmer in the bright breeze. 'Her so-called sister isn't though. She's been turning people against me.'

I heard Harly leafing through my sketchbook. It had my recent Torbeck work in.

'She like a witch?' said Harly, flapping the sheets over. 'Got witchy face, witchy hair?'

I stared moodily at the misty hills. The rusty bracken was all mashed up after the rain. It lay around like coils of soggy steel. I wasn't really listening. I wish now I had been.

'Yep,' I said. 'She's a right witch at times, though maybe she has her reasons. She's put it about that mine's a problem family, so my mate Baz told me. And yet she goes mad collecting all this money for charity. I dunno . . .'

I still had my back to Harlequin. A rainbow had looped itself over King's Cragg in a glorious halo. The violet stripe intrigued me with its intense purple-blue.

'She looks bad,' said Harly. 'Like a wolf.' He turned another page. 'I seen her one time, first night here. She done you bad, Glenn?'

'Bad enough,' I agreed. 'Only I know she ain't all bad.' I was rainbow-gazing still. How could I mix paints to get that eerie violet shade? What was Harly going on about?

He clambered to his feet, dropping my pad. He came over and lifted me up under the arms, my face close to his rough, slender jawline. His blue eyes were twitchy and watery. 'I never drop you, Glenn Jackson,' he said. 'You wait here, be safer here. I not be so long at Skelwith. Two hours, mebbe.'

He lowered me like a precious statue. On the horizon we saw pinky-red clouds in a dark blue sky. It was like hot lava bubbling on a stormy sea.

'Look!' said Harly, pointing a trembling hand. 'Look, Glenn Jackson . . . just *look*!'

He mooched away, eyes on the wild heavens. Then he turned and gave me a final mad grin. He crouched low. He flipped forwards and lay face down. Slowly his resting body began to rise . . . His whole flat figure was in midair, supported by just his palms on the floor.

It was like watching someone levitate. His legs were all taut and straight. They rippled with tension. His palms scuffed about quickly. His suspended body turned a perfect circle, like a merry-go-round. Then, with both hands down, he sprang into a handstand and walked.

I cheered until he finally got tired and stopped.

'Probably see you about half six then,' I called over. I watched him stomp off past the hideous quarry. Segments of slate got crushed under his boots like biscuits.

I tidied away the debris of our lunch. Harly had left my sketchpad open at a drawing of Laura. I frowned and wondered who he'd been talking about moments ago. Not Laura, surely. Why would he say she had a witchy face? It hardly mattered, as Harly might even meet Laura later. Maybe he'd give her a shoulder ride back into Torbeck, the three of us entering the village like heroic outcasts.

The wind got up and blasted over the wintry waste-land. I went into Harly's ratty shack, squatted on a blanket and waited.

FORTY

By two o'clock I'd begun to seriously fidget. I dossed about outside, walking orbits around Harly's animal-shaped slate stacks. When rain began spitting I went inside, in case my carefully gelled spiky hair went flat. I sighed. I was only thirteen and a half, but already turning into my vain dad. I sat in a shady corner of the shack where the wind couldn't coil its cold breath in.

The library books I'd never taken home sat beside me. I flicked through the Van Gogh biography, stopping to study one of his last paintings. It's called *Wheatfield with Crows*, and a print of it filled a double page of the book. The horizon is all slashed in angry blue strokes like the sky is rushing at you. The crows are menacing black flaps. Paths and crossroads cut into the golden wheat but seem to lead nowhere. The whole sensation is like being hemmed in without means of escape. Fear and loneliness haunt the landscape.

Laura had said to meet about three o'clock. At last I was ready to go, and shut the shack's grating door. Hiking down the road, I passed a car bringing visitors to the morbid quarry. And soon, standing on the gravelly bridge, I gazed at the pounding water below. It swept under my feet to smash over the falls just beyond. I went round and stood by the crumbling wall, from where I'd seen Harly bathe one evening. I hurled a dead branch at the nearest waterfall. In a second it got spat out and dashed into the whirlpool. It sped on downstream, tossing and turning. I followed it along, as there was no sign of Laura yet.

Minutes later I stood across the way from Father Charlie's. I watched a car turn off the main road and chug down his track. I could just hear tinkles of laughter from the house. Warm, welcoming lights glowed in each window. I waited there for a whole aching hour, seeing the front door open and shut. But no hint of Laura coming up the trail from the farm. I zipped my jacket tight as the sky went a deeper blue.

At five to four I slogged back up the bumpy sheep trails. There was a chance Laura might've somehow snuck onto Quarry Road, on the opposite side of the valley. She could even be on the bridge or making for the quarry itself if she thought I'd missed her. I squinted over the narrow gulf, with its rushing river way below. The storm had stripped almost every leaf, so you could see Quarry Road through dark trees. But there wasn't a hint of anyone roaming along.

I hunkered on a grassy bank in sight of the bridge, scaring some nibbling sheep. I yawned with weary nerves and closed my eyes to daydream. I rocked back on my heels on damp spiky turf. It was four twenty when I woke, feeling bracken tickle my lower back. I kicked myself hard for dozing off, then it was back down to the crossroads, watching tractors trickle compost onto white road lines. I was desperate for a sighting of Laura, even if she was only trying to signal from the farm.

On my left were fields of bleating sheep. I leaned on a wooden fence where the hedge parted. A lamb's whole skeleton lay a few yards off. Its bones had been picked clean in perfect order. The white ribs curved in as though searching for the missing heart. Head and limbs were naturally arranged, like a real version of Harly's rocky mounds. High above, a kestrel soared in slow, circular flight.

The afternoon was failing beyond Charlie's farm. Laura wasn't coming, I felt sure of it. She hadn't been able to sneak away. A screaming fighter jet blasted my bones and I tried to follow its flight path, but it was gone before my eyes could adjust.

My watch said quarter to five. Once more I dragged back up the lonely sodden trail, straining to hear footsteps anywhere. But there was only the drowning roar of the river. I went up to the bridge, then back down again, until I knew every rut in the path.

Ten minutes later I sat on a knobbly bank, feeling defeated. Spits of rain were coming down. Both hands were clasped behind my drooping head. I was eaten up with tiredness and smashed hopes. I shivered with cold and misery.

Way overhead a kestrel glided as if I were the prey in its vision. I shifted about to prove I was no rotting carcass. I knew it could pinpoint my beating pulse a mile off. Still it wheeled above, giving its pitiful kitten's cry. It hovered with rapidly beating wings. Its head stayed rigid in one spot. The expert eyes examined the ground in detail. Behind me was a sloping shoulder of bank, heading off into scrubby fields.

The kestrel made a sudden steep glide, with angled wings. Its grasping talons were to the front. I heard a deathly squeal as the hawk vanished. My eyes closed in reflex, my body tensed. Minutes passed before the bird took flight again, spreading its tail feathers and fanning the smoky air.

The clocks had gone back last night. Twilight snuck in, making daylight seem darker in a blink. Then something caught my eye over the churning valley. No more than a flick of colour at first, in the shadows. Something flashed behind the bare branches where the sheer river-banks rose up to Quarry Road. It was a person carrying something under one arm. They seemed in a hurry. I edged back down to the pathway.

Looking closer, I felt sure it was Harlequin, his big hat flopping. He was back from Skelwith already. It was way too early; *something wasn't right*. He hiked rapidly up the road. I walked quickly along, in line with him, trying for a clearer glimpse. Something about the shape of the bundle he carried was wrong. Then a break in the tree cover gave me the shocking full view. A second later came the first gasping scream.

Harlequin had Laura dangling under his right arm. Her legs poked out from a blue dress, trailing in mid-air. Her head and body joggled as Harly stalked uphill. Her glasses hung on by one ear. I got snatches of long legs running, of white limbs flapping and struggling. Laura screamed again in jerky breaths.

Something hot and sour bolted up my throat. Then my feet got going, though I stumbled in potholes. I tried shouting but only heaved out cold air. The bridge behind the waterfalls was up ahead. The arrow-shaped river gorge narrowed to its tip there. My lungs worked weakly as I twisted up steep ruts. My yelling voice got sucked into the river, and Harly was plunging at twice my speed.

I was like an old man stumbling uphill in a gale. As the trail evened out I crunched and slithered faster. The bridge was ever nearer. But first came the dry-stone wall where I'd hidden and watched Harly bathing. And then he was right across the watery divide from me. So close I could've lobbed a stone over.

He stood panting and shouting in a frenzy. Laura's glasses had fallen off. A shoe was missing. Her black hair blew as Harly pressed her to his ribs. I heard his frantic words over the watery clamour.

'When you meet him . . . gotta know him . . . you like him . . . he can sing . . . sing again . . .'

I bellowed with straining neck muscles.

'Harly! Let her go!'

He looked round like a startled deer. When his eyes found me in the gathering dusk, his mouth fell open.

'Leave her! Leave her!' I screamed, waving madly. 'That's Laura, not her sister! Let her alone!'

He stared at the wriggling figure in his massive grip. He looked back my way, mouth gaping. He lowered her gently like he'd often done with me. He took a step back, one hand shoved in his mouth. But Laura was in a panic. She pushed away from Harly, tripping down onto a mossy bank. Her eyes screwed up, trying to see me. She leaned forwards, peering blindly. Her right foot was wet sock and no shoe. Harly sucked his fingers, twitching all over. In haste and shame he tried skidding down after Laura. She heard him and shrieked. She stumbled onto a stony ledge. It jutted like a lip over the nearest waterfall. One leap across was the hulking rock-face that split the rapids.

I screamed. 'Stay there, Laura, he'll not hurt you! Harly, get back! Get fucking back!'

I think he understood as he sprawled unmoving on the bank. But to Laura everything was a blur. She can't have heard. I'd never seen her without those cheap glasses. In that second I saw how pretty she really was.

She glanced at the frozen giant behind her. Her arms went out wide like a tightrope walker. She hobbled over the wet craggy ledge. Her mouth opened slowly like she was calling to me. The water raged over the falls. My ears rang with its bedlam.

A light rain fell. My jaws were shivering. Then I was aware of two men on the bridge. They leaned forwards, gripping the iron fence. I darted round onto the bridge. I shoved the blokes aside and shouted into the chaos. Below me, white water roared towards the falls. It drowned each word.

Laura swayed on the ridge over the booming water. She crouched as if to jump, eyes all scrunched up.

Mine widened as I saw she really meant it. Before I could scream at her, Harly slipped on wet moss. He tumbled down the slope onto Laura's rocky shelf. Laura heard Harly moaning behind and wobbled again. She steeled herself and went for it. But her nerve didn't hold. Nor did her left ankle that sagged. Her shoeless foot slipped. She sprang badly, smashing down sideways into the cascade. Her head met a bone of rock. But last night's rainstorm had swollen the torrent. A wave tossed Laura upwards and out. It cushioned the awful blow. With one giant swoosh, Laura lay spinning in the whirlpool. Her face was bloody, her eyes closed. She got whipped around before the current dragged her away like a raft. Then quickly on, down a stream that lay strewn with leaves and bracken like some watery grave. I bent double with a retch, heaving up acid froth.

The two beside me on the bridge moved before I could. They belted through the bridge gate onto Quarry Road. They shouted, and grabbed each other's cagoules.

Harlequin got up clumsily, his mouth a red circle of horror. A thin screeching built in his throat. He bit his hands manically. He danced on the ledge like a monster puppet. He grabbed himself between the legs, wailing like a lost child.

'I done bad again! I never meant it! Tell 'em, Glenn Jackson!'

Now he screamed for real, eyes rolling at the ghostly moon. His howling split the valley open, echoing into the starlight beyond. It sent every bird tearing from the trees.

PART THREE

Blackrigg Farm,
Blackrigg Valley;
Bonfire Night,
five years earlier

FORTY~ONE

Walter Quinn's tractor snarled and pointed its headlights towards home. The two bright beams were spangled with drizzle. They picked out the wooden farmhouse and its glowing downstairs windows. Then Walter got a glimpse of someone running. Someone who flashed across the muddy field ahead of him. Someone heading for the bonfire that Walter's clumsy child had spent weeks building.

He swung the tractor to the right. It rattled onto open ground that lay bordered by grassy ridges. In full glare was the wooden heap that he'd light later. The first proper Guy Fawkes Night they'd had as a family. Just before he grasped the scene before him, Walter hoped the rain would increase. Any excuse to avoid letting off those fireworks. His ten cows, ten sheep and ten pigs would be spared the raucous ordeal.

But then there were three figures trapped in his headlights. They grappled with each other by the bonfire. A red flicker made Walter leap forwards, smacking his head on the window. He cut the engine and killed the lights. His child's awful screaming filled the void. Walter revved his motor, kicking the pedals, and jolted off at speed. Three young bodies leaped into the night, one elbowing another's face. But Walter didn't give chase. He'd sized up his son, straining like a prisoner on the bonfire. An orange flame was blurred in the wet windscreen. He swung the tractor past the woody clutter, clutching its throbbing wheel as the brakes whined. He left the engine running.

Walter took thirty seconds to scrabble up. His boy giant was now lit from below like a shop display. Walter's face felt a lick of heat. His teeth buried into the knots around Haitch's hands. Wet rope tickled his tongue. His knobbly fingers worked furiously. Haitch's big jeans were getting hotter, his cries huskier.

Walter pulled him loose from the pole. But in slippery haste the elderly man went sprawling down. A twisted nail jabbed through his cap and punctured the scalp. Haitch stamped over the stack that crackled warmly as he hit the ground running. He didn't wait for his father but sped home, shrieking in the dark. Badger was pawing the front door in fury at the sound. Haitch fell through it and onto his dog with choking sobs.

He lay on the stone floor, crushing Badger to his

face. Haitch's mother, Jean, hurried in from the kitchen with a steaming dish. She dropped it with a sharp shatter at the sight of her boy's blackened and smoking clothes. Badger hungrily eyed up the puddle of meat and potato. But he let this boy who fed him so often weep loudly into his fur. With a whimper he stretched out, his front paws brushing broken glass.

Half a mile away, three lads barged through a thick hedge. Scratchy thorns bit their blazers and black trousers. They stood, panting in cold sweats, by the dark main road. Tommy's nose was bleeding from a thrust of Donnie's elbow. He was nearly crying.

'Fuck you, Donnie Turnbull,' he blubbed.

'Aye, and fuck ye!' Donnie ranted back. 'The pair of ye. I wasna gonna leave him up there. I was just coming back when Farmer Fuckwit shows up. *He* saw nothing of us. He saw nothing and you'll *say* nothing. OK?'

Tommy touched his tender face, whispering through bubbling lips, 'Fuck you, Donnie Turnbull. And you, Davy.'

'*Me?*' Davy shouted. 'Who was the one tried to put the fire out? And now we've an hour before the next bus. Screw you pair, I'm yomping home. And hey, Donnie, where's all the fancy banter gone now?'

The other two watched him fade into the night along the roadside. Tommy jabbed a stained hanky at his nose. Donnie turned and saw a glow across the fields. He heard the snap of burning wood, then a tractor's angry engine. He could tell by its quick rumble that the vehicle stood still. Its driver was absorbed in saving a life. Maybe even his own by now. Donnie found himself straining to hear the engine rev up and belch back home. At last it did. But even then he had no clue as to the damage done.

Walter was injured. He'd wrenched an ankle falling down the burning rubbish and gashed both hands. The nail jab still bled into his woolly curls.

When at last he limped through the front door, he found Jean cradling their son's weeping head. Badger was lapping steaming mince off the flagstones. Even before he could question his boy, Walter was at the telephone. He'd seen enough to go straight for the police.

'That's right . . . his hands were tied to the pole. Three lads ran off . . . No, I didn't see them properly. You'll call round first thing tomorrow . . . Is that the earliest? Very well. My son's name? Yes, it's Harvey . . . Harvey Quinn. No, for Christ's sake, not Harlequin. Harvey . . . Quinn. Harvey with an haitch, Quinn with a Q. Goodbye.'

Beyond Blackrigg Farm the fire was a red rage. The rain wasn't thick enough to douse it. Walter and Jean spent an hour trying to quieten their son. They soothed and muttered, and stroked his colossal frame. In the end they hauled him off the floor into a chair, with a well-fed Badger jumping into his lap. Even then his tears wouldn't let up, nor the dreadful shivers.

Jean cleared away the dinner mess, her bent back shrivelled at the shoulders. A hobbling Walter brought the animals in for the night. Thirty beasts trooped into three timber barns right by the farmhouse.

Harvey stared at his ruined bonfire through dark rainy windows. He'd blurted out the story of what happened as best he could. Jean got his awkward body into a hot bath and for once Badger was allowed upstairs. Later the family had bacon soup and hot bread by the hearth.

Harvey looked longingly at the firework boxes on the sideboard. He'd only seen their dazzling beauty on TV displays before.

'No,' said Walter firmly. 'They'll save until next year. Or maybe I should just chuck them out.'

'Yes,' agreed Jean, 'get rid of them, dear.' She huddled inside a brown cardigan, looking shattered.

Harvey's misery was complete as Walter took the magical boxes into the kitchen. He heard a creaky cupboard open under the sink. Fresh tears rolled down his narrow red face. Badger whined softly, feeling choked in the boy's crushing grip.

At last Jean got her thirteen-year-old ready to rest. He wanted to hear *Little Red Riding Hood* and snuggled under the blankets as his mother read. He moaned as the little girl found Mr Wolf dressed as Grandma in bed. Jean caressed Harvey's long yellow hair.

'That's all they were, dear,' she whispered. 'Those bully boys. Only wolves from a bad story, dressed up as lads. They won't come back, my dear. Red Riding Hood has just killed them all, right now. Just like she did to Mr Wolf. She cut open their bellies while they slept and put huge stones inside. Then she sewed those wolf-lads back up. When they awoke, feeling thirsty, they dragged themselves to a river. But they toppled off the edge, what with all those stones inside, and drowned in the water. So they won't come back for you, dear. Never again.'

Jean let Badger sleep on Harvey's bed that night. Both she and Walter took sleeping tablets as usual, to ease the backaches which plagued their nights. Each swallowed an extra one – Jean to calm her nerves and Walter for his injuries.

Before sleep came down to smother him, Walter felt an awful stab of guilt. He lay back and allowed this brutal thought to show itself . . .

. . . that his own son's death might have been a blessing.

No, not on that bonfire, for God's sake! No, never like that!

But he and Jean were fifty-eight, worn out, and ready to retire. Harvey would only be an increasing burden the older and bigger he got. Who would care for him when they no longer could?

His body went rigid with anger at the memory of those three lads legging it. His chest flooded with shame and pity. Tomorrow he would take the boy somewhere remote and burn off a few fireworks. Let him scribble some silly sparkler patterns into the dusk.

Jean touched her husband's shoulder, as if she could read his thoughts and understood. They were both deep in slumber by ten thirty.

FORTY~TWO

An hour later, Harvey awoke from jumbled night-mares. A scream choked in his throat as a furry face nuzzled him. But it was only his sheepdog on the duvet, not some wicked wolf in a shawl. Badger licked the boy's hot, sweaty brow.

There had been fireworks in Harvey's bad dream. Fireworks making flower patterns in the darkness and three boys tearing the cloak off a little girl. They tied her to a bonfire as Harvey sped by in a bus that wouldn't stop. He hammered the bus bell until it sang like a church tower. He woke sharply as the red-haired driver turned round. It was Donnie Turnbull.

Harvey played with Badger's velvety ears and thought longingly of Roman candles. By morning those myster-ious boxes would be thrown out like junk. The binmen were due first thing on their weekly call. They always let Harvey hurl Jean's rubbish into their truck's munching machine. It made him giggle and clap and jump.

His bonfire was ruined. The stuffed Guy Fawkes lay in Walter's cold cellar. All that Harvey could save of the party was a few fireworks. Not even that, for he knew what a waking noise they'd make outside. Nor did he know how to light them. So maybe a quiet sparkler then. A shiny magic wand, like the ones on TV shows.

The more he yearned for it, the tighter he grabbed Badger's lugs. And when the boy got up five minutes later, in big black pyjamas, his dog padded downstairs after him. The wooden steps groaned like a haunted house, but Walter and Jean were drugged up with sleeping pills. Harvey's feet were soon freezing on the kitchen floorboards. He took the fireguard away, letting dregs of heat reach his curling toes. A few orange coals lent the room a sinister light. Harvey nestled a log among them, picked out of the wood basket. In the padlocked barns next door he heard restless grunts and snorts.

Kneeling under the sink, he undid a cupboard. Stacked among the cloths and boot polish were two boxes and two packets. Harvey carried them to the table. He lifted one box lid, picking out a blue tube with a pointy red tip. He sniffed the smoky gunpowder inside. His hands trembled as he held each firework and fingered its coloured cardboard.

Harvey grabbed a sparkler packet. He couldn't read its instructions, but knew vaguely what to do. He tore the end of one pack and slid out a brown stick. There were matches in the kitchen drawer. At first he tried to light the metal tip. When this didn't catch he changed ends. Holding the strip in two fingers, he sparked the furry twig into life.

Badger watched with spinning eyes as streaky patterns danced above. Harvey couldn't write his own name, but stroked animal shapes through the air. He looked gleeful now in the dim firelight, the horrors of earlier forgotten. The first sparkler burned out before he was ready, singeing his fingertips. He dropped its glowing end into an open fireworks box. It sizzled and smouldered.

This was too much fun to stop after one go. Harvey ripped the packet wider. Now he pranced around the kitchen, waving another flickering wand. Badger jumped up at him as Harvey circled the table. He waggled the sparkler at the dog's leaping limbs.

'Abatadaba, Badge!' he whispered. 'Make you little piggy!'

He flung up the hissing stick, feeling like a wizard. Catching it clumsily, he shouted with blistered pain. He dropped it into the box that smoked with his other fallen tip.

The impact was terrible. Raw gunpowder flared from a Cherry Bomb. Its blue-red bang was a cannon blast. Harvey screamed and flinched. He swept the whole box from the table, launching explosives into the fireplace. He bounced back against the oven, bashing his spine. A yelping Badger ran from the room.

Now the coals had fresh fuel. Two Catherine wheels, two rockets and four Flowerpots.

A rocket squealed in its burning frenzy. It ripped from the grate, past Harvey's face, denting the wall. The Flowerpots flared together. Sparks showered over Pinwheels on the floor. They whizzed and spat. Now the second rocket was ready. It was caught under the log Harvey had chucked on. Its red cylinder exploded. It spewed a boiling blast onto the wood basket. The logs inside caught quickly. The floorboards began steaming as Badger howled in the doorway.

Harvey wasn't trapped, but his body froze in frightening heat. His lanky legs buckled by the oven. His head shook rapidly. Badger pawed the dining room's scrap of carpet. Upstairs, Walter and Jean stirred from violent dreams. Right below them their kitchen was burning. The old wooden farmhouse was a tinderbox.

With black smoke in his throat, Harvey at last grew bold. He swung a frying pan at the window by the stove. As cold air gushed in, the fire shuddered louder.

Badger bounded upstairs, snarling at the bedroom door. It sounded like his throat was cut. When a woozy Walter responded, the steps below were fiery. His dog squeezed in with choking fog. The dining room was dense with fumes. Walter saw Harvey's empty bed across the landing.

Badger scratched at the door to go back for Harvey. But Jean heard her gangly son screaming on the grass outside. He'd squeezed through the bust kitchen window and run round the house. His dark pyjamas were ripped and bloody.

Walter was dulled by deep sleep, but he bashed open the window. Some notion hit him of tying blankets like a rope. Then the first wave of smoke sneaked under the door. Walter rammed the double bed against it in what he knew was a hopeless gesture. His feet were baking on the floorboards. Harvey shouted something outside . . .

'*Keys . . . keys . . . barn keys!*'

His frantic chant rose above the burning roar.

'Keys . . . keys . . . barn keys! Dad! Dad!'

'Walter!' cried Jean. 'Where are the keys?' She could have answered herself and they both knew it. The barn keys lived in a mug behind the wood basket downstairs.

Badger's howls and the rocket explosions had roused the farm's animals. They smelled fire and fear. Hooves and trotters paced anxiously. Then came the noise of beasts who sense their own death. A squeaking and stamping that shook their timber prisons.

And one voice above them all, now mad with dread.

'*Keys . . . keys . . . barn keys! Dad! Dad!*'

FORTY~THREE

The only option was to jump. As Harvey flapped below, Walter urged him to stay calm.

'Come closer!' he yelled. 'Harvey, come . . . closer. Your mother's going to throw herself out. Try and catch her. Try and break her fall. Be brave, Harvey. Badger's here.'

'Barn keys, Dad! Dad, Dad!'

'Leave the animals. Listen. Catch . . . your . . . mother. Stay there, she's coming now.'

Jean spluttered in the cloudy room. She hooked frail legs over the sill, her nightdress all grey. Harvey's face glowed in the orange night, his black pyjamas a shadow. A window shattered in the room below. It gave Jean the final shove she needed. She pushed away, legs and arms wide open. Harvey moved a step forwards. He caught his thin mother, though the impact floored him. Jean rolled onto wet grass, heaving hoarse breaths.

Walter flung open the cupboards and chucked out

any clothes he could find. Shoes and socks, trousers and jumpers went raining through the window. He tried coaxing Badger to the ledge, but his dog lay shrieking under the bed. As the bedroom door rattled with heat, Walter saved himself. He tied Jean's pink dressing gown tight, shielding his face from the fumes.

As he jumped towards his son, a burning plank slid from the roof. Harvey's eyes flicked from his father. Walter ploughed into him, cracking Harvey's right shoulder. The bone there jutted as Harvey screamed in murderous pain. The family lay wounded and winded. More of the farmhouse roofing tumbled onto the locked barns. The fire spread like a gale through them.

Walter ran to the padlocks on each door, tugging until his hands burned. A bellowing and bleating burst from the furnace. The hot air quickly went rotten.

Harvey writhed on the ground, sick with shoulder agony. Smoke wafted from the window above where Badger scraped at the sill. With scrabbling hind legs the dog heaved its belly onto the ledge. As the bedroom door caved in, Badger dived headlong into the night. His flailing paws caught Jean in the face, splitting her nose.

Walter gripped his woolly hair with mad fists. He staggered around the burning barns like a drunk street preacher. He raged at the hellish fire. The stench made him double up.

Badger clawed the earth, howling at the prickly heat. He stepped all over Harvey, jabbing the boy giant's wrecked shoulder. As Blackrigg Farm yielded to the blaze, the Quinns dragged themselves to a safe distance. They lay watching like injured survivors of a bomb blast. Somewhere behind, the last flickers of Harvey's bonfire went slowly ashen.

A passing motorist raised the alarm. By the time fire crews arrived there was nothing to save. Ambulances took the family away in their odd array of clothes. Harvey had to be sedated for his panic and pain. The police took details of events leading up to the fire. They got little out of Harvey, whose brain drew a blank describing the three lads. Even the red-haired ring-leader was forgotten for now.

The matter was quickly pieced together. But for Walter the most crushing blow was of his own making. Over the years very little of the farm had been insured. Why would it be? They'd always lived off what the land gave and nothing had gone wrong before. Walter applied for a farmer's hardship fund, but he wasn't in the union and his claim took ages. The aftermath of a Foot and Mouth crisis was still being dealt with.

Jean was confined to hospital with infections caused by her broken nose. She also caught a fever brought on by cold and shock. With his livestock lost, Walter was given shelter in a hostel. In time he would return to Blackrigg Valley and rebuild his ruined life.

But the authorities moved quickly onto Harvey. He had no education, no family who could cope, and suspicion lingered over his part in the fire. So they sent him away to a special school near Carlisle, with a jumble of youngsters who didn't fit anywhere. Learning difficulties, broken homes, orphans, druggies, abandoned immigrant kids.

The order of classrooms and lessons was a torture. Harvey sat pining for Badger. For muddy walks in wellies, and trees that changed colour all year round. He couldn't bear being stuck indoors each day. His fresh rosy face turned ghastly white in weeks. At first his gawky height and clumsy manners alarmed the others. They watched him sit alone and contort his pulpy body into frightening postures. But the story of Blackrigg Farm had made the northern papers, and a small gang at the school got busy. They made deathly cow and pig noises outside his room at night. They shoved burning papers under his door, jamming chairs at the handle to lock it. One November they even managed to smuggle some fireworks in. Under the pretence of showing Harvey a sheepdog puppy, they bolted him in the garden shed. A ring of Whiz-bombs erupted by the door that he hammered on.

By the time he'd been there nearly five years, the school was at a loss over him. He'd learned very little apart from basic reading and writing. His only efforts had gone into working on the school gardens a couple of hours each week. The youth had made no friends. His changing moods could snap quickly from violent spells to staying withdrawn. The doctors put him on pills for what they saw as 'depression'. They took blood tests for research on his bones, which had shot him up to way over seven feet.

They'd let him go once, for his mother's funeral three years back. Jean had never made a full recovery and died of bronchitis. Walter gradually built up a small farm again, near his original Blackrigg holding. His hardship fund allowed a fresh start with a small slate cottage and a few animals. He made occasional visits to the school near Carlisle, but they were mostly silent and pointless.

Just after Harvey turned eighteen it was agreed he'd visit Walter for a fortnight. In mid-October, a taxi took him thirty miles home to his native countryside. The second he saw Blackrigg in its yellow autumn glory, something stirred inside him and he knew what to do.

He didn't know much in life, but he knew he'd never return to Carlisle. Walter wasn't at the farm when his son arrived. He'd either forgotten Harvey was coming, or had the wrong date, or was too shattered to care much.

The taxi steered away, leaving the boy giant with an old rucksack. Harvey sank to his knees in the morning drizzle, sucking pure cold air over his tongue. There was no light in Walter's tiny cottage and no smoke from the chimney. Harvey wandered around the ploughed fields nearby, only minutes from his lost childhood home. He found the grave where Badger lay buried. Walter had dug a dog-shaped hole to plonk the creature in two years ago. An outline of slates and stones marked the limbs and body. Harvey added some extra rocks at the back to make a waggly tail.

It was too much for him to stick around so many ghosts. His heart burned with memories of Bonfire Night, five years back. He couldn't stand to see Walter looking at him with despair, and the school expected his return in two weeks. Finding the cottage open, he raided some basic supplies of food and drink. He also nabbed kitchen rolls, felt pens, a big hat and old working clothes.

With a stuffed rucksack he headed south towards Cumbria. He followed his nose and the distant main roads, trudging over muddy crops and through familiar woods where silver streams gurgled. By nightfall he'd reached the English border and took happy shelter in a deserted barn.

The weather picked up overnight and stayed fair. Hiking across hills and rivers, Harvey covered forty-five miles in three days. With no timetable to follow any more he wandered at will, sometimes scaring or surprising walkers with his great height.

One joyful ramble took him to the summit of Scafell Pike. He neither knew nor cared that he stood on England's highest peak. But he rejoiced in just being there more than any climber could ever have before. He jumped about with arms raised, on top of the world, like an innocent god.

The knobbly spines of mountain ranges lay at his feet. Then out of the purple sky behind came a punishing roar. The shocking backlash of a jet engine felled him to earth. When the searing fighter plane made a return pass, Harvey's solitude was ended. He took this as a sign he was being hunted.

From then on he began to ink strange markings on his face. He wore a broad brown hat at all times and stayed on the lower slopes. When the low flying grew more intense he moved around by night, often sleeping rough in dank mountain caves by day. Food was easily stolen from trusting farmhouses with unlocked doors.

Back in Blackrigg, Walter vaguely expected his son some time soon. When at last he contacted the school, a 'missing persons' report went out locally. The police guessed he'd gone north to hide in the bigger Scottish towns, so inquiries were directed there. But Harvey by then was gazing at a rainbow rising over Wast Water; at a hazy blue lake in the sunny rain, and sweet orange colours growing wild everywhere.

By dusk on the following day he'd met a woodland path leading from Skelwith Bridge, near Langdale Valley. This path hugged the main road, then veered up an old track. It led towards disused slate quarries and a deserted wasteland above Torbeck village. There was even a derelict shack sitting empty. It was a seedy shelter, but to Harvey it spelled fierce freedom at last.

A mild Friday night in mid-October. Down in Torbeck, after dark, the first firecrackers of the year banged out.

PART FOUR

Torbeck,
south Cumbria;
five years later

FORTY~FOUR

Someone screamed at me. He shook me by the collar. One of the men from the bridge had returned. He was a blur of blue waterproofs. The other guy was slipping down severe slopes above the rabid river. He clung to tree roots and shinned over sheer rocks. He peered downstream after Laura's body.

The other bloke flapped madly again as if to break my trance. This time his words dug into my petrified mind. I was to *run, run, get help, get someone!* I must've put blind faith in adult logic. They'd save Laura somehow and I was to fetch aid. It was that simple. Just put my head down and tear back along the tracks in tatty trainers.

I fell only once, cracking my spine and getting badly winded. Then I was up and running, sniffing rapidly through spilling nostrils. My cheeks were streaming with tears of cold and horror. But what I remember most is the pummelling water below. That and the thick yellow leaves clagging my way. There were mountain bikers down on the woodland path. If they saw my distress they didn't stop. Nor did I cry out to them, on their swift machines, to fetch help. I thought only of Dad, or Val. At last I collapsed into Torbeck. Someone gave that mocking whistle when I tumbled by the bus shelter.

But then I saw Val walking quickly from our house. She looked back there, all hurt and puzzled, then turned left for her place. I hurled myself at our front door, yanking the handle. My forehead whacked on the paint. The door was locked. As I battered with both fists it swung open, sending me flailing inside. Dad grumbled something about the Yale slipping shut, bloody thing. But I hardly saw him. There in the living room was my mum. She wasn't coming until midweek, she'd said so. Now she stared at me, rising from the settee, her blue eyes filling with dismay.

Dad was holding something and paging through it. My diary sketchpad. I saw a naked Harlequin, a murderous Beefwits and my own angry face flick by. Then I saw stars. Dad thwacked the book round my head.

'What in Christ's name is all this muck?' he shouted. He threw the book at me. He tensed up, clenching his fists, then sprang forwards. 'What the . . . *hell* you been drawing round here, or doing? What's been going on you ain't told me?'

He couldn't read the real shock on my face. But Mum could. 'What is it, Glenn?' she cried, barging Dad out the way. She gripped my shoulders. 'Glenn, what's happened?'

I spoke fast as my whole system screamed. 'It's Laura, the girl I told Dad about. She's fallen in the river up in the hills. Harlequin, that massive guy, did it. But not his fault. Get the car, Dad. *Go!*'

He moved so fast that Mum got left behind, open-mouthed. On the way I blurted all I could recall of the incident. Minutes later, Dad screeched his motor to a halt in wet gravel on Quarry Road.

He started scrabbling down ferocious slopes, his red jeans getting smeared. I lay on the edge, watching him struggle over ripping rocks. There was no sign of those two blokes from earlier. Maybe they'd already saved the day. Before Dad went out of sight somewhere on the banks, I saw him follow the river along. I yelled out for anything he might see, but he can't have heard for all that thudding water.

I was desperate to get down there and search. There were boulders way downstream that could've blocked Laura's flow. It was half an hour since the disaster.

With hands on the road I lowered myself backwards off the edge. Then I got up again as a vehicle approached. A battered Land Rover sped up the lane.

It slammed to a halt by our car. The engine was left running. Father Charlie got out, leaving his door open. He wore a black anorak over his blue suit.

He gripped an old shotgun. A second later it was pointed at my face. I smelled the bitter metal of bullets. It tickled my throat. I tasted it sourly.

'Take me to him,' said Charlie, his dark eyes on mine. 'You know where he is. He's killed my granddaughter.'

I realized where those men on the bridge had gone. They must've tried searching first. I stared at the double-barrelled blackness before me. Blood was blasting in my ears.

'She isn't dead,' I said, nearly sobbing. 'My dad's down there, he'll find her.'

Charlie pressed the gun to my temples, belching loudly. His breath was heavy with birthday beer and whisky. 'Laura's dead, or she'd have come home to her family. She loves us. Two men just told me what happened.' He steered me round with his rifle, poking it into my bruised back.

'Let the police find the body,' he slurred. 'Get in the van. We're going giant hunting.'

FORTY~FIVE

W e didn't bother with seatbelts. It was less than
two minutes up to the quarry. I grabbed the
rattling door and thought quickly. Harly would be in
his old shack, I felt sure. He'd be shivering with fright
or going mad and butting the walls. I had to steer
Charlie away from that slate hut. Anywhere would do.

Charlie braked at the top of Quarry Road, throwing
me sideways. I shouted the first thing that came to
mind.

'He's got this tent I gave him!' I said. 'He's pitched
it in the woods on the far side. That manky hut started
caving in. He'll be in his tent . . . getting ready to run.'

The quarry's vast socket lay before us. To the west,
way beyond the shack, that massive alien-friendly face
grinned from Wrendale Bank. Its carved outline glowed
even at nightfall.

Next thing I remember, we were both outside the
van. Sprouting away on my right was a thicket of

woodland and fir trees. Fallen pine needles glittered like golden pins.

'Charlie?' I begged. 'Please, let's go back. Please. Let's find Laura.'

'Show me this tent,' said Charlie. He jammed on a cap, his tipsy nose a red bulb in the evening. Right hand on his rifle, the left one round my neck.

Dry twigs crackled in the forest beside us. My heart froze, then fluttered like something trapped. Charlie swivelled, the gun's butt on his breast. And standing dead still in the dusky woods was a male red deer. The bony branches of its antlers blended with those on the trees. It stared us both out with immense black eyes, never twitching a muscle. Its handsome head rose from a thick red-brown neck. But its velvety flank was badly ripped. A gouge of dark flesh was visible. Maybe some wire fence had cut in, though the beast gave no sign of pain. Finally it lifted a foreleg and galloped into the undergrowth.

Charlie watched it through his gunsights, then lowered his rifle and grabbed my shoulder. He pushed me on a few steps. I sneaked a glance over to the shack. No sight or sound of Harly. Just the usual peppery boulders.

We trudged past the quarry's near edge. Way over from there was the rim where Harly had saved me. My brain was whining, making both ears ring like I'd been boxed. I took smaller footsteps to play for time. There was a chance Harly had just fled, so he'd need every second. I scuffed my trainers on slate slivers, then bent to my laces.

'Look lively!' said Father Charlie sharply. 'You can't save him now.' He tapped a nostril, snorting snot from the other. 'I reckon he's bust out of prison or summat. I told the police about him last night and they were meant to nab him near Skelwith Bridge today. He must've seen 'em and took off. He'd been thieving stuff out of our kitchen. We leave the door unlocked 'cos we believe in people's good natures.'

My tongue was thickening and I sounded dried up. 'He's not a thief,' I rasped. 'He takes people on real trust. That's more than you and your lot ever do.'

Charlie's cheeks went veiny and purple. 'He came into my home,' he said shakily. 'He put our food and money in his grubby pockets. Then he pissed it all away on cider. Right under my nose. He snatches my grand-daughter and throws her in a river. And you talk to me about—'

'He threw no one!' I bawled back. 'She fell. He thought she was Lavinia. The one who's been gobbing off. The one who—'

Charlie swung his gun again. Something had snapped in the bushes ahead. They guarded a path around the crater where twisting trees clung to the edge. Yellow leaves fell in slow spirals to the pit far below.

Father Charlie advanced, his rifle out front like a hunter. I snuck behind him, eyes locked on the trigger. He slunk through the shrubs, head jerking left to right. I picked up a lump of rock. Charlie stood still, listening, blowing foggy breaths. Evening had settled among the silvery trees. The watch on my wrist felt cold. The damp early dewfall was like a whispering death. A distant church clock tolled the hour. Sunday, six p.m. The woods to my right were hushed except for one songbird. Its trembling trill came in bursts like a warning.

I closed in on Charlie, who waved me back. He put a gnarled finger to his thin lips. He crouched and peered at the tangle of trees ahead. I did the same, but my young eyes were the stronger. It was me who saw Harlequin first. His blond head poked out behind a birch trunk, right on the edge. When he turned towards me and Charlie, we both drew breath. Harly had rubbed some chalky mix over his face. It was whited out and glared ghostly in the dark. His eyes had black circles marked around them. His mouth was a shocking shade of red.

Charlie's gun blasted wildly into the air. A warning

shot at the dark heavens. Uproar in the bird-filled branches. Harly hid again as the chaos of wings slowly died.

'Come out!' Charlie bellowed. 'I've got you.' He knelt down, taking aim at the birch's glinting bark. I inched up behind, rock raised in my fist. I heard Harlequin moaning and caught the words he flung out in protest.

'Tell 'em, Glenn Jackson. Tell 'em what I done for you.'

I shouted over Charlie's kneeling body that was all arched and tense.

'I'll tell 'em, Harly. They'll never take you back. I never told 'em where you were, honest I didn't.'

'Tell 'em now, Glenn. Tell Charlie I never meant *nothing*.' His voice grew hysterical to the edge of madness. 'Tell him now, *tell him now!*'

I tried to. I tried to make Charlie listen, but his purple face was a blank. I wondered how drunk he was. I remembered my dad, back in the gushing valley. My jacket had a loop of Laura's green ribbon pinned on. Not once had I thought of her as dead.

Harly was quiet now but for the occasional whimper. He flung out his big hat. Charlie shot it like a clay pigeon. My teeth chattered out of control. Charlie's finger was on the trigger again, squeezing softly. I edged beside him. And that's when Harly burst from hiding.

I punched my rock on Charlie's head. His gun fired as he fell aside. Again the trees were in turmoil. Charlie butted me in the guts, knocking me flat. Face on the ground, I looked up. Harly staggered towards me. He stumbled in the dipping earth, among flowers. His overalls were seeping a dark stain. He swayed closer, like a drunk. I lay, unable to rise. Charlie stood slowly, one foot on his gun.

Harlequin turned a circle, holding his chest. He looked like a clumsy clown. His laces were flapping. His big legs got mixed up. Tripping down a slope, he met thick tree roots. His body crashed onto its right. The jutting shoulder bore the impact and snapped. Harly squealed, rolling over. His lower half swung off the quarry's rim. Its weight sucked him down. He grabbed the mossy edge. His right shoulder collapsed. His left fingers tore at chunks of turf. The earth crumbled in his grasp.

I sprang out of my numb terror. I flapped and balanced on the edge. No sound came from Harly's yawning red mouth. It sank below me in a tortured face. The chalky skin was flecked with blood.

I could say he took as long as a stone to drop. The full nine seconds that I counted once. But stones don't grab in despair at knife-edge rocks. They don't clutch at thistles on a sheer slate cliff. Prickly bushes don't slither through their plunging hands. Nothing slows down a stone. Not like a wounded hunted giant. For he survived moments longer by slapping the cold cliff. His body found crevices to break the fall. His wrists and fingers snapped, gaining split seconds of life. A stone would just shoot away. At the very bottom it would bounce off at an angle. It wouldn't slam onto slabs and rip open. It wouldn't gush blood and guts like a slaughtered beast. It wouldn't wear a white face all smashed and staring. The loss of a stone wouldn't break your heart till it burst.

Charlie spoke softly, but with menace. 'You little toss. I wasn't aiming at him, I wanted him alive. You killed him by shoving me. You've shot your precious, dumb donkey friend. I wouldn't take a life on the Sabbath.'

Still holding that hard lump of rock, I sped from the quarry's black tomb. Charlie's Land Rover's lights were burning. A sticker on the windscreen said IN GOD WE TRUST. I pelted my chunk through the front window, leaving a splintered circle. Then I bounded over stacks of rubble, across the stream where Harly always washed before eating, and into the dark drizzly hills beyond.

FORTY~SIX

I crouched in a bed of bracken, shivering terribly, gnawing my knuckles. Cold rain and hot sweat made rivers down my face. Charlie's Land Rover roared away in a slam of doors and engines. My eyes were running but I focused on a distant bird's nest. I could see its twiggy shape in a solitary tree near the shack. I fixed on this nest as the whole world shrank to that one point. I hardly blinked until my eyes burned and I'd got a searing headache.

Standing up, I could see a twinkle of lights, two miles away down in Torbeck. Cottage chimneys blew smoke into the bruised sky like a trail of dying campfires. Cosy family scenes in the village below; murder and mayhem in the valley above.

Back at the quarry I scrambled on all fours and peered over until I just made out a gangly, crumpled body. It lay at the farthest edge of dark green water. *The Great Harlequin Grim. Finally at poor peace. No one to hurt him now. Nothing to run from.*

I found myself cradling the tree-swing, swaying against it, knowing I should race back to my dad. Back to Laura. But I could only slouch there and gently rock. Then a car revved up the hill with a whirling blue light. A stocky copper with closely cropped fair hair got out. A solid figure with his crackly radio and thick truncheon. He looked around until he'd got where the creaky swing noise came from.

He crunched over in black boots like Harly's. I managed to croak a single word.

'Laura?'

He nodded with a tight smile. 'Alive,' he said, 'but only just. Your dad found her. She's on the way to hospital. I'm PC Slater.'

I closed my eyes, clinging to the swing. My broken mind and legs both crumbled. Soft moss wet my trouser knees. PC Slater helped me up and walked me over to the quarry, a strong arm round my shoulders.

'Down there,' I whispered, pointing into the abyss. 'Right below those birch trees. You can just see his white face.'

'Right,' said PC Slater, 'I've got him. OK . . . Glenn, isn't it? I'll take you to the station in Ambleside and sort things out as best we can. You ready?'

'Ready,' I said. There were needles of fire and chunks of ice in my veins. 'No . . . wait.' I bombed off round the shrubby path, then onto the far ridge where Harly fell. I picked every wild plant growing there, snatching and tearing up savage clumps. I lay close to the quarry's dark edge, throwing them out like confetti.

'Careful!' shouted PC Slater, hurrying towards me. But I was very careful. I made sure every flower floated down right where I wanted it. They told me later that Harlequin's body was covered in them. White daisies, orange dandelions, rusty ferns, yellow buttercups. And finally I flung the loop of Laura's green ribbon over, plucked from close to my heart. I sent it spinning down to earth, with a silent prayer from Glenn Jackson.

They gave me a cup of hot and tasteless tea at the cop station. With shaky fingers I put five sugar sachets in to pep me up. Dad came out of an interview room wearing a dark blue police shirt and jumper. His face was cut and his hair all bedraggled. He can't have been near a mirror recently.

I waited by the main desk where phones never stopped ringing. Dad came over and hugged my face to his chest. I was too numb to cry, but my heart flicked in jumpy rhythms, making me short of breath.

'Hell on wheels, kidder!' Dad breathed. 'What's it all about?'

I rolled my head against him. 'You got Laura?' I whispered.

'Yes, mate, I found your girl. She'd got snared in some big rocks downriver, her mouth just above water. She was unconscious. Her lips were all blue so I did that kiss-of-life thing. I took my tops off and wrapped her up. I think she's got a fractured skull and pneumonia. She was frozen stiff, Glenn . . . a block of ice. So now we just wait, and we even pray if you feel it's right.'

PC Slater touched my elbow. 'Glenn, are you OK to talk? Your mum's just got here and she gave us this. Is it important?'

It was the diary sketchbook, with its spine all bent where Dad had whacked me.

'Yeah,' I said, taking it back. 'The stuff inside it is.'

They found us rooms in a guesthouse nearby. I'd never been to Ambleside before, with its twisty steep roads, warm lamplight and cosy shops. Back at the station two officers got ready to swoop on Torbeck, to charge Father Charlie with manslaughter. In my hot vengeance I'd told them Charlie had threatened to kill me, and fired at me when I ran off. It was something I never retracted, despite Charlie's denials. Beefwits was later picked up for air-rifle misuse, and animal cruelty to my beautiful Goldeneye.

I had a room of my own and a bed with stiff white sheets. Dad tried to make me eat a sandwich and glug hot coffee, but my stomach was churning too much. Mum drifted about in a daze, looking at me like a stranger. I stood outside their room across the corridor, hearing them row.

'How long's this weird shit been going on?' Mum shouted. 'What's happened to my son in two weeks?'

'Strewth!' Dad thundered. 'You tell me, Janet. I've been coping the best I can.'

'Well how would I know, Nick? I haven't—'

'You haven't been here. Damn right you haven't.'

'Oh . . . right! Well, it didn't look like you were missing me. You were all over that Val woman when I turned up.'

'She's been a friend! A good friend! She's been there to help me *and* Glenn.'

I shivered back to my rectangle room. I felt frozen still and crawled into bed, putting the TV on. I can't recall a single image I saw on any channel. The bright light still pulsed in the darkness when I woke at three a.m. I prayed into my pillows for Laura and wept on them for Harly. An hour later I tiptoed downstairs and found a phone number in the Yellow Pages for Kendal Hospital. I was put on hold for ages, then a nurse explained that Laura Delaney was in a critical condition.

She'd survived the worst but it was too soon to tell. Was I family?

'No. I'm . . . her boyfriend.'

'Oh, I see. Well listen, sweetheart, you try and rest up. Call us again in the morning and we might know more.'

But the morning found me back at the police station. By now they'd established Harly as Harvey Quinn, from Blackrigg Valley, near the border of Cumbria and Scotland. His body had been brought up at first light and lay in a nearby morgue.

'I'd take you to identify him,' said PC Slater, 'but he's in a terrible mess and you'd be very upset. You've been through enough.'

'Where will they bury him?' I asked. 'Not in a churchyard or some city cemetery. Please don't. Bury him out in the wilds where he wanted to be.'

'It's out of our hands right now,' said PC Slater. 'But I promise we'll keep you informed. And in the mean-time, maybe you can help us. We've found out where he was for the last five years, but this past fortnight's all a big blank. Perhaps you can fill it in and tell us more about him. A bit simple, wasn't he?'

'No,' I said firmly, feeling my throat swell. 'Very complex. Not simple at all.'

Mum and Dad had come with me, but I asked them

to leave me to it. A few hours later I spotted them in a coffee shop over the road. I stared through its window, standing on the pavement as they linked hands over steaming cups. Then they saw me there watching and both smiled together. I couldn't remember the last time they'd done that.

FORTY~SEVEN

Home-baking smells in the café made me hungry for the first time in ages. I'd shared a picnic with Harly about this time yesterday, his last meal, and had been running on empty ever since. Mum got me hot chocolate, veggie burger with chips, and strawberry cheesecake.

'No change in Laura,' I told Dad. 'The police rang earlier to check.'

My parents' faces were knitted in concern as I tried to relate so much that I could hardly understand myself. I told them about discovering the quarry and this huge figure that stopped me toppling off the edge.

'Looks like I didn't hear his name right,' I said, slurping the soothing cocoa drink. 'But I think he quite liked having a new one. Wasn't a harlequin like . . . some sort of comic figure in old pantomimes?'

Dad pressed his cheeks up into a smile. 'That's right,' he said. 'Same as what your old man's become recently. So, did anyone else get to meet this Harvey?'

'Loads of people saw him,' I said as a plate got plonked before me. 'Even though he was running away and tried to disguise himself. God, I don't know where to start really.'

'Take your time, love,' Mum said, stroking my hand. I stabbed at fat chips.

'Well, he'd been living rough for a fortnight after leaving this special school. Sounds like he once destroyed his family's farm by accident, killing all the animals. Something to do with fireworks indoors. And then he started noticing fireworks over here, coming from the mountains. He seemed to think they were a message, or a warning from dead-animal spirits. He had a useless telescope that he looked for them with.'

Mum and Dad stared like I'd been brainwashed by a cult.

'But it was only my mate Baz trying to attract alien life. I told you about him, Dad. It was Baz and me who cut that gigantic face into the hillside.'

Mum dropped her teaspoon with a clang. She stroked her temples like a faith healer until Dad touched her breezy blonde hair. 'I'll go for a wander, love,' he said kindly. 'You talk to Glenn.'

Mum nodded as Dad rubbed the top of my head and left. I bit into my burger, all tangy with relish and cheese.

'Are *you* OK then?' I said, swallowing hungrily. 'I thought you'd been with Ray, that smart guy from Booths' wine department. I met him once with you at the cinema, remember? Just before you . . . went away.'

Mum frowned slowly, her head drawing back in surprise. '*Ray?*' she said. 'Oh, you mean Ray Woodrow? God no, love, it was nothing like that. Ray's not, er, really into women. I always got on well with him though – even confided in him. But I've not been staying with Ray. I was with someone else. Someone you don't know and don't need to know about. I can't really expect you to understand, despite your strong feelings for this Laura. I hardly know what I'm going through myself.'

Mum stroked my cheekbones, holding my face like a precious eggshell.

'But the thing is, Glenn,' she sighed, 'you've got your whole life stretching out. I'm getting towards middle age, and there come certain turning points. Certain . . . moments when you question everything you've been living for. But I'll always live most of all for you, sweetheart. You're the thing I actually gave life to. The most important thing I've done on this earth.'

I swallowed my food, which had lost its taste. 'Don't you love my dad any more?' I said.

'I do, which makes it hard for you to understand why I left,' Mum said. She bunched paper napkins in her fist. 'Maybe one day you might, but right now I know you've been through hell. And so . . . I think me and your dad can make it back together. At least we can try. Booths have offered me a position in a new store up in Carlisle. It's an assistant manager's role, decent money and prospects. It would mean leaving Torbeck though, and starting again. How would you feel about that?'

My heart told me how I felt about leaving Laura. A cold stone dragged it down like a weighing scale.

'I feel it could have been different there,' I said. 'Or better maybe, without certain people who'd bust their own guts to make trouble. But I know we can't really go back and I think Dad wants out. Torbeck cramps his style too much, though he can still look the part when he wants.'

Mum tufted my spiked hair and smiled. 'I know he can, love. Right from the off he could cut it for me. But he got worn down by work and didn't know how to get the best out of life any more. You and me know he's funny around the kitchen table, but it don't always come off in other places. He'll find something that satisfies his hopes and dreams. I bet it's been some rotten fortnight for you both.'

'It has,' I said, attacking the strawberry cheesecake. 'But Laura's hanging on in there, thanks to Dad. I'll ring the hospital every hour until they let me go over.'

'She'll make it through,' Mum said, stirring an empty cup. 'Something good's gotta come out of all this.'

I learned it was Mum who'd been phoning our home those times when the line went dead. She'd called me after school, hoping I'd answer, but kept getting Dad instead.

'I thought he'd have found a job sooner and been out more,' she said. 'Still, at least he tried making new friends, from what he's told me. I'm not surprised it didn't come off though. I never really fancied Torbeck myself. Those titchy places ain't always like they seem on the pretty postcards.'

A special church service for Laura was held in Torbeck that evening. The place was packed for a girl who had no obvious friends. But everyone wanted to catch up on the gossip and scandal. They crammed onto cold pews, whispering and fidgeting, hardly hearing a word the vicar said. When he mentioned that my dad had saved Laura from certain death, a disgruntled murmur broke out. Then the full house was scolded at from the Bible. The vicar wasn't fooled by the sudden gush of godliness in Torbeck.

'Many have fallen by the edge of the sword. But not

so many as have fallen by the tongue. May we consider this, as we move about our daily lives with grace.'

The crowd sat quietly after that and took its teaching on the chin. One or two even had the decency to blush, and believe the vicar was gazing into their souls. But no prayers were said for my other friend. Harly, Harvey, Harlequin. Whoever or whatever he was, no thoughts were offered up. At least Father Charlie wasn't present at the sermon. He was in police custody at the time, answering some tough questions. They later released him on bail, pending further inquiries.

The same nurse answered yet again when I phoned Kendal Hospital for the sixth time. She went a bit quiet when I told her my name.

'I'm sorry, erm, Glenn. The family have asked that you don't visit. Laura's at a critical stage right now and they'd rather be alone with her. Sorry, love, I'm sure you understand. But the news is no worse today, so keep everything crossed.'

It wasn't until four o'clock that I realized I should've been at school. There was no way I'd be going back just yet, if ever. I imagined Baz kicking around the mountains, deep in thought, but couldn't find the heart to ring him. It might be awkward if I did, anyway. He wasn't a great talker when the subject wasn't his cosmic concerns. And I'd not forgotten how he'd backed away from meeting Harly once.

So at quarter past one that morning I lingered on the guesthouse phone again. I could hear the normal hospital sounds in the background — phones ringing, keyboards tapping, a drunken shout, coughing, complaining. At last a Scottish nurse came on, speaking briskly between sips of a drink.

'Laura Delaney . . . Ward Sixteen B . . . Recent severe concussion. That the one? She's through the worst and we expect a full recovery. Could take some time though . . . but she's made it this far and might well be out within a month. Anything else?'

Nothing else.

FORTY~EIGHT

'In case there's an inquest on Harvey's death,' said PC Slater as I gave another statement next morning. Mum sat outside while Dad sorted our council-house affairs. PC Slater, who seemed to work round the clock, handed me a photo sent down from his colleagues in the Scottish Borders. It showed a man of about sixty, with woolly white hair and a flinty face.

'Walter Quinn,' he told me. 'Harvey's dad, who comes from around here originally. Thought you might be interested to see it. We had a suspicious death up in his part of the country recently. Everyone in that area's being questioned, including Walter. You ever seen him before?'

'Never,' I said. 'But he reminds me of Father Charlie. Maybe that's why Harvey trusted Charlie when he came calling that Saturday, offering work. He thought he was safe among farming types, even though he was on the run. I wondered why he came down to the country fair that time. If farming folk were all he knew, I guess he never thought they could betray him.'

PC Slater scribbled in a notepad. 'We can't release the body yet,' he said. 'Not until Walter gives permission. Apparently he nearly fainted away when he was told what happened. The poor sod's lost everything in life. Anyway, how are things with you, Glenn? Is there anyone here you'd like to talk with, in private? We can arrange a counsellor . . .'

'No thanks,' I said. 'It looks like we're moving to a place called Brampton, up near Carlisle. And the hospital told me I can't visit Laura 'cos her family won't allow it.'

PC Slater stood up and stuffed pens in a shirt pocket. 'I'm popping over there this afternoon. If Laura's people are around I'll put them straight on a few things. You deserve better luck, Glenn. Your dad OK?'

'He'll get through it,' I said. 'If anyone can find some humour in all this, it'll be him.'

'We're going back with our heads held high,' Dad explained. 'If someone's got owt to say they can say it to our faces.'

The three of us drove back into Torbeck on Wednesday morning. Sleety rain slanted across the windscreen of a hired car. Dad's motor was up on Quarry Road still, though its wing mirrors had been smashed since Sunday. The police were towing it in for repairs.

The Village of the Year was cold and quiet. We shivered around the house, packing things into the boxes they'd arrived in nineteen days ago. Nobody turned on the lights. It was like we had to do this grim task in silence.

'Good job I never took a lodger in,' Dad laughed. 'Imagine being turfed out after a fortnight 'cos the landlord's gotta flit.'

Neither me nor Mum raised a smile. We just bent our backs to cardboard crates, stacking them with plates and pans. I balanced Rembrandt bear on a clothes bin bag. Maybe if I dropped him on the pavement again Laura might spring up to dry his rainy fur. Just like that first afternoon. I pressed my face to the hailstormed window for an aching stare at the spot where we'd met. I'd chalk mark it with an X before we left, and let the filthy rain do its worst.

Dad wanted his music stuff kept safe until we moved properly. I dashed outside with him, lugging record sleeves and CD cases to the car. Then we both fled back to the house, pelted by stinging pearls.

And then there was a girl on the pavement, coming our way as we stood in the door. Only it wasn't Laura;

it was Lavinia. She wore a brown poncho over a black top and trousers, like a young widow in mourning. Without a trace of awkwardness she came up the soaking path towards us. Her silky sweep of hair was plastered in thick strands. There was a touch of red in her cheeks, but that might've been the sharp weather. She stood before us, looking only at Dad when she spoke.

'I'm sorry if I've said anything that caused your family distress. I realize that you acted bravely on my sister's behalf and we are all grateful. Laura continues to make a slow and steady recovery. I hope you'll understand I was only trying to protect her interests. That is the truth, although I may have spoken hastily at times.'

It was like she'd written it down first then rehearsed it to perfection. Dad looked rather puzzled by the apology, which was offered to him but really aimed at me. He nodded, hooked thumbs in his belt and sauntered inside. I wasn't feeling at all gracious and did the same, after kicking the door to.

'Who was that?' asked Mum, sellotaping a box.

'Nobody,' I said. 'Just another sad stranger we never knew.'

'Walter Quinn's had a stroke,' PC Slater informed me over the phone. 'He's too ill to oversee any funeral arrangements, but he heard how you'd looked after

Harvey. The thing is, Glenn,' PC Slater went on,
sounding awkward. He lowered his voice. 'Thing is,
right, we may have to exhume the body at some stage.
It might be needed for a separate inquest. I can't say
any more on that, so if we can lay him to rest somewhere local for now . . .'

'Up in the hills,' I said. 'Somewhere near the quarry
where his last days were. Then at least it's away from
prying eyes if you have to . . . dig him up.'

I heard the rattle of a pen on teeth. 'Might be for
the best,' said PC Slater. 'Leave it with me. Oh, and
I've cleared your absence at school, in case you were
worrying. A Mrs Broughton sends her sincerest
thoughts to you. And a Mr Garner, who I also talked
with, sends best wishes to . . . Glynn. Or maybe I just
heard him wrong.'

So they lugged Harvey's eight-foot coffin up in a police
van. Among the slatey animal graves he'd made out of
tormented guilt, we laid him into a long hole. It was
a warm Friday morning at the end of a black week.
There was the local vicar in jeans and sweatshirt, PC
Slater, me, Dad and Mum. We didn't sing any hymns,
but the birds getting ready to fly south for winter
offered a chirpy requiem. A simple white cross was
rammed into the rocky earth.

Everyone left me alone for a while when we'd finished. I creaked open the door of Harly's hovel, where my three unreturned library books lay waiting. *Little Red Riding Hood*, *Kes* and *Van Gogh: A Biography*. And stuffed in a crevice, near the roof, was that old charred newspaper. I still had a bruised knee after Harly had flung me out for trying to burn it that time.

Reaching the soiled paper down, I quickly found the reason he'd kept it so long. It was a copy of the Scottish *Daily Record* from five years back, with a story on page nine about the fire at Blackrigg Farm. A picture showed Harvey looking about twelve, though his unnatural height made guessing difficult. His parents on either side were lanky but hunched. A dark wooden house loomed in the background, maybe a year before the tragedy.

Someone had penned a thick black arrow by Harly's face. Its tail sneaked back to the margin, where four clumsy words were scrawled: *Is this you, Freak?*

Perhaps some kid at the special school nabbed hold of a copy and shoved it Harly's way. It was probably the only reminder Harvey Quinn ever had of his family life.

The report noted that local police had questioned three schoolboys about the farm incidents. All had later been released, without any caution or juvenile charge.

PART FIVE

The following year

FORTY~NINE

Crooked Row, Brampton, nr Carlisle
April 15th

Dear Baz,

Sorry I've not written before now. Yeah, I know it's spring already, but we left Torbeck last October in rather a hurry! Then there was the usual upheaval and settling-down period. We're still picking up the pieces really. Funny how no one saw us arrive in Torbeck and no one watched us leave.

I'm at a far bigger school where you don't stand out being new. I turned fourteen last week and we went to a comedy night in Carlisle. They kept asking the audience if anyone wanted to come out and do a turn. Dad tried shoving his hands up, but me and Mum pinned him down.

Mum's OK, a bit moody. Dad's got a job with the local council, dealing with the same kind of madness he did back in Burnley.

Last week he got called to a council flat above a bakery. No one had seen the old couple who were living up there

337

for ages. Their rent got paid by standing order so maybe nobody looked out for them. When Dad busted their door open he found the pair dead on the sofa. They were so far gone he couldn't tell who was who. Dad asked the baker when he'd started getting suspicious. The guy said it was when yucky stuff began dripping from the ceiling onto his apple slices.

It took ages for me to face up to drawing again after all that happened. But I'm painting props for the school play, and my Torbeck charcoal landscapes are up in the IT room.

I heard from the hospital that Laura got released before last Christmas. Wasn't sure if it was safe writing to her. Can you suss that one out for me? Oh, and I'm going to see Harly/Harvey's dad at some stage. Wish me luck, it could be gruesome. And what news from the crackling cosmos beyond?

Thanks for being my buddy. You really should get a school award, even though it was only for two weeks. Sorry it couldn't have been longer.

Glenn

32 Furness Road, Torbeck
April 19th

Dear Earthling,

If only I could feel the same shockwaves up on King's
Cragg that you left behind! Sadly not much to report,
though someone's been up Wrendale Bank to attack our
'Mr Smiley'. They've cut a scar down the face, probably
with a lawnmower. I suspect your Beefwits wally was
involved. When the aliens come I'll make sure they cart him
off for spiteful experiments on the privates. It's probably
'cos he got done over that sordid duck incident. And got
a caution for illegal air-rifle use. Old Mr Guthrie recovered and won damages off the family. He gave some to the
youth-club fund. Bloody big-hearted, I say. Beefwits is
banned from attending when it opens.

Father Charlie had his gun licence removed, so no more
grouse-bagging for him. He's taken to carrying a puppy
around instead. I reckon he's after a change of image. I
heard someone did a nasty black 'n' white sketch of him
with a gun up his arse. Copies of it got sent to dozens of
houses in Torbeck. No name on it, no nothing. It surely
wasn't quiet little Glenn's doing!? Yes?!! No?!!

Well now, I know you're impatient for news of
. . . HER!! Yeah, she got free of hospital back in December
and returned to school in January. But most of the time she

stays far apart from everyone. Even at break she wanders moodily around the field, sketching little birdies in the hedgerow. Lavinia tells us it's delayed shock, but I reckon Laura's pining away for something, or someone . . .

Oh, and I let her in on the Big Secret! She searched me out a while back, asking how to contact you. I was on the Special Website at the time and I trusted her on instinct. It drives Lavinia mad to see us confabbing in private. Think it best if we three stay in touch by email. I'll put mine and Laura's details at the end, so get online and get back to us. And, as if you couldn't guess, The Girl sends her luurrvve.

Your briefest of buddies,

Baz

PS: If you're serious about nominating me for a buddy award, write to Mr Minor, the head. Don't wanna sound too pushy, but it might look good on a CV!

FIFTY

From: Laura Delaney <adora-laura@aol.com>
To: Glenn Jackson <vanglenngogh@ntlworld.com>
Subject: Happy landings!
Date: Thursday 12 July

Hey you,

Well here I am down in New Zealand. Flew in yesterday.
Am staying with a cousin of my real mum's. They found
out about me when the adoption agency contacted them.
Back when I was fighting for me dear life in hospital. Even
these guys don't know where Mum ended up. She was an
Aussie called Sylvia who was dead brainy and came to
England, to Oxford Uni. On her gap year she went travelling, got preggy, went back to Oxford, had me, gave me
up, buggered off. Last heard of in India, maybe. So I've
got piccies of her and whatnot and she also had moppy
black hair. Not so drop-dead gorge as yours truly! It's pretty
cold over here but there's wine and walks and cute guys (not
really!). Soz, but I'm out here most of the summer as Mrs

Delaney ain't coping too well with any of us, or anything. Lavinia's staying with her big sis for a while in Edinburgh. Will try and snuck up to see ya, but it looks like being autumn, like you said. Miss you and think of you and wanna be you . . . and be with you. Wot news lol?

Gbh&k

Laura xxxxxxxxxxxxxxxxxxxxxxxxxxxxxxxxxxxxxxxxxxxxxxxxxx
PS: Have kept all your emails in a private folder. My password's 'glitterglenn' btw, if you're feeling nosey!

From: Glenn Jackson <vanglenngogh@ntlworld.com>
To: Laura Delaney <adora-laura@aol.com>
Subject: UN-Happy landings!
Date: Saturday 14 July

Hey yourself,

   Miserable that you're a zillion miles off and not coming home till bleak midwinter. Got some summer work at this modern-art college in Carlisle, helping with equipment sorting, bit of decorating and studio designing. Lots of natty girls about, but none bold enough to take a header into two waterfalls. So I resist 'em all. Things cracking up at our home too. Dad stayed out all night on Tuesday and Mum refused to call the police. In the end he crawled home on Wednesday with the father of all hangovers. Mum gave him soup and bread, and I saw her sitting on the bed nursing him, but I know they're close to the end. Mum's other bloke phones her mobile when Dad ain't around. It must be love 'cos I know he made her a CD compilation. She borrowed my portable to play it in private.

Miss you, funny face. Can't believe it's eight months since everything happened. I have your 78 emails in private folder too. My password's 'Harlequin'. Sorry, I'll change it to something with your name. Am learning web design too. Gonna create a tribute site to Harly one day, with a sketch of Father Charlie's neck in a noose. Hope the sick sod's crops all fail. Have a great summer (but sounds like winter there) and don't forget yours truly.

Gbh&kb
Glenn
xxxxxxxxxxxxxxxxxxxxxxxxxxxxx

FIFTY~ONE

From: Barry Crookes <blackholebaz@secretsun.com>
To: Glenn Jackson <vanglenngogh@ntlworld.com>
Subject: November visit
Date: Friday 27 October

Hiya Jacko,

Soz, I somehow wiped your last message. Didja say you're coming down next week, in early November? Not been able to see Laura in private recently so couldn't check. Pity your secret attempts to meet her over the summer failed. She got whisked off to some long-lost relative abroad, yeah? Guess you know more about that.

What news? Well, dear Lavinia's youth club finally looks set to open. She did raise a fair wad for it. Thing is, now she needs someone young 'n' arty to do the murals and decor inside. And you ain't here and there's no other takers! How gutted is she, eh? Very!

Beefwits got taken on by the local builders, so I intend to move six counties away before ever buying a house. He's also, oh Lord, got a crappy car and zooms it round the village like a Ferrari. Last week his wing mirror pinged off on the church wall. Saddo.

Having said that I popped up to Harly's grave last week. There's a rumour going round (natch!) that his body was dug up recently. Anyway, I hiked up there and saw Beefwits gawping at the grave. He had a baseball cap in hand, like he was paying last respects. Weird. Wasn't it his gang who did a catapult job on the shack that time? Maybe they saw Harly head there after the country fair and thought he was easy meat. Wrongo!!

But . . . even more astounding than a repentant Beefwits!! Yesterday evening I lay near the summit of King's Cragg. And . . . I got a definite deep rumble down the spine. It rippled through me five times. Such tingles are pretty rare on a sacred landing site, so I'll sign off now and report to the higher powers.

All best, Baz.

PS: Mrs Broughton's back next term. She had a baby girl named Willow!! Arty hippy.

PPS: Val in Henderson's shop says thanks for the postcards, and how she's dead sorry about everything.

From: Glenn Jackson <vanglenngogh@ntlworld.com>
To: Barry Crookes <blackholebaz@secretsun.com>
Subject: Re: November visit
Date: Monday 30 October

Dear Dr Spock,

Yep, I'll be boldly returning on Friday November 5th. I'm bunking off school and telling Mum we've got a class day trip. I'm staying with her at the moment. Things haven't worked out between Dad and her, so she's got her own place. There's something I've promised myself I'll do on Bonfire Night, back in Torbeck. And me and Laura are meeting on the Quarry Road bridge after school, where we never got a chance that evil Sunday.

The new Booths branch is doing well and Mum's chuffed. Haven't met her other bloke yet, though I think he's in catering. Guess we'll have to meet one day if it's for real. Dad's mate Geoff came to stay, and he got Dad looking at Singles ads in the paper. In the end Dad went upstairs laughing, but I heard him crying through the bathroom door.

Anyway, he's joined a writers' group led by local novelist Murray Johns. We bumped into him in Brampton once — he's like a yokel prophet, with long silver hair flowing. Dad said if he had hair like that, then he too could write great stuff. But I reckon if he ever lost his quiff he'd lose the will to live. So he's given up on comedy and learning to get stories down on paper. Remember that bomb dropping near the quarry? Dad's heard that two coppers caused it, firing a traffic speeding gun at the jet. Reckons it sent the delivery system haywire. He's written a radio play about it and got some literary agent interested.

I went to see Harly's dad, Walter. He wants his son buried back in Blackrigg now the police have finished mucking about with the body. Even Walter wasn't told what they were up to. I gave him the story of Harly's death, though I made out it was accidental. He wept a bit, and cursed the police for never catching the three lads who started it all. Said some youth called Donnie Turnbull was probably behind it, but has no proof. Harvey was thirteen when all his horrors began. He would've been nineteen last month.

'Harmless as a great baby elephant,' Walter said. 'Gentle as a dove's white wings.'

I'm glad he remembers him that way.

Yours, going mad waiting for Laura,
Glenn

FIFTY~TWO

I took an early bus to Carlisle, then the West Cumbria train down the coastline. November 5th was a clear, cold morning, and the Solway Firth rolled in distant dark waves. The two-carriage train chugged through steely Workington, down by the beach at St Bees and past flaky FOR SALE signs in Sellafield, where they process nuclear power.

I was a jumble of romantic nerves and all fidgety. I checked my house keys, wallet and train tickets like an obsessive. I delved into my small rucksack in case things I knew were there had somehow jumped out. After that there was nothing to do but watch golden landscapes and a sombre sea through my grimy window.

Two hours later I arrived at a small town where buses run to Torbeck. It was lunch time so I got a chip cob and watched school kids mooch by. Seagulls scolded me from above for my truancy.

The buses went every few hours and I was close to

Torbeck by two thirty. And it was on the quiet main road leading in that I suddenly seized up. A bolt of nervous cramp kicked my stomach. I had hot shingles and rubbed my face on the cold window. I got out before the village, to walk and think about this panic attack.

Was it Torbeck I couldn't face, or just anxiety over seeing Laura after so long? I guessed it was both and so hiked up to Wrendale Bank past The Moon pub, into the valley. I avoided the village centre with a shudder, though I'd have liked to see Val again.

Like Baz reported, someone had been busy with our alien-friendly face. A wonky scar ran from its eyes down to the swanky cigarette. It had looked so cool and now it was mangled. But whatever beauty you try to build, someone always wants to rip it up. The trick is to keep on building until there's too much to destroy. I know that now.

I had an hour to kill before meeting Laura. Once more I joined the flat woodland trail leading out of Torbeck. One year on and a fresh layer of dead leaves made a crinkly carpet. A tree had giant fungal mushrooms embedded in its trunk, like dinner plates. I passed the spot where Harly did that mighty piss, with me watching from his crooked shoulders. Maybe I hoped a giant beanstalk might've sprouted there. But the only trace of Harly was planted in my memory. That was enough.

At the crossroads I took a hard look down at Father Charlie's place. My hands grew hot, thinking of his freedom and Harly's loss. I stared at his farmhouse, almost willing him to come out and fight. But there was no sign of the former priest and his new puppy dog. No sound either, now that his forbidden gun was rusting away.

Further on up, and I could hardly look at the water-falls. They thundered before me as if outraged. There'd been recent flooding in south Cumbria, so the white rapids were bulging. I used to hate the rain back in Burnley, when it swept over the sooty inner city. But I was thankful for the downpour that had swelled the fountain Laura fell into. It softened the blow and spat her out with half the injuries she might have got. I'll never forget that moment. There's a lot I'll never forget.

Up in the hills I heard a rumble of mining and ex-cavation work. It sounded like the mountain's metal guts had just swallowed a scrapyard. I had to smile. No wonder Baz felt strange stirrings up here with all that commotion.

I wore my red jacket with a green ribbon looped at the breast. Above me the sun was fighting to stay awake. Apart from the rousing water everything felt calm and hopeful. I checked my watch again, counting down the minutes. *Quarter past four*, Laura had emailed. *Expect me about then and we'll meet on that flat bridge over the river. Let's tempt fate*, she'd written. *Let's dare it to spoil things this time.*

At four o'clock I paced on the bridge, tapping at the gate that led to Quarry Road. I went through my mental checklist of things I'd talk about: my mate Gary at school, who was Cumbria's teenage tiddlywinks champion; Dad's radio play, *Cops and Bombers*, being accepted by the BBC; a large-scale graffiti painting I was involved with to decorate a youth club. I must have things to tell Laura. There mustn't be any clumsy gaps after so long apart.

I stood with my back to the gate, rehearsing these casual speeches. The waterfalls boiled away down on my left. The struggling sun gave a warm whisper. Then came a pinch to the back of my neck. And there she was, right behind me, in her dark blue school gear and denim top. Laura swayed on the spot, grinning widely. I felt a warm wave shudder through me; my green eyes were suddenly wet at the edges.

The gate stood between us like a prison barrier. I spoke first.

'Hey, you've got new glasses. Very dinky and modern.'

'Sorry,' said Laura shyly. 'I had an accident somewhere round here with the old ones. Don't you like these?'

'What? Oh, I do,' I said, rubbing my hands on the gate. 'You just don't look quite so . . . quirky in trendy ones. I mean, very nice though. And your hair too . . .'

It was shorter now, cut neatly and curled around the shoulders.

'Don't you like that either?' asked Laura. 'I had it done yesterday.' She touched her black locks, going red at the cheeks.

'Yeah, course I do. It doesn't matter or anything. You're here now, aren't you?'

'Guess I am,' said Laura, the smile fading. Her lower lip trembled over a dimpled chin. She poked at the gate I was still leaning on. 'Are you going to open this thing and come over? Or shall we stay on opposite sides and swap news?'

I fumbled with the iron latch, snagging my fingers. 'Ouch. Sorry,' I mumbled. 'I'm not thinking.' My checklist of great chit-chat went zipping downstream. And I noticed my fly was undone.

'What's in your backpack?' she asked as I lugged it onto my shoulder. 'Is it the stuff you're using later?'

'Yeah,' I said. 'I've got my heart set on doing it, like I wrote you. You can take part if you want. I was kind of hoping you would.'

Laura shook her head firmly. 'No. It's something you need to do on your own. Nobody else should be there.'

My heart sagged for the third time in a minute. I fiddled with a loose strap on my pack.

'That's OK,' I said, staring at dancing leaves. 'It probably sounds mad anyway.'

Laura drifted a few steps away, her arms folded over denim. 'Not mad,' she said. 'Just something that's not for sharing. Shall we take a walk up there? To the quarry?'

'We should go somewhere,' I said. 'Me having come all this way.'

Laura fiddled with her new hairstyle. We strolled upwards to the sound of water on solid stone. I was tongue-tied and kept stealing glances at Laura, who stared ahead. Her gorgeous face was rigid, like the slabs of drizzly rock beside her. I watched the plummeting river down on my left. To my right I felt Laura look at me nervily, but I didn't know how to break this awkward ice. Even the news of Dad's radio play felt toothless just then. Laura carried a black shoulder bag, running her fingers through the stringy strap. Finally I muttered about maybe seeing Baz before I left.

'What's that?' said Laura, leaning across. 'Did you say Baz is coming?'

'No,' I sighed. 'Least I hope not . . . not right now.'

'He's heard strange rumblings in the hills,' Laura said, stepping over a rutted puddle. 'And spotted a blue light over King's Cragg at midnight through his tele-scope. We're fairly sure something's trying to make contact.'

I hitched up my rucksack. 'Sounds like you make a good team,' I said. 'Happy for you both.'

Laura stopped on the crooked path, turning to me but looking at my green ribbon.

'Glenn . . . don't you want me here?' she said. 'Shall I leave you alone?'

I stepped forwards, splashing her trouser legs from a watery pothole. 'Didn't you want to see me?' I asked. 'Only . . . I thought you did. I know we've never been alone for long before. And I've got things to tell you, but they don't seem interesting now. And I've waited so *bloody long* for this . . .'

Laura smiled, put down her bag and loosened the top. 'Right,' she said, fumbling inside. 'Here you are, my big squeeze. Have some of Laura's sweet medicine, and let's start over . . .'

FIFTY~THREE

*I*t was a full bottle of ginger wine with a screw-cap top. Laura opened it, had a good glug, then passed it over. She fanned her mouth, taking cold breaths. I grinned, kissed the rim where her lips had drunk, and swigged. Fiery spices poured into my throat, warming me all over. I thrust the bottle back at Laura, then lifted it out of her reach, standing on tiptoes. She tugged my jacket and tried to press my shoulders down. Then the shine in her eyes made me grab her for a fierce hug. My left hand pressed the bottle into her back.

'Little wino,' I murmured. 'Did Lavinia's charity tins pay for this?'

'No,' said Laura, nibbling my neck. 'It's my private comfort these days. For when Lavinia drives me mad, or when I'm wanting to see you the most. Someone brought me a bottle in hospital and now I'm addicted. Keeps the chills away from one so fragile.'

I held her even tighter, feeling a year's load of

troubles roll free. 'You're not fragile,' I whispered. 'Most people wouldn't have survived what you did.'

Laura pulled away but held my wrists. 'A nurse said that when I finally spoke again, the first person I asked for was you. I don't remember but I believe it.'

When we started kissing there was no gentle build-up. It was manic from the off, with chewing lips and lovebites on the jugular. Then we stood in a tangled knot, swaying to the water playing its way downstream.

If you've ever waited a year to snog someone's mouth off, and finally done it, you'll know what a rampant state I was in. Total arousal kicked in, big time. I had to turn away in shame and hear Laura giggling. When I could stand and face her again she shivered, with arms wrapped around herself. She ran her pink tongue over those so-red lips, and smiled wickedly.

We carried on up Quarry Road, with a dark blue chill in the afternoon. Fumes from distant cottage chimneys drifted up the valley. The air grew smoky sweet with burned toffee and baking potatoes. Bonfire Night cooking.

'So, how is dear Lavinia?' I asked.

Laura's voice went moody. 'Oh, she's all right,' she said, booting a stone along. 'She keeps trying to get me to *talk* about things. About being adopted, about Ronnie dying, about what happened last autumn. She's been seeing a counsellor and wants me to do the same. She can stuff that though. I've got all I need right here, with you.'

I kept sniffing the breeze, filled with woodsmoke and burning leaves. I was kind of missing all this wildwoods malarkey.

'And mad Janice, your replacement mum?'

Laura dug her nails into my knuckles and I squeezed back. 'She's on pills now for all her various traumas and trembles. Hardly dares go outside these days, poor lamb. Thinks her family is the talk of the village and she ain't far wrong. She got a break from me in the summer though, when I went to New Zealand. Still, two more years and you and me can be at some sixth-form college together. That one in Carlisle sounds good.'

'It *is* good,' I said. 'Reckon I can find you a spare bedroom. Right next to mine.'

Then we were up at the hideous crater itself. The light played glumly through silver trees on the far side. We trod carefully to the edge where Harly clung on for those final seconds. Laura kneeled on the same patch of moss where he tumbled. She threw a stone over, listened for its long fall and imagined. I shivered at the vicious memory and hauled away to the shack.

Laura caught me up at the door that still hung on a

single bolt. Mouldy blankets lay bunched in a corner. I spread them in a shabby carpet so they made something to sit on. We finished the ginger wine with gulps and gasps. I was thrilled right through with love and alcohol. I tickled Laura's tinny ribs and let her slump against me.

'I knew you'd come back one day,' she said. 'When I recovered I came here all the time. I cycled up Quarry Road every day. Just waiting and wishing. I felt closer to you, knowing you'd hung out up here. It was like a part of you hadn't left and I could talk like you were right beside me. So I did. I did that often.'

She put her head on my shoulder as I bundled her up in my arms. My throat was lumpy. 'Do you think everyone's life has a moment like this?' I whispered. 'I mean, even some grotty old street wino's? Was there a time someone felt this way about them?'

Laura played with my watchstrap then gave me a gingery kiss. Her breath was warm and spicy. She said, 'I reckon everyone has a secret someone. Maybe it's all that keeps us going. Once you've known the feeling, you live in hope it might happen again.'

She shoved her shoulder bag down, then lay back on it like a pillow. The stuffy stained blankets were crumpled beneath us. I saw a spider the size of my palm spinning cobwebs in a dark corner. The stony earth was damp and smelled of old soil. Grotty walls killed off the last cracks of light.

Laura pulled me forwards, right onto her. She shifted about until my arms cradled her neck. 'So,' she said, nibbling my chin, 'what are these things you've got to tell me?'

'Forgotten them,' I whispered. 'You got anything to tell?'

'Later,' said Laura. 'It can all wait.'

Then my mouth was too busy to reply. My lips were silent and soft over Laura's. My hands felt warmed with wine as I searched her all over. I got away with every daring tweak or touch. I took off her nifty glasses, kissing eyebrows, lashes and lids. It was twenty minutes before I lifted my numb left arm away.

'Such an innocent orphan,' I sighed. 'Or you were once.'

Laura sat up, shaking with cold now that I wasn't wrapped round her. She buttoned her jacket and smartened her clothes. 'I need a wee,' she said. 'All that wine's trying to bust out. It's your fault for pressing in sensitive places. You wait here, mister, and no peeking. Girls don't find the great outdoors so easy.'

I did peek for a few seconds, then ducked back inside. A minute later Laura called me from somewhere beyond. I took our bags and found her by Harly's

grave. Someone had erected a small white cross with
HARVEY QUINN carved on.

'No one's owned up to paying for this,' said Laura.
'But I reckon it's Father Charlie's doing. Maybe it's his
way of squaring things with God, or he really regrets
what happened. He wants us all to spend Christmas Day
with him. But I can't face the thought, and so . . . so-
oh . . . I reckon I should spend Christmas with you!
It's only seven weeks away. What d'you reckon?'

'With me?' I said. 'What, you mean come up to
Brampton?'

'Why not?' said Laura, kneeling to arrange some
rocks on the grave.

'Wow, I don't know,' I said, dropping our bags.
'Aren't you meant to be with your family? Won't they
cut up?'

'But they're not my family,' said Laura, standing to face
me. 'Not really, so what does it matter? Lavinia's got an
older sister called Elaine who went off to college and left
home years ago. Lavinia was only six then and I was
adopted as a sort of playmate. But it was Ronnie who
arranged it. He was great with me, always treating me like
an equal to the others. After he killed himself, Janice
seemed to forget I was there and went all dippy. But I'm
a survivor. I've a right to go after what I want. And I
wanna be with you. How else we gonna see each other?'

'Dead right,' I said, snaring Laura round the waist. 'Consider yourself invited. I know Dad wants to see you and get to know you. You didn't say much last time you met, just choked up some river water. And Mum still feels guilty over what happened, so we can play on that. Spend some time with her. If you're serious . . .'

'I'm serious,' said Laura, pulling me close. 'I'm fourteen and a half and com*pletely* serious. I'm also dead hungry now and want my tea. Walk me back to the bridge? Does that leave you enough time?'

'Just. I'll get the last bus out of Torbeck at half six, and there's a train at seven forty. Ring me tomorrow night and we'll start planning.'

I dumped my rucksack back in the shelter and grabbed Laura's hand. On the way down, in cloudy darkness, we nattered our news at top speed. Laura wanted a part in Dad's radio play and I made out she was having a fling with batty Baz. We threw rocks at the waterfall that nearly claimed Laura's life, hurling insults at the blasting cascades.

When we finally let each other go, I watched her drift away down the scraggy road. She turned and gave a last wave before rounding a rocky precipice. I waited hopefully in case Laura changed her mind and ran back. My right foot sneaked forwards, tempting me to plunge into the dusk after her.

But my conscience knew there was a promise to fulfil. One that I'd made when I learned the full truth of Harly's tragic childhood. I was going to give him the fireworks party he'd never had, yet wanted so badly. The display he for ever missed out on, after one night of carnage exactly six years ago.

FIFTY~FOUR

I approached his grave again in the grey stillness, feeling haunted. It was just after half past five. A flock of birds flew in two prongs, like the hands on my watch. There was no clue that Harly might have been dug up recently. Only a long smooth mound scattered with nuggets and soil. I banked up the borders with more flat slates, overlapping them like roof tiles. He deserved a proper shelter at last. One that wouldn't let the dark nights in, or the cold Cumbrian rain.

It was getting too gloomy to see properly and I scrabbled about, knocking into blurred boulders. But by ten to six I was ready to start the show. I scooped a series of holes along the strapping tomb and wedged a line of fireworks in. Stashed in my ready-made kit was a long-burning portfire stick. This would light the fuses from a few yards off.

I lit the blue touchpaper of a Roman candle and stood well back. In the few seconds of waiting I felt a childish thrill. Then out shot a brilliant shower of sparks, coloured bangs and flashes. My eyes were dazzled and mesmerized. When the candle was dead I held a flame to three cones, jammed together. Each one released a bright orange plume, fizzing like flares in the blackness. Next I fired up something called an Armageddon. This kicked out red and green spinners, revolving into the night at dizzy speeds. Then came crackling stars, coloured bouquets and ten loud thunderclaps to finish. God! I'd forgotten how much fun these things were. It was years since I'd been so close to fireworks.

I dug excitedly in my selection box for the next wonder. More luminous tubes brought green stars and silver whirls to the cloudy wasteland. Gushing fountains changed colour every few seconds, blazing through the whole rainbow. Blue pearls whistled and banged; golden tails raced away like burning comets; rockets guided themselves into perfect flight, bursting into a flood of pink petals; tiny volcanoes erupted with lakes of red lava; Catherine wheels whizzed around, spitting sparks like a woodcutter's cog.

With each barrage of noisy colour I thought of Harly. I opened a packet of sparklers, lighting a furry tip. With big tinselly strokes I wrote a name in the darkness before me.

The . . . Great . . . Harlequin . . . Grim.

I waved the twinkling stick over his grave, showering it with hot glitter. I moved like a shadow among the beast-shaped heaps that Harly built, guided by a sparkler's light. And suddenly, from the horizon away over King's Cragg, came another tribute. A rocket shot gaily above the mountains, melting into multi-coloured hearts. Out of this beauty came a bang that shook me up from a distance. Then a final shower of crackling dragon eggs.

It could only be Baz. He must have been waiting for me, not wanting to intrude on my time with Laura. This was his greeting and his own salute to Harlequin. I waited to see if anything else came. One last special effect for final glory. And it did come. Baz had told me once about a firework called Dark Fire, Falling Leaves, and here it was. Bright stars fizzed against the dirty heavens. They burned in one colour, seemed to burn out, then lit up again in a different colour.

Red stars . . . *blackness* . . . orange stars . . . *blackness* . . . green stars . . . *blackness*.

It was like the gods were spray-painting them in a fresh coat each time.

I had nothing more to fire off in response, yet between us we'd done the boy giant proud. But there were still three sparklers left. I stuck two of their silver spikes into the cold grave. With a thread of string I tied the third one onto them like a crosspiece. I quickly set the trio alight, then jumped back to admire. A shimmering capital 'H' stood burning merrily.

I brushed off angry tears and sprinkled the burned sparkler bits over Harly's body. Walter had told me he wanted his child brought back by New Year, to lay him to rest on home ground. I could visit there with Laura when she came to stay in future. The thought of her being so close, under the same roof, thrilled me right through. I was ready to go home, to own up about where I'd been, and mention there'd be company for Christmas.

I gave Harly a last lingering wave and backed off past the dark shack. The door's rotten timbers creaked in the November night breeze. It was time to move on.

I hurried down Quarry Road, led by the peaceful lights of Torbeck far below. Back in the village, Henderson's shop was locked in darkness until morning. I heard the measly whine of a few back-garden fireworks. There was no organized bonfire display anywhere.

I strode towards the bus stop, expecting to find some pillocks lurking and whistling at me. I was armed with Laura's warmth and a year's worth of new confidence. But the night was too dank for even Torbeck's losers to mope miserably out there. The shelter's inside walls had been cleared of graffiti, insults and scribbles. Old love hearts were washed away under a clean sweep of white paint. No place even for romance there now. A bus timetable was ripped on the stone floor that was strewn with empty crisp bags, fag papers, alcopop bottles. A poster advertised a new youth club in the village, with urgent requests for help in decorating. Contact Lavinia Delaney for details on 23980.

Five minutes later the last bus trundled up, trapping me in its headlights like an escaped prisoner. Nobody else got on board and I fled from the village like a phantom.

FIFTY~FIVE

I made the train with minutes to spare, chucking myself into a nearly empty carriage. The two coaches grumbled away past acres of black sandy coastline. We called at small deserted stations, where golden lanterns held back the night.

Only three other people were aboard my half of the train. One was a sharp-suited guy speaking loudly into a mobile. Finally he got up and threw a newspaper aside, still yakking.

'Yeah, Juliet . . . coming into Sellafield now. You in the car park? Be there in a sec. Love you too, angel. Right . . . just getting off . . . Here I come, babe . . . don't move your sweet ass . . .'

As we jolted on again I got up to nab Romeo's newspaper. It was a copy of the *Daily Record*, the Scottish paper I'd found in Harly's hut. I read through the national news, war reports from overseas, Celtic's dealings in the transfer market and a story about an award-winning blind sheepdog in the Borders. When I'd finished poring over all this we'd reached Wigton, with ten miles to go. The light was dim in the carriage and I was drowsy from the day's emotions.

I only started reading one last small feature item because of its headline: THIEF REMANDED IN CUSTARD-Y! It told the bizarre tale of a burglar from Longtown, somewhere north of Hadrian's Wall, on the Scottish border. This guy, called Tommy Pepper, had a history of petty crimes. He'd been DNA tested by the police while serving a two-year prison sentence.

The night after his release from jail, Pepper had broken into a council house in Longtown. He'd spied the owners, a Mr and Mrs McPopple, being picked up by a taxi earlier. Pepper broke in at their back door, nicking a peacock statue and a set of silver candlesticks. But before stealing back out, he'd spotted a freshly baked custard tart on the kitchen table. A rich brown crust, the court was later told, filled with Mrs McPopple's thick yellow mixture.

Unable to resist after years of prison grub, Tommy Pepper had bitten three tempting chunks out. His teeth marks were printed on the pie like tiny battlements. When the police were called they found no fingerprints, for Pepper had worn gloves. But his DNA, in the form of saliva, was all over Mrs

McPopple's pudding. A quick test and match led the cops to Pepper's bedsit, where he was busily spraying the candlesticks gold.

He was given a four-month sentence and an £80 fine. All for the sake of three greedy chomps at a home-made custard tart. A photo alongside the story showed Pepper in all his grisliness. He was cock-eyed, with two dark pupils looking down a crooked nose. His hair was a short black fuzz. Curving up from each corner of his mouth was a smiling scar. He'd been slashed on both cheeks, so the wounds had healed in a wide grin.

Laughing at Pepper's luckless daftness, I nearly threw down the newspaper. But something about a connected story below caught my eye. It was another piece about DNA testing that contained the word *Blackrigg*. The valley where Harlequin had grown up.

The report concerned an unsolved murder in that area, dating back just over a year. It had taken place last October, in a woodland on the edge of Blackrigg Valley. The time of death was estimated at between midday and two p.m.

The victim was named as Donnie Turnbull, aged eighteen, from near Canobie. He was known to be a minor drug dealer who had flunked out of university, studying history. The college commented that a brilliant career had been ruined by misadventure. Turnbull had also served a youth sentence for arson once. Of above average height, with long red hair, he was last seen leaving a nearby pub around noon. At some stage in the next two hours he'd been strangled to death, his neck broken. The body was found in a shallow river, making DNA testing more difficult. No attempt had been made by the killer to hide the corpse. Three large stones were jammed into the victim's mouth and throat. A fourth was found lodged in his windpipe.

I slammed down the paper. My brain wrestled with a chaos of memories. October last year. *October . . . October . . .*

We'd arrived in Torbeck in the middle of that month. I'd first met Harly the next day. Like me, he'd been travelling with all his worldly goods. Unlike me, he had nowhere special to go. And all his gear had fitted into one old rucksack, not a white van.

So if he'd left Blackrigg the week before . . . Could he have . . . ? Would he . . . ?

I quickly read through the rest of it. The police confirmed that, despite forensic testing, no arrests had been made. A body was exhumed in south Cumbria recently, but the results were not conclusive. Inquiries would continue, said a spokesman. They were, however, disappointed by the response from

Turnbull's community. Very little had been learned from talking to residents there. Many were afraid to speak out, fearing his connections with criminals. The case remained open.

I dropped the paper onto the table.

'I done bad, Glenn Jackson. I never meant it this time.'

I shakily tore out the item with hands that wouldn't steady.

'Tell 'em I saved you. Tell 'em when they come.'

I heard Walter Quinn's croaky voice in my exhausted mind.

'Harmless as a great baby elephant . . .'

Only Harly wasn't always harmless. I'd seen that.

'Gentle as a dove's white wings . . .'

But he could have been. If left alone to be free and happy.

'Red Riding Hood knows. She killed them wolves with big stones . . . She clever and brave, like me.'

The case remained open, it said. I read the report through again, then three times over.

Closing my eyes, I dreamed up this nightmare scene . . .

Leafy wet woodland. A cold October day. Through golden trees, two young men approach each other. One is on the run, the other forever drifting. One's a gawky blond in rough overalls. The other has flaming hair, a leather jacket. In a forest clearing, by a river, they draw near.

As they pass, the tallest one stops and swivels. A burning memory awakes. The other youth turns in mid-stride. An arrogant shake of red hair; he smokes and smirks. He strolls on, as clumsy footsteps crackle behind. The first thing he feels is a brutal blow to the neck. The last thing he sees is Harvey Quinn's fierce face. Crushing hands throttle him.

I came to with a jolt. The train was braking with an awful shriek. It screamed like a fighter jet . . . like Harly in his terrors. My ears ached with squealing metal.

'We are now approaching Carlisle,' crackled the guard's voice overhead. 'This train terminates here. Please take all your possessions with you when you leave.'